MY NAME is
Sloan

by

E. Compton Lee

Lavender Press
an imprint of Blue Fortune Enterprises, LLC

MY NAME IS SLOAN
Copyright © 2024 by E. Compton Lee

This book is a work of fiction. Names, characters, businesses, organizations, places, events and incidents either are the product of the author's imagination or are used fictitiously. Any resemblance to actual persons, living or dead, events, or locales is entirely coincidental.

For information contact :
Blue Fortune Enterprises, LLC
Lavender Press
P.O. Box 554
Yorktown, VA 23690
http://blue-fortune.com

Edited by Stacia Chapman
Cover design by BFELLC

ISBN: 978-1-961548-14-5
Second edition: June 2024

Dedication

For Rob and Chris

Acknowledgements

I would like to thank my publisher Narielle Living; my editor, Stacia Chapman; and my friend and support system, Alma Kendall. I also want to thank the members of the Silver Quill and the Williamsburg critique groups. Their input was invaluable.

Elizabeth

Chapter One

*N*othing John Avery had learned in school or in life was any help to him now. He fought an instinct to step behind Dr. Wittcomb's enormous back. She was the clinical director of the Columbia County Mental Health Clinic, and ten minutes earlier John had mistaken her for a patient.

They were in a large, well-appointed office where an eight-year-old girl keened a high-pitched cry that rose and fell while her mother, Clare Raffienne, held the girl on her lap and stared straight ahead with a look so intense John prayed she would not turn it on him. A plump woman in a dress too small for her sat next to them looking as though nothing was happening, even though she was the social worker who had taken Sloan Raffienne from her home and mother.

Dr. Wittcomb swayed forward a step. "Clare, I am so sorry about this. We will do everything we can to make this for as short a time as possible."

Clare Raffienne reached up, took her daughter Sloan's arms, and forced them away from her neck. The child grabbed a fistful of hair in one hand. Clare pried it loose with her fingers then in one quick motion she stood, handed Sloan to Dr. Wittcomb, who took hold of the child and held her against her chest. The mother never paused. She walked past John as though he didn't exist, out the door, down the corridor, and exited the building through the back door. Sloan stopped crying. She peered straight into Dr. Wittcomb's eyes then threw her head back, arched her torso, wailed, and kicked her feet. John stepped forward and lifted her into his own arms. The child brought her knees up and bent toward his neck with her teeth bared.

"Put her in a chair, cross her arms, and hold her wrists behind the back of the chair. Otherwise you'll get bitten or worse." Dr. Wittcomb's voice was flat, professional, and only broke on the last word.

John Avery looked up from the struggling child.

"I don't want anyone to get hurt," Dr. Wittcomb said. She inhaled deeply through her nose and pushed a chair toward the young man.

"Move behind her, take her arms and cross them and keep your head low so she can't headbutt you."

When he had secured Sloan, John leaned his head against the back of the chair and nearly wept.

Ms. Platt, the social worker, straightened in her chair and pulled her dress closer to her knees. "We should have taken her directly to her foster home. At night. No need to bring her here with her mother. It only makes things worse."

Dr. Wittcomb eased herself onto the edge of the desk. Her gray hair had come undone from her bun. She had been in this position for thirty years, and this was the worst yet. It was getting harder and harder to keep herself under control and find a way to ease the pain of the people passing through her office, client and staff alike.

They had to wait over an hour for the psychiatrist to arrive. When he did, he gave the child a shot that, in two minutes, stopped her struggles, and in five left her unconscious. He wrote a prescription and handed it to Dr. Wittcomb. Sloan would not be causing any more trouble. The dose could stop a train. Dr. Wittcomb thought about saying something but had been down that road before.

Clare Raffienne did not bother to pull into a parking place at the Jolly Roger. She stopped the truck in front of the door and jumped out, leaving the engine running. She went straight for the bourbon and put a half gallon of the cheapest on the counter. Roger Downs, the owner, was arranging cigarettes against the wall. He turned around. "Hey, Clare, how's it going?"

She didn't answer. She fished around in her pockets, brought out a ten and a five, which she placed next to the bottle.

"Do you think spring's ever going to get here?" Roger said.

Clare glanced up then dug deeper in her pockets. She found two ones and added them to the pile. Roger watched as she pulled quarters and a dime loose from her jeans and dropped them on the paper money, then continued to fish around in her pockets. He reached into his own pants, brought out his wallet, and put three ones on the pile. Clare grabbed the bottle around the neck and turned to go. "I owe you," she said over her shoulder.

"Take care," Roger called after her.

Clare turned the truck onto the road that passed by Hozelroad Holler on the way up the mountain. She drove by a solid mass of rusted metal, busted-out cars, and tar paper dwellings that had collapsed into various stages of decay. If I'd moved in with them pigs, she thought, I would have Sloan now. The debris gradually diminished as she drove into the woods. Clare pressed the truck as hard as she could, bouncing around the turns. She slammed on the brakes in front of a battered two-story house, turned off the engine, threw the keys on the dash, took her bottle of bourbon, kicked the front door open, and flicked on a light. The wood stove had gone out and the house was colder inside than out. Clare took a plastic cup from a table in the room that served as a kitchen. She filled it with the liquor, went into the next room, and sank into the springs of the couch. She put her head in her hands. Thank God Pap wasn't alive to see this. Of course, if he was alive, it wouldn't have happened. She took a long pull on the bourbon. How had she not seen it coming? Clare pulled a dingy comforter around her shoulders and took another drink. It was almost dark in the room, the only light coming from the bulb in the kitchen. It was good to keep it dark. That way Clare did not have to see Sloan's things: her books, her paper and crayons, her dolls, her dirty socks, and especially her ragged blankie lying around the room. She wouldn't go upstairs to the bedrooms, she wouldn't light the wood stove, wouldn't turn on any more lights.

She would stay in the dark; the morning sun would arrive soon enough. The light would come through the bare windows and she would have no choice. But for now, she would sit here on this couch, in this room, and drink this rot-gut liquor until everything went black.

Chapter Two

John opened and shut the kitchen door as quietly as possible. The other boys were out, and his father would be at the mill in Coleton, Pennsylvania, where he seemed to stay for days. His mother, of course, would be in the parlor. John took three beers from the refrigerator, two chicken legs from the stove, and what was left of a loaf of bread from the counter. He went up the back stairs to his bedroom. The beers were cold in his pockets. When he shut the door to his room, he felt relief followed by guilt, but not enough guilt to go see his mother.

People were fond of saying that when Maureen Avery was a young woman, men bumped into lampposts when she walked down the street, she was that beautiful. One of John's earliest memories was strolling along a busy sidewalk holding his mother's hand while she pushed a stroller with the other. They were stopped so often by various men it seemed to the little boy that this behavior was part of the excursion, part of the reason for the outing. "Hello, Mrs. Avery," the men would say in voices so eager that even shy John looked up at them. "What beautiful children," they said. "But what else could they be with you as their mother?" Sometimes they patted his head. One knelt down and looked him full in the face, smiling. "You look just like your mamma," he said, and John looked up into his mother's face. She smiled down at him and he buried himself in her skirt, his chubby arms wrapped around her legs. He wanted to climb her like a tree, encircle her neck, and put his cheek against hers, lose himself in the milky, talcum, yeasty scent of her, but, of course, he couldn't because there was the stroller and his little brother in the way and, anyway, you didn't do that in public or even at home.

After her fifth child in six years, Maureen began to recede. She pulled further and further away with the next four pregnancies. She had all but disappeared into a world that held no place for John or her other sons until she gave birth to her last child, a baby girl. Then the presence from John's early years returned and he turned toward its long-missed glow. But at four years old, when it was clear that baby Colleen was not going to speak to anyone, not even to her mother, Maureen disappeared faster and more completely than before. She left the parlor only in the afternoon to fix supper: spaghetti, meatloaf or chicken, which she left on the stove. The boys came at various times during the night and helped themselves and presumably fed their little sister. Maureen stayed in the parlor watching TV until eleven, when she returned to the kitchen to put the dishes in the dishwasher before going to bed. Over the years, a film of grease covered every exposed surface in the room.

John dropped the chicken and bread onto his desk. He pulled the beers from his pockets where they had left damp spots. He put them next to the food and placed a magazine underneath them. He opened one, sat down, and finished half of it in a long swallow. He could still hear the inhuman sound the child made. That social worker was a cool one. She just sat there through the whole thing and when the girl passed out, let John carry her to the car.

John drank some more. I didn't do well today, he thought. Practically hiding behind the director's skirts. He opened the second bottle. Where had that mother come from? What a face. Wild. But what do you expect when you are losing your child. John put down the beer and went across the hall to his sister's room. She sat on the floor playing with dolls, her black hair falling in front of her face. She looked up and smiled at him. He felt tears for the second time that day.

"Hey, what you doing?" John sat on the edge of her bed. Colleen went back to her dolls. Autistic was the first psychiatrist's diagnosis. The second said she was "intellectually challenged." John had tried to erase from his memory the look on his mother's face, wide open with hope, when she had come back from Dr. Wittcomb's.

"The doctor says she's selectively mute. That means she can talk, John. She will talk. She's not retarded. She's not crazy."

John had hugged his mother. "I'm happy for you. I'm happy for Colleen, but I'm very, very happy for you."

Now, Colleen went back to playing with her dolls. She rarely cried and she smiled often, and because she never made a sound, her brothers frequently took her with them. She had been to pool halls, restaurants, bars, baseball games, R-rated movies, and even sat in the back seat during some dates. As he watched Colleen, John pictured Sloan. She'd still be asleep from the meds. In a strange bed, in a strange house, among strangers. What would she feel when she woke? He looked at his watch. Seven o'clock. He couldn't wait to get to work tomorrow.

Chapter Three

Dr. Wittcomb watched John Avery carefully. She was surprised at his early arrival this morning. She wouldn't have hired him. He was too young and too good-looking. He was not as beautiful as his little sister Colleen, but almost. Beautiful people were a distraction in therapy. And his family was dysfunctional. Not blatantly so. They didn't rob banks or murder people, though she did suspect one of the eight other boys was a thief in order to support his drug habit. And there was the conflict-of-interest thing. Colleen Avery was still Dr. Wittcomb's patient, even though her mother hadn't brought her in for over a year.

No, she wouldn't have hired this boy. However, she hadn't been asked to sit on the interview panel despite the fact she was the clinical director. It was just one of the ways that the new administration was trying to get rid of her. They had made one very serious and open effort, but Dr. Wittcomb happened to be friends with the best lawyer in town. She and Marshall Tiege often had lunch together. An exquisitely written letter by him implying, but not actually threatening, an age-discrimination suit put an instant and permanent stop to the official push to rid the clinic of Dr. Wittcomb. The indirect methods, however, continued. Now, looking at this boy, she wondered if she shouldn't take him off the case and assign it to someone else. But whom? All the therapists were green as grass.

"This is an unusually difficult case," she said not unkindly and motioned him to the chair next to the desk. "What is your plan?"

John had no plan. He didn't know he was supposed to have a plan this early in the case. He had hoped Dr. Wittcomb would have helped him develop one. "I was going to go up the mountain and visit the mother."

"And what will you say to her?"

"Well, I'll ask her if she understands why her daughter has been taken away."

"Do you know why?"

"According to the Children's Protective Service report, for emotional and physical neglect."

"What does that mean?"

John cleared his throat. "I don't have the chart."

"And you think that the details of the emotional and physical neglect are in the chart."

John hesitated. "I'm assuming so."

"They may or may not be. Read it carefully. For starters. If the report isn't clear, call CPS and ask for clarification. Then arrange a meeting between Ms. Raffienne and CPS and you to make sure everyone is on the same page. In the meantime, go on up that mountain and see for yourself what it's like up there."

John read the report and it stated that the child went to school dirty, was often absent, and then it went on to say something about a bear. Apparently, someone had reported seeing a bear hanging around Clare's house. They had called the police, who called The Department of Social Services. Ms. Raffienne had not responded to the Department's suggestion that she make arrangements to have the bear removed. Furthermore, when Animal Control arrived at the cabin to capture or shoot the animal, Ms. Raffienne had chased the officers off with a rifle. At that point, they said it was a Child Protective Service issue and closed the case. The report did not directly say why a bear hanging around the cabin was reason for removing the child, but John could make the connection.

It took half an hour to arrive at the turnoff to Clare's house. John wished he had taken the clinic's one SUV instead of a sedan. He checked to make sure the doors were locked. He absently noted the debris in some of the yards and looked from one side of the road to the other. The homes became indistinct, their beginnings and endings disappearing into tacked on buses or vans or mounds of gutted appliances and cars. This must be Hozelroad Holler. He'd heard of the Holler but was not prepared for the wanton dissolution. This supposedly was where the mountain people went when the law or CPS came after them. Why, John wondered, hadn't Clare?

The metal and debris gradually diminished until there were only woods again. John drove two or three more miles until he came to a clearing and the road stopped at the back of a two-story house. Some horses were fenced in by a few strands of rusted wire and grazed on hay thrown among the trees. The house had long since lost its paint and John was certain it leaned to one side. He looked right then left. No signs of a bear. Still, he walked smartly to the back stoop. He tested each rotting step before he put his full weight on it. He knocked on the graying door. Silence. He knocked again while looking over his shoulder, then he pushed, and the door swung open. The bitter smell of cold ashes filled the room, which contained an iron wood-burning stove, an electric stove, a refrigerator, and a wooden table with two chairs.

John called out. "Ms. Raffienne. Hello? Is anyone home?" He heard a moan from another room. "Ms Raffienne, is that you? I'm John Avery. You know. From yesterday. At the clinic."

"Get the fuck out of my house."

"Ms. Raffienne, I'm here to help. To work with you to get your daughter back. May I come in?" John stepped into the other room before the woman could say no. She was lying on a couch with a ragged blanket pulled over her and her arm across her eyes. A half-gallon bottle of whiskey lay on the floor.

"Are you all right?" he asked.

"Christ, no." Clare rolled off the couch and staggered out the door. John heard retching sounds and looking out the window, he saw Ms. Raffienne crouching on the bottom step of the porch, her head between her knees as she vomited onto the ground. He went outside and sat beside her. She continued heaving, and the brown liquid splattering around her feet smelled like pure alcohol. John reached over and held back Clare's hair. Eventually, she had the dry heaves and then finally was still. Tears rolled down her cheeks. She took a deep breath, wiped them away with the back of her hand, stood up, and walked back into the house where she took a can of Pepsi from the refrigerator, turned around and gave John the full force of her stare.

He reached for the back of one of the wooden chairs. "May I sit down?"

Clare nodded without interest.

"Please," he said. "Sit with me."

She remained standing and drank from the Pepsi can. Her hands were shaking.

John pulled out the chair and sat. "Ms. Raffienne, I work with Dr. Wittcomb. I'm an in-home therapist."

Clare said nothing.

"Do you know why CPS took your child?"

A muscle twitched on the woman's jaw, but other than that, she didn't acknowledge the question.

"The report said something about truancy and going to school dirty and then something about a bear. Do you have any idea what they would be talking about?"

"No."

"Um, how many days has your daughter missed school?"

The woman went to the only cupboard in the room and took out a glass, put some ice in it and poured in the Pepsi. She went to the living room and came back with the bourbon, which she added to the soda. She sat down.

"Maybe you should go easy on that stuff."

Clare stared at him then took a long drink from the glass.

"I'm sorry," John said quickly. "But it won't help your situation."

"Get out of my house."

"Ms. Raffienne, I'm here to help."

"Well, you ain't."

"It's my job to get your daughter back to you as fast as possible. And drinking before noon won't help."

"I told you to get out of my house. Now I suggest you do that."

John watched her carefully. What would she do if he remained sitting where he was? What could she do? He remembered the report and the mention of a rifle. He wondered where she kept it. He kept himself from glancing around the room. Anyway, she was pale and shaky. How quickly could she move? Pretty damn quickly, he suspected. He reached into his pocket and put a card with his name and phone number on it on the table then rose to his feet. "Please, call me," he said. "I'll talk to CPS and find out what they want you to do to get your daughter back. Then you and I can make a plan. I'll come back." He let himself out and looked around again for the bear. As far as he could tell there was no sign of one. He unlocked the car and sat for a moment before starting it. What the fuck, he thought.

Clare poured more whiskey into her glass. She'd known it would be trouble when she'd run Animal Control off. She'd raised that bear from a cub, though. She and Sloan had found it not far from the house, no bigger than a large pup. They'd bottle fed it and kept it in the kitchen near the stove through the winter until the next spring when it went off one morning and didn't come back. "To find a boyfriend," Clare had told her daughter, and she'd thought that was the end of it until a few nights later they saw a dark, familiar form in the twilight at the edge of the yard. They put out the scraps for her. After that, the bear hung around in the woods close to the house, sometimes coming right into the yard. Soon it ventured onto the porch and bawled until they fed it. Sloan named her Sister and looked for her every morning as soon as she came downstairs and again every afternoon when she arrived home from school.

When the first hard days of winter settled in and Sister wasn't on the porch in the morning or in the afternoon either, Sloan sat on her mother's lap and cried.

"She's just hibernating," Clare said. "She's taking a long nap 'cause it's so cold. She'll be here again in the spring, you wait and see, maybe even with a little one alongside."

The bear did return, but not to the house. They saw her walking along the wood line with her cub, and Clare took food up the mountain, leaving it where they had seen her. Mother and cub appeared nearly every night until late fall when Clare walked outside to find Sister reaching through the fence for some hay. "Here now," she said and poured the bucket of feed she was carrying onto the ground. "Your cub grown up, is she?" Sister wandered over and buried her nose in the grain. She was a black bear, not very big but ravenous, her body trying to prepare itself for the winter months of hibernation. "You come here every night and I'll have dinner for you," said Clare. "Sloan will be thrilled."

Sister was back the next night and the next. Sloan wanted to hug her, but Clare wouldn't let her. They spent many evenings watching Sister amble, with her funny rolling gait, down the mountain and then help herself to the food Clare had put out. Sometimes after she had eaten, she would get down and roll around, scratching her back and playfully batting at the shadows made by the leaves drifting from the trees. Occasionally, she rolled up onto the porch and stood stock still while Sloan scratched her behind the ears.

Now, Clare put her head down on her folded arms and felt the wood of the table against her cheek. I ain't gonna cry, she thought. But I might puke again. Where was Annie? After years of nothing, Clare had gotten a short note from her about a week ago, saying she was coming back to Coleton. Three years after Annie left, Clare had stopped hoping. After five, six, or maybe seven, she stopped being angry. Then a note. A fucking note. Clare didn't raise her head because things were beginning to spin. The table smelled faintly of bacon and maybe peanut butter. She rubbed it with her hand, noting the roughed-up places. She let her eyes close. Eventually, she fell asleep.

Katie B. Sloan

Chapter Four

Sloan woke with a terrible headache and the feeling of falling. A woman yelled from the bottom of the stairs, "Breakfast!" The last thing Sloan wanted was food. She wanted to go back to sleep and stay that way, but a boy popped his head into the room and said, "Better get up or you won't get breakfast or lunch." Sloan pulled the covers over her head.

The woman called again. "Nathanial, you git outta that girl's bedroom." The boy stepped into the room and pulled the covers off Sloan. He looked her up and down then moved lightly behind the door and with his brown skin and silent, quick movements he seemed to Sloan like a wild thing. She could hear the heavy steps on the stairs and then the woman was in the doorway and the boy slid behind her and down the stairs.

The woman stood next to the bed, fists on her hips. "I'm Mrs. Grafton. Your foster mother. Come on now. You got to get up." The woman took Sloan's hand and pulled her out of bed. She handed her a new set of clothes. Sloan was wearing the same outfit she had on the day before. She stood holding the new clothes and not moving as the room tilted and turned.

"Here, I'll help you this morning but after that you got to do it yourself. Put your arms straight up."

Sloan didn't move. The woman took Sloan by the wrists and lifted her arms over her head. When she let go, Sloan flopped flat on her back on the bed, her eyes closed. The woman put her hands on her hips again and stared at her. "Hey, you. Wake up. Come on now, you have to get up." Mrs. Grafton took hold of the girl's hands and pulled her into a sitting position, grabbed the bottom of her shirt and wiggled it overhead and off. With a great deal of tugging and grunting, she managed to pull the clean shirt over the crown of Sloan's head, settled it around her neck and then stuffed her arms in the sleeves. As soon as she let go, the girl slipped boneless and prone back onto the sheets. The woman stood with her fists on her hips. "Has anyone ever combed your hair? And those jeans, they're at least two inches too short for you." Eight years old, she was supposed to be. At eight Mrs. Grafton had been milking cows at four thirty in the morning, but it seemed to her this child had been raised with no direction. She didn't agree with drugging her to the eyeballs, but maybe it was the only way to control her. What good was controlling her, though, if she was turned into nothing but a rag doll? She pulled her into a sitting position. "You can leave them pants on but just this once. It's dirty wearing the same panties more than one day. Look at you with that mess of red hair. You're a regular Raggedy Ann. Can you stand? There. Now hang onto me, we'd better get you downstairs before them boys eat everything in sight."

There were five boys at the breakfast table, the brown boy called Nathanial and four smaller white ones. The woman placed a bowl of Corn Flakes and milk in front of Sloan, who tried to put her head down on the table.

"You sit up now," Mrs. Grafton said, "and eat." Sloan didn't respond and a strong hand pulled her into a sitting position. A man she hadn't noticed came from behind her and sat across the table. He was gray. Gray hair, gray face, gray clothes. "Everybody, I'd like you to meet our new sister, Joan. Say good morning to her," he said. The other children didn't look up but mumbled something around their cereal.

"Joan, this is Nathanial, Jeremy, Michael, Laremy, and Joe. You can call me Father and my wife Mother." Sloan looked from him to Nathanial, who was bent over his bowl spooning in the cereal.

"We are very glad to have our new sister here with us. We've been praying a long time to get a little girl, haven't we Mother? Now, Joan, say good morning to everyone." Sloan continued to stare, wishing she could put her head down and go to sleep. She felt like she might be sick. The man turned to talk to his wife and in the time that took, Nathanial switched cereal bowls with the girl and bent over the food, spooning quickly. "Mother, go get that stool and we'll comb Joan's hair. She's much too pretty to go around with rats in her hair." He faced the children again. "Now you boys take your bowls to the sink and go outside."

The boys went out, banging the door behind them, and Mr. Grafton half carried, half dragged Sloan to the tall stool, which Mother had placed in the middle of the kitchen. The child's head hurt, and the falling feeling had returned. Images of her mother floated through her mind, but she couldn't hang on to them. She started to slide from the stool, but the gray man put his hands under her armpits. Mrs. Grafton worked at the tangled hair with a brush, bringing tears to Sloan's eyes.

"You're hurting her."

"Well, I can't help that. These rats ain't goin' to come out any other way."

"She's got tears in her eyes."

"I don't know what you expect me to do. We should just cut it all off."

"Not that beautiful hair. That would be a sin."

"Hair is a woman's sin."

Sloan started to whimper.

"Oh, for pity's sake, Mother." The man took the brush from his wife. "Just put it in a braid for now."

Out on the porch, Sloan stood blinking in the sunlight. She noticed a swing hanging from the ceiling and headed for it, but the brown boy, who had been sitting on the steps, jumped up next to her and took her by the arm and dragged her stumbling down the stairs. "Can't sit there. We ain't allowed to stay on the porch. Come with me. I got a good place to go. You'll like it. The other kids won't come around and they can't see us from the house." He took her to the back of one of the outbuildings and pulled her down on the ground next to him. A watery sun was out and the thin warmth spread across Sloan's face and lap. She laid her head against the shed and let her lids slide shut.

"Don't go to sleep. It's the meds makin' you so sleepy, but I'll show you how to take care of that. We only got ten minutes to play before we got to go work in the greenhouse. It's hell in there. I put poisons in the dirt so the plants will die. You won't have to do the heavy liftin' I bet, but they'll make you do the plantin' and weed pullin' for sure. The boys got to carry them heavy sacks of seeds and dirt and mulch. Sometimes it's a hundred degrees and more. We all pass out nearly every day. Those other boys don't have to do as much as me 'cause I'm black." A farm bell rang. "That's that Nazi bitch. They'll be lookin' for us soon. She won't come back here on her own, so we got some time. They won't give me lunch if I don't show up, but I know how to pick the lock on the refrigerator, so I could give a shit."

The boy's words were unintelligible to Sloan; they blurred and blended together in a sing-song that soothed her enough to slip into a twilight sleep in which she was still aware of the comforting sun, the smell of the earth coming alive, and the sound of birds returning from the south.

Chapter Five

The therapists got younger and younger. Since the new administration, the turnover was high and the quality low. Most of them were fresh out of school and took the job only to get some experience on their resumes and then moved on. Dr. Wittcomb chose not to be irritated by this, but instead thought of these youngsters as various fish, pretty creatures that floated into the eddy that was her office where they stayed for six months, give or take, then floated away to be replaced by others. The trick was not to upset them, not to throw rocks and alarm them from their graceful, detached, and languid selves as they moved blandly in front of her every week for supervision. To upset them would mean they would lose their nubile ease, their youthful magnetism, the thoughtless assurance that allowed their clients to hope. Supervision was the only time she saw most of them. She took each case they presented, got their attention in the most beneficent way she could, and gave them as much support and knowledge as they would tolerate. They did in-home therapy and the majority of their work was in the field. There were six of them, all women, which was not unusual. Only one showed any interest in developing the skills to be an effective therapist and she looked twelve years old. Chrissy had a master's degree in counseling psychology from a good university, but the lack of credibility her looks engendered was beginning to take its toll. She had developed a sullen demeanor, and Dr. Wittcomb heard her snap at a client on the phone. The girl worried her, but she worried more about John Avery. He was presenting yesterday's case, and even though his voice shook, he didn't spare any details as he recounted his visit to the Raffienne home. His intensity and the facts: the vomiting, the cursing, the condition of the woman, the getting thrown out of the house, were enough to rouse the other clinicians gathered around Dr. Wittcomb's desk and they stopped doing their nails or doodling or staring out the window. Instead, they looked at John. Actually, now that Dr. Wittcomb thought about it, they had been looking at him under their lashes off and on since he'd walked through the door.

"You'll have to go back and apologize," she told him, and the look of surprise and dismay on his face almost made her smile. She leaned forward as far as her belly would allow and said, "Look, John, you went to her house uninvited. You are a stranger. The 'system' just took away her baby. Why should she trust you? And then you sit down and tell her to stop drinking."

"But the drinking won't help her get her child back."

"Of course, it won't. You know that. I know that. She knows that. You just don't want to hit her with it right from the get-go. What kind of support does she have?"

"Support?"

"Yes, support. Family? Friends?"

"Ah… I don't know."

"Well, we'll want to find out. Listen, I have some information for you that may help. I happen to know Marshall Tiege's law firm just hired a new attorney. If I'm not mistaken, the woman used to be a friend of Ms. Raffienne's. Look into this. Clare doesn't have any family that will help. Her Pap is dead."

"And this friend would do…?"

"She needs a lawyer and a friend; someone she will talk to. Believe me, the Raffiennes don't talk to many people."

"What about the child's father?"

Dr. Wittcomb sat back. "No idea who he is. Ms. Raffienne… Clare, I'm going to call her Clare, that's what I'm used to… always liked men. I think she kept more to herself after the child, and once her Pap died, she had no one to babysit so her social life was curtailed, but at one time she was… very popular."

John looked uncertain. "Shouldn't we try to find out? DNA or something?"

"Clare's not interested." Dr. Wittcomb reached for a Post-it and wrote a number on it. "Here's the number for the law firm. See if you can find out the whereabouts of this friend. I think she is going by her maiden name of Voight. When you go back out, ask Clare if you can speak to Ms. Voight on her behalf. Take a release."

"I'm not sure she'll let me back in the house."

"Go back out there and knock on the door. Don't go in unless you're invited. Talk through the screen if you have to. Say you are sorry about criticizing her drinking. That you were out of line. That you want to start over. Ask her to tell you what she wants you to do. Remember, you work for her. Her and the child. This child doesn't belong in foster care. Believe me. Tell her that your job, *our job*, is to get her baby back as fast as possible. Tell her you will work with DSS to do just that."

As usual, Dr. Wittcomb's small house was cold when she arrived home. Chukchi jumped off the bed in the downstairs bedroom and greeted her owner by touching her nose briefly on Dr. Wittcomb's hand on her way outside. The woman touched the top of the dog's head. That was the only physical contact the animal would tolerate. Though a full-blooded Siberian Husky, she looked more like a wolf than any dog should. Dr. Wittcomb turned on the gas fireplace and heard, with satisfaction, the whoosh as the fire came on. She had given up the woodstove two years ago, deciding she was old enough to stop chopping logs. She made herself an egg salad sandwich with plenty of mayonnaise and poured herself a large glass of wine. She sat in front of the fireplace and ate her meal. The egg salad spilled out of the bread, and Dr. Wittcomb licked the excess from the edges. The wine was a full-bodied, dry red that maintained its flavor well. She ate and sipped until everything was gone, then she filled the kettle and put it on the stove to boil. Her kitchen was at one end of the room, and she could see the fire from where she stood. When the water boiled, she made instant decaffeinated coffee with plenty of real cream, poured another glass of wine, and opened the door to let in Chukchi. She filled the dog's bowl with food and put it on the floor. Then she returned to sit in front of the fire with the coffee and wine. Eventually, the dog lay down next to her chair, her head on her paws.

Dr. Wittcomb had noticed the peaked look on Chrissy's face this morning. It would help, she thought, if the girl stopped calling herself by that silly name. No one past the age of three should be called Chrissy. Perhaps she should take to wearing sophisticated makeup, the urban look, or maybe no makeup at all, and fringed clothing, an ethnic appearance. Or slacks and a jacket. Probably nothing would help. The girl would either tough it out until she got some miles on her or she wouldn't. John Avery was a different matter. Not only too beautiful, but, she suspected, tender-hearted as well. She sighed. This was a good time of day. She would have to make a pumpkin pie this weekend. Pumpkin pie would be good with this wine.

Chapter Six

Annie Voight spotted Lonesome immediately. He had gone completely white by now. When she called to him, he raised his head from the flake of hay, looked straight at her, and pricked his ears in her direction. He nickered and trotted toward where she stood at the fence. His lips were not as firm and the skin around his eyes not as tight, but these were the only signs of age. Clare had taken good care of him. His solid confirmation stood out among the poorly put together training horses and rangy colts from which Clare eked out a living. Annie rubbed him between the eyes. "Oh, hell and damn, Lonesome," she said. She leaned her forehead against his and breathed deeply the warm pungent odor of a horse. "Hell, and damn," she repeated.

The house was the way Annie remembered: the simple kitchen, the acrid smell of the woodstove. But not Clare. Her dusky skin had gone ashen, and her upward slanted eyes were swollen and bloodshot.

"Well, don't you look fine." Clare leaned against the sink with her arms folded. She didn't smile. It had been eight years since she had seen her friend. Annie had brightened her pale blond hair with highlights and wore it pulled back in a severe and sophisticated ponytail. She wore a business suit tighter than her own skin and even held a briefcase in her right hand. She was a stranger. Clare turned away from her and ran water into a glass, which she drained in several deep swallows.

"You don't," said Annie. "You look like hell." She put her briefcase down. Clare turned around abruptly. They faced each other across the distance. Eight years. At first Annie had written a few letters, then cards at Christmas and Clare's birthday. Then promised herself that she would write, but she hadn't until two weeks ago, when she'd dropped a line saying she was coming back.

Clare straightened away from the sink, held Annie's gaze for a moment, then tilted her head and smiled that familiar, mocking smile. "Well, shit, Annie, why don't you say what you really mean?" She went to the refrigerator. "Can I get you a drink? I was just fixing one."

Annie shook her head.

"Well, sit down, anyway. That is, if you can move in that suit. I can't imagine how you can get anything done in them clothes. And heels, even. Jesus, I swear. You're even wearin' pantyhose." Clare waved a hand toward a chair. "Go on wiggle your ass over there while I fix a drink." She filled a water glass with ice, whiskey, and coke and sat down at the kitchen table. "So, why the hell are you here after eight years?"

"Your girl. I mean … ah, hasn't anyone told you? I work for Marshall Teige. I'm here to help you get your daughter back. And to see you, of course. I've missed you." Annie pulled a chair from the table, scraping it along the floor, and sat across from Clare, who was staring at her.

"Her name is Sloan," Clare said. "Do you even remember that?"

"Yes, of course, I do." Annie remembered only because the name was so unusual for a girl. Clare had sent her a snapshot, years back, and Annie had wondered about the reddish gold hair that stood out from the baby's head in a curly froth. Where had that come from? Not from Clare, whose dusky coloring came from a mixture of French and Native American. Annie folded her arms across her chest, determined not to look away. "I've talked to John Avery, Dr. Wittcomb, and that woman from social services, Ms. Platt I think her name is. And Marshall. We have three things to deal with. The truancy. That should be easy—you just have to make a commitment to get her to school every day unless she is sick. They also say she is dirty. I'm not sure that even is legal. I don't know of any statutes that say it's against the law to be dirty. DSS would have to make a case that she is living in conditions that are a danger to her health. Then there is the question of the bear. That seems to be the biggest concern. Social Services is making the case that Sloan's life is in danger. You will probably have to go to parenting classes. That's standard. And…ah…you will have to do something about the bear. We could call the ranger and see if he will help."

As Annie talked, Clare's skin drew tighter around the bones in her face. She drank her whiskey and coke. "Who did you say you'd been talking to?"

Annie hesitated.

"I mean, ain't all that my personal business?"

"Sometimes people, the professionals working on a case, can share information," Annie lied. "And, anyway, you and I are friends."

"Really?"

Annie looked around. "Do you have anything to eat?"

"Don't try to take care of me."

"I'm not. I'm hungry. I haven't been to the grocery store yet. I went straight to the office once I arrived."

Clare stood up. She got a jar of peanut butter and bread and jelly and put them on the table. Her hands were shaking. She eased carefully onto her chair. Annie went to the cupboard and took out a knife. Everything was familiar, but there was no comfort in it. She found a plate and began making herself a sandwich. "We will get Sloan back."

"What makes you so sure?"

Annie wasn't a bit sure, nor was she convinced she could take on the deep and profound indifference the establishment felt for the people from Hozelroad Holler. The fact that the government had taken the child in the first place was extremely strange. She couldn't imagine why Clare and Sloan had drawn their attention. Even so, she said, "Because they don't have a case. We just have to jump through some hoops. It may take a month or two, but even Marshall said he didn't understand why this had happened. We'll sit down with DSS and find out exactly what they are asking for. We could even go to court and claim this is bogus and screw DSS. I think it's best though not to take an adversarial role immediately. Someone mentioned to Marshall that you might be drinking too much. I know that's false, but we have to be careful. You want to be sober when we meet with Child Protective Services. And when we go to court. Can you promise me that?"

Clare stared at Annie. "If you think I'd let any of them people see me drunk, you've changed more than I thought."

"I know. I don't know why I said that. I'm a little nervous, I guess. Coming out here as a lawyer and not just a friend."

Clare raised her eyebrows.

Annie started to sweat. Soon she'd have circles under her arms. "Lonesome looks good," she said finally into the silence.

"Yeah, well."

"I don't know how to thank you. I wouldn't have trusted him with anyone else."

"He's a good horse. You gonna be takin' him back now?"

"I told you he's yours for good."

"Yeah, well."

"Clare? I'm sorry about Pap."

Clare said nothing.

"What happened?"

"It was a training colt, nothing special. Neither real good or bad. He'd handled millions like it before. This one wheeled around and clocked him in the head. He went down like he was shot. Caught him right on the temple. Doctor said he was dead before he hit the ground. Pap never got caught off guard like that. Did this time, though. And this colt wasn't fast or nothing. Just an ordinary, run of the mill, worthless colt."

"I'm so sorry."

Clare looked at the wall over Annie's head, then at the liquid in her glass. "He wouldn't have liked growing old, anyway. He was already complaining about his knees from all those years in the saddle. He even begun to limp a little." She pushed the hair away from her face. "I can just imagine what he'd have to say about this mess. Course I doubt I'd be in this mess if he was here." She sighed.

Chapter Seven

The sun, which had been comforting while lying next to the shed, was uncomfortably warm in the greenhouse. The gray man had carried Sloan there. She remembered that. He placed her on some burlap sacks in a corner where she lay dozing and sweating and then sometime later he carried her to the house and put her in bed where she fell into a sleep so deep she did not remember dreaming. She woke in the morning to a cold clarity that took her breath away. She tried to scream, but her lungs were empty and though her mouth was open, she could only gasp, choking on the dryness of her throat. The woman from yesterday grabbed her by the arm and pulled her out of bed. "Don't you start crying. It won't do you no good."

It's all right, thought Sloan, I'll run away before the night. Mama hasn't come to get me, but she will and if she don't, I'll run away.

The brown boy sat next to her on the school bus. "They don't give all the meds on the days you go to school. That's cause the teachers complain if you act all doped up. I'll show you how not to take the meds at all." He held her hand. "Then we can have fun." Sloan tried to pull her hand away.

"What's the matter? Don't you like me?"

Sloan pulled until her hand slipped free. "You ain't my mother."

"You better forget about your mother."

Sloan looked out the window so he wouldn't see the tears forming in her eyes.

"I'm the best friend you got now. You'd be smart to remember that. Them other boys won't watch out for you like I will. Here's your school. I'll sit with you on the way home."

"That's not my school."

"It is now."

A young woman who was barely bigger than Sloan took her hand as soon as she got off the bus. "Hello, Joan, and welcome to our school," she said. "My name is Miss Sally and I'll be showing you around."

"My name is Sloan."

"You will be in Ms. Durham's classroom. She's very nice. Now here is the office and then we go down this hall. The bathrooms, boys and girls, are down that hall. Over there is the cafeteria, but you'll be going with your class so don't worry about finding it. Here we are now. This is where you come every morning." She led Sloan into the classroom and to the desk where a stout woman with short mousy hair sat. Children milled around small desks looking over their shoulders at the new girl. "Everyone, this is Joan Raffienne." Sloan's guide dropped her hand.

"Thank you Miss Sally." The teacher rose from her chair. "Come with me, Joan, and I'll show you your desk." Sloan didn't move. "My name is Sloan," she said. Ms. Durham stopped and peered down at the girl. "What did you say?"

"My name is Sloan."

The woman looked closely at the roster. "It says right here that your name is Joan Raffienne."

"No, it ain't."

Ms. Durham hesitated between a rebuke and taking the girl seriously. She looked into her green eyes. Sloan stared back, and the teacher decided she would check at the office later to see if there was a mistake. In the meantime, she settled the girl at a desk in the front row, being careful not to address her by name. The bell rang and the universal routine of schools across the country began. As soon as Ms. Durham was busy at the blackboard, Sloan slipped from her seat and out the door. Once she was in the hall, she broke into a dead run. She passed several doors before she heard a commotion behind her and, in front of her, heads popped out of classroom doors. "Stop her!" someone yelled. Sloan pelted around a corner. A pleasant-faced matron in a navy-blue suit stepped out of the office into Sloan's path. Behind her, the wide glass doors showed green grass and the road to freedom. Sloan dodged, but the matron proved surprisingly quick on her feet and caught her around the waist. The girl's legs kept pumping and somehow got tangled up with the woman's and the two tumbled to the floor. The matron held on despite the fall, and Sloan was aware of a pleasant smell and the sounds of panting. She struggled, pushing with her fists and kicking her feet, but it was useless. Several other adults took hold of her and held her still. The matron, born and raised in the South, sat up and began patting her white, bouffant hair back into place. There was a great flurry around her, people trying to get her upright, asking over and over, "Mrs. Clark, are you all right?" One woman put her hands under the matron's armpits and tried to heave her to her feet. Mrs. Clark, without seeming to move, disengaged herself from this grasp and said, "That will do." There wasn't the slightest hint of stress in her voice. She took the hand of a man standing in front of her and allowed him to pull her to her feet. Once on her feet, the principal tugged her jacket into place. "Miss Sally, would you walk this little girl back to her classroom?"

"But she knocked you over," someone said.

"We knocked each other over. Stay with her until she is settled, Miss Sally."

Sloan was sent back to the classroom two more times and two more times she attempted an escape. The last time, she barely got out of her seat before Miss Sally, who was amazingly strong for a woman so small, snatched her back into her chair and held her there by her wrists, her arms crossed over her chest.

"Shit!" This from Sloan, loud and clear.

The teacher told Miss Sally to take her to the office. "Maybe Mrs. Clark can do something with her. Her foster father should be here soon." Sally, with a grip of iron on Sloan's wrist, walked her to the office. Mrs. Clark was waiting for them at the door. She had been the school principal for fifteen years and no one could remember ever seeing her lose her buddha-like calm. "I see the Graftons finally got their girl," she said.

"And we get the fallout." The young woman shut the door behind her and locked it.

"Where is she from?" Mrs. Clark went to a file cabinet and opened a drawer. She pulled out a manila folder and flipped through it, reading here and there. "That's strange," she said finally. "Apparently, this little girl is from near Hozelroad Holler." She looked at Sloan, who was watching her steadily. The child didn't resemble the people Mrs. Clark had seen who were raised in that place. She was a strawberry blonde, for one thing. And where did those green eyes come from?

"I've never heard of a child from Hozelroad Holler being in foster care," said Miss Sally.

"My thoughts exactly." Mrs. Clark was too gracious to ask the child questions. She wanted to, but now was not the time. She leaned down, supporting her upper body with her hands on her thighs. "Would you like some crackers? Sally, why don't you go and get Joan a carton of milk." The principal put her hand on the girl's shoulder. "Would you like something to eat and drink, sweetie?" Sloan, her face solemn, nodded. When Miss Sally unlocked and opened the office door, the gray man was standing there, hat in hand. Seeing him, Sloan ran behind the principal's desk and ducked into the cubicle underneath. Mrs. Clark smiled and nodded at Mr. Grafton then moved to sit down at the desk. She tucked her feet under her chair so as not to step on the girl. "Come in. Please. Do sit down. You made good time, I see. Joan is a little nervous after all the changes. It's not a bit unusual." She ducked her head to look at Sloan crouched in the cubby hole and mouthed, "It will be all right."

The man sat holding his hat on his lap. Mrs. Clark laid her plump forearms on her green blotter and folded her hands. "Normally I wouldn't have called you, but we are afraid that Joan might actually make it outside. She's very fast and very determined. If she were to escape from the building, there is traffic to be considered among other mishaps that could befall her. Perhaps, after a night's rest and some reassurance, she will be more prepared to face school tomorrow. She will need lots and lots of reassurance. And just plain tender loving care. It is not unusual for a child in these circumstances to have a rough time the first few days of school." Mrs. Clark leaned under the desk and smiled at the girl. "We will be looking forward to seeing you tomorrow."

Sloan didn't move. "I want to stay with you."

"Will you go back to your classroom and stay there?"

"I want to stay here with you."

"You can't stay here, sweetie. You'll have to go back to your classroom."

Sloan didn't take her eyes off the principal's face. Mrs. Clark put her hand on the top of the child's head. "Why don't you go home now, and we'll start all over tomorrow."

Mr. Grafton leaned in closer and looked down at the desktop. "You come along with me now, Missy," he said loudly, "like the principal told you."

Sloan moved back until she had pressed herself hard against the wood then wrapped her arms around her bent knees.

The man straightened and said crossly, "Can't you make her come out from there?"

Mrs. Clark looked at Miss Sally, who dropped to her knees and scooted toward Sloan. "I'll be waiting for you tomorrow and I'll stay with you all day. Do you like to color? We can color tomorrow. But you have to come out of there now."

Mr. Grafton grabbed Sloan's hand as soon as she crawled into the open. She pulled back, but he dug his fingernails in hard. "I want to stay here," Sloan said, planting her feet and pulling away harder, but the man gave her a quick, effective yank. He thanked the principal and before she could answer, he walked Sloan out the door then through the double doors into the sharp sunlight, holding tight until he picked her up and put her into the front seat of the truck and buckled her in. He slammed the door shut and locked it. When he was sitting behind the wheel, he said, "We will have no more of this behavior, Missy. There will be no supper for you. It will be straight to bed. Consider yourself lucky. If you try this again, I'll have something for you that will make sure you never even think about being so naughty again."

Sloan stared straight ahead. I'll fix you, she thought. I'll be gone by tonight.

At the house, his hand on her shoulder, Grafton propelled her upstairs. When he handed her the pill, Sloan shut her mouth tightly. The man took hold of her jaw the way his wife had only harder and when he had the pill in Sloan's mouth, he stuffed it with his finger toward the back of her throat. His nails scraped her tongue and she gagged. He put one hand under her chin and the other on the top of her head and held her mouth shut. "You swallow that now, you hear me. Do you want some water?" Her mouth was parched, and she gagged again. The man smacked her hard on the ear then held a glass of water to her lips. "Drink," he said. After he took the glass away, he stroked Sloan's hair, petting her as though she were a dog. "There, there, now Missy. Everything will be all right. You just have to learn the rules. This medicine will help you sleep, and tomorrow is a new day." He pushed her gently by the shoulders down onto the bed and pulled the covers under her chin. He smoothed her hair back from her forehead. "Night, night sweet angel."

Chapter Eight

*J*ohn Avery adjusted his tie in front of the full-length mirror propped against a wall in his room. Then he stepped back and gave himself the once over. Christ, he looked like a funeral director. He went back to the closet, hung up his suit and gray tie and pulled out a blue shirt, navy-blue blazer, gray slacks, and yellow tie. He studied himself in the mirror. Now he looked like he should be teaching Psych 101. John undid his tie, threw it on the bed, and unbuttoned his top button. No, too obvious. Dressing down for his client. He put the shirt back and riffled through the rest of the closet. Finally, he settled on a plain white shirt that had been worn and washed many times. Wearing it with a nondescript tie and his khaki pants, he thought he looked sufficiently bland, and the aged cotton had a nice drape.

At the clinic, John leaned against the doorway to Dr. Wittcomb's office, playing with the keys to the state car. She flicked her eyes over him so quickly it might not have happened.

"So," he said, "I don't go in unless she asks me to. I apologize for saying anything about her drinking and I try to find out about her support circle. Friends, relatives… if there are any, and that lawyer—I've talked to her. She mostly asked me questions. She's going to represent her. And DSS is writing up a Service Agreement."

"They should have done that before they took the child. But good for you for checking into things so quickly." They stared at each other for a moment, then Dr. Wittcomb smiled and said, "You'll do fine. Call if you have any questions. Have you got one of our cell phones? Yes. Good."

The sour smell of damp earth or rotting vegetation—sharp and nasty— registered and Clare turned in her sleep. Her arm hit the back of the couch and nudged her from unconsciousness enough to remind her of where she was sleeping and why. A thought, uncensored and clear, brought her fully awake. *I wish I was dead.* It was the first time she had ever in her life felt this way, but she knew it would not be her last. She lay still, breathing slowly in and out, waiting for the room to settle. The noise of horses banging their feed buckets eventually opened her eyes. She looked down at the bucket she had placed next to the couch last night just before she slid into unconsciousness. It was the vomit that she smelled. She didn't remember throwing up. Daylight now filled the room. She'd never slept this late. The horses would be banging at the gate next. Clare tried to remember if she'd fed them last night. She had no recollection of it. Fortunately, she had slept in her clothes to include her boots. She could just get up, walk out the door, and start throwing hay. She might skip the grain. Never, in her entire life with horses, had she not taken pleasure in their care. Every morning, every night, moving among them slowly, deliberately, putting out grain and hay, filling water buckets, running her hands over backs, legs, taking in their condition, checking for any mishaps that might have befallen them when she wasn't looking. Now, she walked across the hall into the room Gram had once called the parlor. After the barn had collapsed, Pap had used it for storage, and it was filled with bales of hay and bags of grain. It smelled innocent and sweet, and of days that now felt like a foreign country. Clare climbed to the top of the piled hay and threw a bale to the floor. She dragged it out the front door, letting it thump behind her down the porch steps. She tore the twine from the bale and then threw pads over the fence, spacing the distance between them to prevent fights. The horses flew at the food with their ears pinned. She checked the water trough.

Half full. That would do. She paused long enough to scan the horizon. The trees had just started to bud and between them you could still see into the forest. Nothing there.

Back in the kitchen, she made a whiskey and coke, sipping from it as she rummaged through the cupboard for some bread. She couldn't find even a forgotten slice, so she spooned peanut butter from a jar. She decided she would go to the school and grab her daughter during recess, but then realized she didn't know what school Sloan attended now. She'd find out from Avery. He could be good for something, anyway. She wouldn't ask Annie. Not after eight years. She knew this plan was impossible, that it would only kill any chance she had for getting her daughter back quickly, but she needed to plan something. She couldn't wait for others to do the job for her. She would go into town and get some groceries and call Avery. She picked up his card where he had left it on the table. He probably was under strict instruction not to tell her where Sloan was. She'd get it out of him though. She really should empty that pail of vomit. The whiskey was making her head light. She went into the living room and sat on the couch. Now, let's see. Bread. Milk. Cereal. She propped her elbows on her knees and put her head in her hands. The vomit smelled awful. Clare took the pail outside, where she threw the contents into the driveway. Then she went back inside and sat on the couch again. Bread, milk, cereal, maybe some cheese and Coke. She was almost out of Coke. It was impossible, of course. Going into the grocery store without Sloan begging for candy, running ahead, disappearing around an aisle to get the cocoa puffs or some other dreadful candy cereal, having to be told no, no, no and finally settling on some treat to be handed over only after they had loaded the groceries in the truck. Clare decided to go to the 7-Eleven and buy a hot dog. She could load up on Coke there. She drained her glass, feeling quite lightheaded. She sighed. I ain't even hungry, she thought. She could always drink the whiskey straight. She laid down and put her arm over her eyes to block out the daylight. Let the damn room swim.

John was shocked all over again by the acres of inhabited dump, no earth showing anywhere and the shacks barely discernable. How could people live like this? Where in this mess did they actually call home? Three men were standing by the side of the road, doing, as far as John could see, nothing but watching him approach. He resisted the urge to accelerate. Everything about them was monochrome, and they stood as still as the decaying debris around them. He was careful not to meet their eyes when he drove past.

Clare's house, by comparison, seemed the height of respectability, even though in town it could only have belonged in the nastiest neighborhood. John tapped lightly on the door. He spoke to the peeled paint. "It's me, John Avery, and I've come to apologize." He felt like an idiot, but to his amazement Clare answered him almost immediately. "Come on in," she called.

The house smelled awful, worse than the first time. Clare met him in the kitchen. Her hair was a snarled mess, her face carved and full of shadows, a bony specter. She dropped into a seat. "Well?"

Avery sat down across from her. "I'm sorry I criticized your drinking. I shouldn't have done that."

Clare looked straight at him, her eyes black and with no expression he could read. "I need to know where Sloan is living," she said.

"She's living with the Graftons out on route 301."

Clare blinked and missed a beat. Then she resumed quickly, getting the details of how far out on 301 and was the house right off the road and what did it look like? John answered these questions as easily as he had the first and before she had time to marvel, Clare knew exactly where her daughter was staying. "Well," she said.

Noticing her expression, John wondered if he'd said anything he shouldn't. He frowned. Maybe the mother wasn't supposed to know where her daughter was. He saw no logic in that. She couldn't do anything about it, after all. There was no danger that she would just show up at the door and take the child. The law would be on her in a flash. She must know that. "Say," he said. "Are you doing okay?"

"Sure. I'm fine. The government has snatched my kid, but I'm just fine. And you been telling tales about me to strangers."

John looked confused.

"Annie Voight's been out here."

"Oh, right." He reached into his briefcase on the floor. "I brought a release for you to sign."

"Ain't you supposed to do that before you blab my business?"

John leaned against the back of the chair. "Look. Ms. Voight is your advocate and I'm in a hurry to get your daughter back."

"So you keep saying. You still had no right to blab my business. Anyway, you want to do something for me? You can take me to the grocery store."

"What?"

"You got any kids?"

"No. I'm not married."

"I can't go into Safeway and pick out groceries like nothin' has happened. I can't pick out stuff just for me. If you had kids, you'd know that."

"Of course. I totally understand. I'll take you," John said, standing up. "I'll take you right now."

In Safeway, Clare raced down the aisles throwing corn flakes, milk, bread, frozen dinners, large bottles of Coke, American cheese, mayonnaise, hot dogs, bacon, and eggs into the cart. She moved fast, sometimes doubling back for things she had forgotten. John managed to keep up. When Clare headed for the checkout, he said, "Wait. Do you mind if we go over here to the deli? I want to pick up something for lunch and their rotisserie chicken is hard to beat." He turned toward it without waiting for an answer. "I'll have that chicken, please," he said, pointing. "And some macaroni and cheese." He turned to Clare. "I have a weakness for their mac-and-cheese. I'll have more of that if you don't mind, make it two quarts. Thank you. And some of those green beans. A quart will do." When he turned around, Clare's eyebrows were drawn together and she looked as though she might say something, but she turned away from him and walked over to the cashier, where she grabbed her things out of the cart. She reached into her jeans, paid the bill, and then John paid for the deli items, and they drove back to Clare's without a word. John helped Clare put her groceries into the cabinet, which he noticed had a film of grease over it like at his home. He put the chicken, the macaroni and green beans on the table and began opening drawers.

"What are you doing?"

"Looking for plates and knives and forks. Ah. Here they are." John put a set of two on the table. He put a chicken leg and thigh on each plate, then large mounds of macaroni and cheese and he split the green beans between them. "Come," he said. "Sit down. Before it gets cold."

Clare poured out two glasses of Coke and put them on the table. She poured some whiskey into her glass. Then she raised the bottle toward John and waited. He looked at the amber liquid and at Clare's big-boned hand.

"I ain't got the shakes, if that's what you're wondering."

"I wasn't," he lied. "And sure, I'll have some. But just a bit."

Clare ate the chicken with her fingers and for the macaroni and green beans she leaned over her plate, scooping large forkfuls into her mouth. John had a sudden, strange urge to touch her hair, to straighten out the tangles. They ate in silence. When Clare had finished the thigh and leg, she pulled half the breast from the bones and ate that. John offered her more macaroni and cheese, but she shook her head and burped.

"I'll put it in the refrigerator then." He gathered up what little was left of the chicken and pasta and put them away. There was a slice of stiff cheese lying on a rack and that was it. Clare slumped in her chair as though drugged.

"I'm going to arrange a meeting with Charlene Platt, the social worker, Ms. Voight, you, and myself as soon as possible. Maybe the end of this week. First part of next at the very latest. We'll get the details of the service agreement. Word for word." He said this quickly to avoid objections, but Clare barely seemed to be listening. "Well, then." John stood and smiled. "I'll come by to let you know when the meeting is." Clare put her elbow on the table and propped her head in hand. She watched him quietly. Finally, she said, "You didn't drink your whiskey."

Chapter Nine

The brown boy sat next to Sloan on the bus again the next day. Sloan didn't remember breakfast or getting to the bus stop, but she did remember climbing up the bus stairs with the gray man right behind her. He nudged her into a seat, leaned close, and said, "You have a good day at school, hear?" As soon as he was gone, Nathaniel slipped in beside her. "Look," he said. He tore a small bit of paper from his notebook. He twisted and squeezed it to the size of a pea and put it into his mouth and rolled his tongue so that it disappeared.

"What are you doing?"

"Teachin' you how to cheek your meds."

Sloan jerked her knees apart, leaned over, and retched onto the floor.

"Shit." Nathaniel jumped out of the seat into the aisle, but there was nothing in Sloan's stomach except a watery yellow liquid that splashed on the floor and against her sneakers. When her dry heaves were over, the boy sat down and patted her back. "It's the meds makin' you sick."

Sloan spit several times, wiped her mouth on the back of her hand, and leaned her head against the seat.

"You got to learn to cheek that shit. Now watch." He demonstrated again with a tiny wad of paper. Sloan began to cry.

"Well, now's prob'ly not the best time. But you got to learn soon." Nat lifted a strand of her hair. "How come your hair is wet?"

"It ain't."

"Yeah, it is. You don't know what happened 'cause you was too drugged up." He stared straight ahead. "How old are you?"

"Eight, but I'll be nine in September."

"That's practically a year away, Joanie."

"My name ain't Joan. It's Sloan."

"My name ain't Nathaniel either. It's Nat, as in Nat Turner, but the Graftons, they didn't like that. They change just about everybody's name. Now I know what your name is, I'll call you by it when we're alone. And you can call me Nat. Don't cry. Here, let me wipe your face. There. Here's your school. I'll see you when you get home, and we'll work on the meds thing again."

Miss Sally took Sloan firmly by the hand the minute she stepped onto the ground, but the girl had no intention of running this time.

"Would you like breakfast?"

There were other children in the cafeteria. Miss Sally put a box of Fruit Loops, a carton of milk, and an apple on Sloan's tray. She sat very close to her at the table and poured the milk over the cereal. Sloan slowly put a spoonful in her mouth then spit it back in the bowl.

Miss Sally jerked away. "What are you doing? Heavens, are you sick?"

Sloan kept her head down, blinking back tears. "I'm okay," she said eventually.

The aide wiped Sloan's dress with a napkin. "There now. Are you feeling any better? Would you like an apple? No. Well, that's okay. It's no wonder if you don't feel good."

"Where's the woman with the white hair?"

"Do you mean Ms. Clark? She's busy now, but I'm going to take you to your classroom and I'm going to stay right there with you. Are you all right to go to your classroom or do you want to see the nurse? Are you feeling sick again?"

Sloan shook her head. "I want to go see that woman with the white hair."

"You can't. She's the principal. That means she runs this whole school and that makes her very busy. And you have to go to your classroom. Come on. Let's put your tray away."

"I need my mother."

Miss Sally sighed, picked up the tray with one hand, and placed it on a stack while holding Sloan's hand with the other. "Come on then," she said. "Let's go to class."

Chapter Ten

Annie Voigt sat on Clare's right, John Avery on her left at the Department of Social Services, waiting. They had been waiting for some time now. Clare, in worn jeans, battered cowboy boots, and a flannel shirt, sat still, staring at the door. Annie knew that look. Once she had known Clare Raffienne better than anyone and even after eight years, she knew what she was capable of. Even so, there had been a time when no one felt safe around her except Annie. A time, in fact, when Annie hadn't felt safe anywhere else.

The door opened and Ms. Platt entered. She positioned a chair so she could face the trio. Her skirt stretched and hiked up her legs, revealing far more than Annie cared to see. Ms. Platt spoke to John. "Who is this with you?"

Annie started to speak, but John cut her off. "This is Ms. Voight. A friend of Ms. Raffienne's."

"It's nice of you to come, Ms. Voight, but it really isn't appropriate that you be here. We have to respect the Raffiennes' confidentiality."

"Ms. Raffienne has given permission for Ms. Voight to be here. She wants her here. She is a close friend and support."

Annie looked at John.

"Ms. Raffienne doesn't have custody of her daughter anymore. We do. And it's the child's rights we must be aware of. We have to respect her confidentiality."

John spoke slowly. "Ms. Platt," he said. "We all agree that the goal is reunification, correct?"

"Yes, but…"

"Well, doesn't it make sense that Ms. Raffienne be allowed the support she needs so that she can make the changes that CPS will require of her?"

"Of course, she will need support and should have it, but you, Mr. Avery, are providing her with in-home services and then there are parenting classes that she could attend."

"However, nothing can take the place of a true friend. No professional can do that."

"Nonetheless, we have to respect the child's confidentiality."

"Look," Annie said, "I'm her lawyer. I'm here to represent the family."

"Lawyer! No one said anything about a lawyer being present."

Annie blinked. "I'm just here as support. To help Clare understand what's going on." Clare stared at Annie. "I mean in terms of the law… as her lawyer."

"This is extremely unusual. In fact, it has never happened before. I am going to have to talk to my supervisor about it." The social worker pulled her skirt down as far as it would go then rose. "I won't be long. Please stay here until my supervisor talks to you." She straightened her jacket and left the room.

After Ms. Platt had gone, Annie leaned forward and looked at John Avery, who wouldn't meet her gaze. She sat back against her chair. "I guess I should have called first. Or someone should have."

"You're just here as a support," said John. "I saw no reason to call."

Annie noticed a small, frilly embroidered pillow on the desk. Drawings hung on the walls of smiling adults along with smiling children. From their expressions, there were no cares or worries in their lives that could possibly affect those grins. On the far wall was a large poster with grown-up hands reaching toward smaller ones, some of them already clasped, and the words *Pennsylvania Loves Her Children* in bold letters.

Right. Annie's sigh could be heard in the dangerously quiet room along with the banal ticking of a clock. She had a right to be here, she knew that, but nothing good was going to come of it. Heavy steps approached, followed by the determined click of high heels. Ms. Platt entered the office followed by a thin, sharp-edged woman in an exquisite red suit and matching red and white stilettos.

"This is Ms. Brockett, my supervisor."

John stood and held out his hand. "John Avery."

The thin woman reached her hand toward him, squeezed, released, and folded her arms under a nonexistent bosom. She gave Annie the once over then turned back to John. "Mr. Avery, one does not bring a lawyer to this sort of meeting. This is not a litigious matter. This is the Department of Social Services, not the courthouse. We are not working for the Justice System. In all the years I have worked for this agency, no one has done anything like this before. Is Dr. Wittcomb aware that you brought a lawyer to this meeting?"

"Not to this meeting, no."

"Good." Mrs. Brokett switched her weight to one hip, her tone instructional, and created a smile showing well cared for teeth. "In the future, Mr. Avery, talk to your supervisor before arranging a meeting with us." She sat at Ms. Platt's desk, her eyes still on Avery. "You must be new. We've never met." Her smile softened. "So. How long have you been at the Health Department?"

"A few months," he lied.

"And this is your first case?"

John said nothing.

"There's a learning curve. You'll know better next time." Silence sat heavy while Ms. Brockett continued smiling at John.

Annie thought, why, she's trying to flirt with him. "If it helps," she said abruptly, "I'll leave, and you can discuss the service agreement. I'll just see it later when I visit my client."

Ms. Brokett turned to her. "You see. The very use of the word client implies that you are serving as her attorney not her friend." Ms. Brocket looked back at John and again smiled. "I will let you know when we have a service plan ready to discuss with *your* client. Do you have a card? I will call you."

"I thought the service agreement was finished. It should have been finished before you took Clare's daughter into custody."

"I don't know where you got that idea."

"It makes sense."

Ms. Brockett kept smiling, but the smile had changed. "Ms. Platt will call you when it is drawn up, Mr. Avery." She rose from the desk. "And the next time you come to DSS, there is no need to bring a lawyer."

As soon as the social workers were out of the room, Clare stood. "The next time you two want to help me get my girl back, be sure to let me know."

"Your hired help stinks."

Dr. Wittcomb looked up, took in the yellow skin and the swollen eyelids. "Come in," she said. "Sit down." Clare sat in the chair next to the desk. She was trembling.

"What happened?"

"The lady at DSS wouldn't talk to us cause Avery brought a lawyer."

"Do you mean Annie Voight?"

Clare dropped her head into her hands, her elbows on her knees. Dr. Wittcomb was so shocked, she missed a beat and took a breath. "Marshall Teige is the best lawyer in town by a long shot. He wouldn't have hired Annie Voight if he didn't think she was very good." The older woman didn't know what was or was not going on between Ms. Voight and Clare Raffienne, but it must be bad to get this reaction.

"One thing we know for certain," she continued when Clare didn't raise her head. "You will have to go to parenting classes. That's standard. You're in luck on that score. There is a new round starting this week. Go to it. Don't miss a class. Not one. You won't have to do much except say you're sorry, you'll never do it again, you've learned the error of your ways. That sort of thing." Dr. Wittcomb couldn't imagine Clare saying anything of the sort, but still.

"How long," Clare asked into her hands.

"Twelve weeks."

Clare snapped into an upright position. "Twelve weeks! Are you kidding me?"

"No."

"I can't leave Sloan with strangers for twelve weeks. You know that! Jesus!"

Dr. Wittcomb felt that sick feeling again, the one that came when she was confronted with the death grip of bureaucracy. Most of the time she could follow the tracks of an agency's thinking, ruinous though it might be. This time she couldn't even get that far. With someone else she might have tried to smooth things over, make the whole thing seem less bizarre, less… well, sinister. "I agree with you, this is a mess," she said, looking directly into Clare's eyes. "I've been at this job a long time and thought I had a handle on DSS, but this doesn't make any sense to me. I can promise you I'm going to do the very best I can to get to the bottom of it and move things along as soon as possible. In the meantime, go to those classes. And let Avery come to your house every week. Be there and don't throw him out even if he says something stupid. He really is on your side. So is the lawyer."

The gray man petted Sloan's hair. They were in the kitchen, standing next to the sink. "Now Joan, I want you to call me Father. You don't have to call me Father Grafton. Just Father will do. Now open your mouth, please." He held the pill in his free hand. "Open your mouth, please." When Sloan hesitated, he tugged lightly on her hair. "Open, please." Sloan opened her mouth, and he placed the pill on her tongue then reached for the glass of water and held it against her mouth and before she realized what to do, she swallowed. "Good girl. Now Mother will get you ready for bed. Mother," he called, "Sloan has taken her medicine, and you can put her to bed now." His wife came into the kitchen and motioned for Sloan to follow her. "I don't know why you think I can't give her the meds."

"I just want to be on the safe side."

"On the safe side. What's that supposed to mean?"

"Mother." Mr. Grafton flicked his eyes at the girl. When his wife continued standing stubbornly in the doorway, he said, "You can do it next time, all right?"

Mrs. Grafton led Sloan through the room where the boys were watching TV. When Nat saw her, he caught her eye, said, "Saved," to the other boys and then followed her soundlessly up the stairs. He caught her by the hand just outside her door. "Did you do it?" he whispered. Sloan shook her head.

"You get outta here, Nathaniel," said Mrs. Grafton.

"I need to talk to Joan a minute."

"Well, you can't and you know that."

"Stay away from that boy," she said after she led Sloan into her bedroom and shut the door behind them. "He's a bad one. Now get in your pajamas." Sloan began to undress, turning her back to the woman.

"You don't need to do that. Ain't like I never seen it before. That boy ever touch you?"

Sloan didn't know what she meant but shook her head anyway.

"You come tell me if he does. He's a bad one. Stay away from him. You tell me if he touches you funny. Now get in bed."

"How come I have to go to bed before the boys?"

"Cause you're younger, you know that."

"I want to watch TV."

"Ain't nothing on there for a little girl to see."

"Pleeease." Tears formed on the edge of Sloan's lids.

Mrs. Grafton stood with her hands on her hips, looking at her. "You can't sit with them boys. But maybe some afternoon you and I can watch something. Now don't you dare cry." She held the covers up while Sloan, not wanting to push her luck, hustled into bed. The woman pulled the blanket awkwardly under her chin and smoothed it flat. Before she turned the light off on the way out, she said over her shoulder, "Night Miss Raggedy Ann."

Annie returned to her apartment and changed into jeans, a turtleneck, and windbreaker. She pulled on footwear that could, maybe, pass as paddock boots, then took them off and put on sneakers instead.

She didn't knock, instead stuck her head in Clare's back door, called, and stepped inside. Her friend entered the kitchen from the living room and said nothing. She pushed her hair away from her face, went to the sink, and washed out the glass she'd been carrying and turned around. "You've changed your clothes," she said.

"Clare, listen. When I left, I left everything. I put it all behind me. You know what I mean. Stewart. Lydia. Jack. The farm. All of it."

"And I was part of it?"

"No. Of course, not. Look, I know I let you down. I have no excuse. I guess I couldn't separate things out."

"So why did you come back?"

"It just wasn't working. I got my law degree. That was okay, being in school. Then a job with, as it turned out, some very bad people, so I got a different job, and they were just as bad only pretended not to be. I dated. A lot. Lots of men. I didn't like any of it. Then one of them tried… well, you know, but I remembered something you taught me and got out of it. Then I got mugged in a parking garage just like out of some B-list movie. That was it. I just wanted to come home, so here I am. Maybe I'll buy a little piece of land, keep some horses on it. Pay for it by working for Marshall. Get into the business again, maybe with you. That's what I've been thinking."

Clare moved her hands to her jean pockets, crossed one leg over the other, hip against the sink. "The Norton farm… I mean your place, or your ex's place, sold about five, six years ago."

"Yeah?" Annie knew this but wanted to keep Clare talking.

"It's all fancied up now. Some doctor bought it. Kinda funny, huh. Guess he knew your ex's parents. Lives out there with a friend. They keep to their selves. Have some horses, but don't seem to do nothin' with 'em. I go by it on my way to town. They even paved the damn driveway."

Annie smiled. "Can you believe it? That old place all gussied up." She reached into her briefcase, brought out some papers, and held them toward Clare. "It's the service agreement."

Clare retrieved the documents from Annie's hand, held them between thumb and forefinger, but didn't look at them. "Dr. Wittcomb says I have to go to parenting classes."

"Uh huh."

"And let that Avery come out here any time he wants to."

Annie nodded again.

"If I do, will I get Sloan back?"

"If you do everything written there, they shouldn't be able to keep her from you." Annie stopped.

"What?"

"Look, Clare, I'm going to be straight with you about this. Technically, they should have to return Sloan to you once you do all those things. But I don't get why they took her in the first place. You practically have to kill your kid to get Child Protective Services to take action. This doesn't make sense. I have no idea why they've taken an interest in Sloan, a kid from the Holler. You may have moved up the mountain, but they're still your folks down there. You know what I mean. It's just weird. CPS never gets involved with people from the Holler. And not certainly for the reasons they list."

"Then I shouldn't have to do what they say."

"But you do."

"But even if I do, I might not get her back?"

"I'm lead counsel on this. But Marshall will help if I need him. He's the best. They don't get any better. But it may not even come to that. It's just that I can't figure out why they've taken her."

Clare straightened, moved away from the sink, hummed a tuneless melody, and went into the storage room. Annie followed and watched as she dug behind the hay in the far corner of the room. She pulled out a shotgun and cocked the barrels open, sighted down them.

"What are you going to do with that?"

"Shoot a deer," Clare said without looking up.

Annie started to say it wasn't even near deer season but thought better of it. Clare returned to the kitchen, rummaged under the sink, pulled out a rusty can, a rag and stick, and sat at the table. She continued to hum as she oiled the gun then fell silent. Annie sat at the table with her. The evening shadows turned long and came in through the window. The two women remained in silence for a timeless period, and in that silence and half-light, with the smell of burned wood and gun oil, and Clare bent over a task in the bare room, Annie felt it happening. As fine and delicate and breakable as the veins in a new leaf, the thing that was between them drew breath and began to live again.

That afternoon, as soon as the children jumped off the bus and crossed the road, Nat pinched strands of Sloan's hair in his fingers, keeping her from following the other boys as they ran up the hill toward the house. She stood obediently by his side for an instant, glanced at the Greenhouse, pulled her hair from his grasp and started up the road. From behind her, Nat took her hand and broke into a run, pulling her along. He yanked her behind the outbuilding where they had sat her first morning here. He reached into his jeans and pulled out two pieces of red licorice wrapped in clear plastic. As soon as she saw them, Sloan's mouth began to water. The Graftons didn't believe in sugar, not on cereal, not in the form of cookies, cakes, pies, soda, candy, not in any form at all except for a-king-sized-loaf of white bread, jelly, and plain Corn Flakes. Nat waggled the licorice in front of Sloan, who kept her hands at her sides. "They'll miss us," she said.

"No, they won't. I told you that. We got some time. Let's sit down. Don't you want your candy? I stole it from the treat tray at school cause I was thinking of you."

Sloan kept her eyes on the candy and her hands at her side. Nat peeled back the cellophane, pulled out one red stick, and held it toward the girl. She took it. Then he held out the other stick. "For the other hand."

"Don't you want any?"

Nat reached into the other pocket and pulled out an identical package. He grinned and slid down the side of the shed, settling into a cross-legged position, his back against the wall. Sloan put a stick of licorice in her mouth and closed her eyes. Nat took her fingers and pulled gently. She plopped next to him still concentrating on the candy, pulling off pieces with her teeth and chewing, saliva filling her mouth. She sucked, swallowed, started on the second stick. "I'm going to run away," she said.

"Oh, sure."

Sloan put her fingers in her mouth and pried the candy from between her teeth. "I am. I just gotta figure out how to get by the Graftons."

"There ain't no place to run to."

"You're just chicken."

Nat gave her a sharp look. "I sure as hell ain't."

"Come with me?"

"No way."

"Why not, if you ain't chicken."

"Cause it's just stupid, that's why. Look around. Ain't nothing but woods."

"Ain't nothin' wrong with woods. I live in the woods. It's fine in the woods."

"There's bears in the woods."

"I know. I own one. Her name is Sister."

"You're going to sit there and tell me you own a bear. And people call me a liar."

"I do."

"The hell you do."

Sloan looked at her pink stained fingers. She kept her eyes lowered, breathed through her mouth, and would not look at the boy when he nudged her. He nudged her again then shoved her, nearly knocking her over. "Don't get all sulky just 'cause I said you don't own no bear. Look, you're getting dirt all over your sticky hands."

Sloan looked up into Nat's face. "I do own a bear."

"Course you do. You've got the most beautiful eyes I ever seen, you know that. Green like water."

Sloan began to cry.

"Hush. Stop now or someone will hear you."

"My mama's dead."

"Really? Is that why you're in foster care?"

"No. She was alive when they took me."

"Then how do you know she's dead?"

"She hasn't come to get me."

"Oh, that don't mean she's dead. Our parents ain't allowed to get us. The government won't let them. It's taken us away from our folks so they can pay people like the Graftons to take care of us. My papa sold drugs and mama used them. She was high most of the time, but when she wasn't, she was a good mom. Hell of a lot better than the Graftons."

"My mama didn't sell drugs."

"Maybe not, but she must have done something the government could use."

Sloan blinked, rubbed her eyes with the back of her hand. "Use for what?"

"Like I said. So, they can pay people like the Graftons. It's a plot. You know, I think I will run away with you. Do you know which direction your home is?"

"Yes," Sloan lied.

"Good. I gotta go change and get to work now, so do you, but tomorrow after school we can plot our escape."

When Mr. Grafton held out the pill for Sloan that evening, she put it on her tongue, shut her lips and held it against the roof of her mouth while sipping at the water. As soon as the man turned away to place the glass on the table, the girl put her hand to her mouth and eased out the pill. During her turn in the bathroom, she dropped it into the toilet and flushed.

Lying in bed, Sloan stared at the ceiling. So her mama wasn't dead. The government was keeping her away. Sloan had no idea what the government was, but whatever or whoever it was, they were paying the Graftons to keep her. But Sloan knew her mother. She couldn't imagine anyone or anything being able to take her away from her mama. She would ask Nat tomorrow exactly what this government thing was. She laid in bed and tried to picture it. It must be some kind of enemy soldiers or boogey men. Criminals of some sort. She had seen lots of men shooting each other on the TV when the Graftons weren't looking. Her mother would never let them take her without a fight. Maybe she was dead after all, shot through the heart trying to rescue her. Sloan began to shake. I'm going to be sick, she thought, and she threw up into the wastepaper basket. She flopped back on the bed, held still until her stomach stopped heaving, and then got up and went to the window. She leaned her forehead against the cool pane, resting there then looking down until her eyes adjusted and she could make out the porch roof below. She was pretty sure she could make the jump. The problem would be to not roll off. It didn't look like there was much to grab to stop from tumbling onto the ground below. But the roof would break her fall, anyway. She considered getting Nat, but it was too risky. What if one of the boys he shared a room with woke up? Sloan tiptoed to her closet, felt around like a blind person until her fingers made out a pair of pants and shirt. She pulled them on over her pajamas. Who knew how long a trip this would be. She found her sneakers easily, but the socks were on a shelf in the back of the closet. It took her some time to move soundlessly through the clothes without rattling the hangers until she thought to drop to all fours and then made straight away to where the socks lay, tucked into tidy balls.

Fully dressed, Sloan put her hands against the window frame and shoved upwards. Nothing happened. She pushed harder. The window wouldn't budge. The girl tried the latch. It resisted movement too. Acid tears sprung to her eyes. Sloan decided to risk turning on the light. She would beat the lock open with a shoe. It was shaped like the maple leaf pods that drifted through the air in the spring. She would have to be very careful not to make too much noise, so she covered her sneaker with a sock and tapped carefully. The wings shifted slightly, and the girl tapped harder, pushing against the resistance as she did so. When the lock broke free, she gave a little gasp. She grabbed the bottom of the frame and pushed. Nothing. It was then Sloan noticed the nails, one in each corner of the window and two in the middle. She dropped onto the floor and bit her lip to keep from crying out loud. Sitting with her arms around her legs, head on her knees, tears and snot soaked her pants. She sat rocking and rocking, murmuring, "Mama" over and over. What a coward she was. Her mother would never let a little thing like a nailed window get in her way. But Sloan could not bring herself to make the terrible noise of smashing it apart, shattering the glass. Not in this deathly quiet house. Not with Mrs. Grafton and her square immobile face and Mr. Grafton's long, strong, and bony hands.

A dirty gray light came in the window before Sloan took off her pants and shirt and returned them and the sneakers and socks, rolled into fists, to the closet. She crawled into bed and fell into a sleep so deep she might as well have taken that pill.

Chapter Eleven

The weather had turned warm, and through Clare's screen door John Avery could smell bacon cooking. She beckoned him in as though she had been expecting him. Her skin was paler than ever, but her eyes were clear, and the puffiness was gone. She was tall, almost as tall as he, and the white skin accentuated her dark eyes. He abruptly sat at the kitchen table. He didn't say a word while Clare finished her cooking. He watched her add eggs to the bacon grease, flip them, and put slices of bread into the toaster. Her hair was pulled into a thick braid down her back and out of the way. She moved without effort, her mind seemingly elsewhere. She slid a plate of food across the table to John and sat opposite him.

"I brought you some honey," he said, taking it out of a paper bag. "From that stand down the road."

"Perfect." Clare slathered it on her toast, which she dipped into the egg yolks. The honey and butter glistened on her lips. She ate steadily, four pieces of toast, six slices of bacon, and three eggs. Occasionally, she licked the honey from her fingers.

John had only had a cup of coffee on his way here and was suddenly famished. They ate in silence. When they both were finished, he washed his hands in the sink to get rid of the sticky honey and then he leaned against the counter. He watched Clare as she washed the dishes, squirting soap from the container onto an old washcloth, running it around the plates, into the glasses, scrubbing the knives and forks, then holding them under the water letting it flow around them and over her hands. Finally, she put them in the plastic dish rack to dry. She looked up, only to glance out the window over the sink. John kept his eyes on her hands, never her face.

"So, tonight is the first parenting class."

Clare did not indicate she had heard.

"I'll take you if you want me to."

"I know how to get there." They still didn't look at each other.

"I was thinking since this is your first time you might like someone along for the drive." John shifted his gaze to the floor.

"I guess that would be okay, for the one time." She rubbed her wet hands on the back of her jeans. They watched each other. "You're not married, right? No kids?"

"No."

"Sisters? Brothers?"

"Actually, I have eight brothers and one sister."

"Eight brothers. Wow. Is it fun? I'm an only child. I always wanted a sister. Or brother."

"It's okay. We're not so close. They're all into different things."

"What about your sister?"

"She's only five. The baby."

Clare dropped her head then looked back at John. "Bring her here. I want to meet her."

"What? I can't do that."

"Sure, you can. What harm would it do?"

"I think it's against the rules."

"Do you know how good it would be to have a little girl running through the house again? Nothin' bad will happen to her, if that's what you're thinking. Does she like horses?"

"Ahhh… I don't know. Probably. She likes a lot of things. But Clare, it's a boundary issue."

"Oh, for God's sake." Clare pushed away from the sink. "Boundary issues.

Here you are comin' to my house three, four times a week and you're talking about boundaries. I bet she'd love a pony ride and I got just the pony for her."

"She's different, Clare. She's not like other kids."

"How so?"

"She doesn't talk."

"Not at all?"

"No."

"Is she slow or something?"

"No. She just doesn't want to talk."

Clare held still, let the idea fill her. "Well," she said. Then finally, "Bring her here. I think she'd love it."

Eight or nine people were hanging out in the parking lot when John Avery pulled in. They were smoking and drinking cans of soda and Clare thought she saw someone with a can of beer in a paper bag.

"I see I got dressed up for nothing," she said. She wore her flannel shirt tucked in, had a belt in the loops of her jeans, and her hair was brushed.

"You look fine," said John. He guided her through the stares of the men and women and the haze of smoke hanging over their heads and inside to the reception window. Clare paid her fifteen-dollar fee and sat next to him to wait. She crossed her legs, uncrossed them, folded her arms across her midriff.

John looked at her hands then up to her profile, which resembled a Greek head on a coin. "Are you nervous?"

"No."

By the quickness and firmness of the reply, John realized she was lying and was surprised by his surprise. It occurred to him suddenly he was slightly afraid of Clare Raffienne. He glanced away, embarrassed. She was the client, he the professional. How could he be afraid of her? It was this in-home therapy. Going into her house. He wished now he had held out for a regular therapist's job. One with an office. Yet, he wasn't afraid of his other clients. He looked down at her boots. They must have been for wearing in town, he thought, since they were without any scuff marks and clean. He blinked at the surge of tenderness caused by this thought and resisted putting a reassuring hand on her knee. "You will be fine," he said instead.

Clare flicked him a look.

The group from outdoors wandered into the lobby, though they did not sit down. An extraordinarily short and round young woman opened a door and said, "Nurturing Parent Group." John nodded and Clare followed the others down the hall. She couldn't take her eyes off the young woman's behind, which seemed to have a life of its own bobbling up, down, and sideways. In a large room, chairs were arranged in a semi-circle, with one facing them, presumably for the leader. Clare sat at the very end and glanced around the room, realizing with a stir that she recognized all the men. It was nice to be here with some familiar faces. She smiled at a tall young man who looked like Tom Sawyer grown up, but he quickly turned away, pretending he hadn't noticed. The young social worker took her seat facing the group. The sides of her thighs extended so far off the chair Clare knew it had to hurt. She was so short only her toes touched the floor.

"We'll start by going around the group and introducing ourselves. I'm Shahanna Soffee," the social worker said. She was young, maybe mid-twenties, with black, thick, wavy hair, eyes almost as black, and a rose bud red mouth. Clare thought she was beautiful and that it was too bad this culture had such a thing about being fat. She must have been staring because Ms. Soffee looked at her and smiled. "Why don't you start? Tell us your name and a little about yourself."

Clare's chest tightened. She had never spoken in front of a group before. "I'm Clare," she said.

A scrawny woman about Clare's age put her hand beside her mouth and whispered to the woman next to her, "I told you that was her."

"What?" asked Shahanna, her eyebrows raised and her smile encouraging. The thin woman looked down at her hands in her lap and said nothing. The room remained uncomfortably silent.

"We share all conversation here," Ms. Soffee ventured uncertainly. The group members looked carefully at nothing, avoiding eye contact. No one spoke. Clare glanced at each of the four men then at the group leader, whose cheeks were growing pink. Shahanna smiled at her. "Go on, Clare. Can you tell us a little about yourself?"

"Ha." This from the woman who had whispered.

Shahaana turned toward her. "What?"

"Nothing."

The social worker's cheeks were crimson by now. Clare shifted in her chair. She was pretty sure she knew the cause of the silence. She looked at each of the women carefully. Two looked vaguely familiar but she didn't really know them. They all gave her heavy, sullen looks while the men looked everywhere but at her. It was all ancient history, water under the bridge. It hadn't meant anything back then, or not much, and it certainly didn't mean anything now. It was obvious this strange young social worker with flaming red cheeks and lips hadn't a clue about the people in this town or their histories. With her coloring she could be middle eastern. At any rate, she definitely wasn't native to the area. Clare decided to help her out. "Ms. Soffee," she said. "It's just that I been with every guy in this room, but it was a long time ago so it don't really matter."

The social worker's eyebrows rose. "Been?"

"Like in having sex."

Shahanna's face went utterly blank. She looked like she'd been shot with a tranquilizer gun. She didn't move or blink for so long Clare looked at the others to see if they knew what was happening. No one appeared willing to help the situation along and the men were trying to become invisible. The room became as heavy as Shahanna Soffee was still. Was she having some kind of epileptic fit? Caused by shock? Finally, Clare said, "Miss, it's okay 'cause I ain't involved with any of them now and don't intend to be. So, it's okay,"

"Well." Ms. Soffee inhaled, let her air out with a small huff. "Is this going to be a problem for anyone here?"

What could the group do but laugh? And in so doing, any control the social worker might have hoped for was gone and Clare realized that until she got her daughter back, she would spend one hour and thirty minutes every

Wednesday night in this room for no reason she could possibly figure out.

John watched the group straggle down the hall in clusters of two or three to wait outside for the public bus. Clare came last and walked alone with a bemused expression on her face until she saw John and then she smiled, catching him off guard. She came and stood in front of him, and he rose awkwardly, careful not to bump into her. "How did it go?" he said, taking a half step back.

"Um, I'm not sure."

John stretched his arm in the direction of her back without actually touching her as he turned toward the door to the parking lot. "What did you talk about?"

"Nothing."

"You're right. I shouldn't have asked."

"Mostly people talked to each other or made stupid jokes. There was a lot of laughing."

"Jokes?"

"Not from me. I minded my own business."

John held the door open for her. "It's only the first session."

Clare looked at him gravely. "Twelve weeks is a long time."

"It will probably change once people get to know each other better."

"I don't plan on getting to know them better."

John started to say something but changed his mind. He guided her through the door with his hand poised just behind the small of her back, only a tiny strip of air between them. In the parking lot he handed her a can of Pepsi.

"You're sweet," she said.

"It's just a Pepsi."

"No, I mean you're a nice person."

Avery turned to unlock the car, said so low she wouldn't hear it, "Don't be too sure about that."

They made the trip back to her house in silence. When John stopped in the driveway, Clare did not get out of the car. She turned to face him. John turned off the engine. He knew what was coming and he knew he would not say no. What he did not know was how light those fingers would be when they touched his neck, how distinct would be the shape of her mouth, how her complete lack of guile would turn him tumescent at once and leave him that way when she stepped out of the car and disappeared into the house, and he was alone looking through the windshield into the moonless dark.

A cold front had come through during the night and when Clare turned on the light in the kitchen at six in the morning, she could see her breath. She pulled on sweatpants over her jeans, an army jacket over her flannel shirt, and a stocking cap over her hair and went out to three inches of snow and still falling. The bluebird snow they called it. Schools might be closed.

Once off the mountain, though, the roads were clear, and Clare drove through the pre-dawn to the Grafton's house. She passed the driveway several times looking for a place to park that would keep her truck out of view. She finally settled behind a bush draped and turned solid by a heavy covering of snow, but over top of it a clear enough view of the bus stop. The sun came up and shortly after four boys ran down the driveway and then there was Sloan. She walked beside a much taller boy and, clearly, they were together. When they reached the field near the road, the boy took her daughter's hands and with arms outstretched, twirled her around in circles until they flopped onto their backs and waved their arms up and down in the snow. The boy jumped to his feet, pulled Sloan along with him, and they looked back to survey their work. Snow angels. One big. One small. The boy and girl bent back their heads, mouths open, letting the snow fall onto their faces and tongues. The bus appeared through the gray light blinking its red lights, stopped, opened its doors to receive the children who disappeared inside, Sloan's hand still in possession of the tall, dark-skinned boy. Clare laid her forehead on the wheel and wept and wept, though she had not cried since she was five. She wept until she felt hollow and then she remained with her head against the steering wheel and faced the fact that she was up against it all right. She straightened and stared, her eyes on the angels in the snow. Eleven more weeks. A lot could happen in eleven weeks. Clare put the truck into reverse, backed out from her hiding spot, and turned toward home.

Once there, she brought logs into the kitchen, laid them in the woodstove, scrunched up some newspapers, and started the fire. When she was satisfied it had taken, she shut the iron door, poured Coke into a glass, splashed in a dollop of bourbon, drank the mix down, and went outside to do what had to be done for the horses.

First, she put grain in the feed buckets, which were attached to the trees forming the fence line. The horses lined up, some flattened their ears, snaking their necks out with bared teeth. She clipped their halters to the ropes attached under the buckets. While the horses ate, she dried off the two leggy colts with a saddle blanket. The snow had stopped, but the wind picked up and the youngsters were shivering. She brought two turnout blankets from the feed room and secured them around the yearlings. The older horses had good winter coats and enough fat to keep themselves warm.

Next, she dragged five bales of hay from the house and spread them in piles, taking her time, shaking the hay loose. She didn't hurry. She fluffed the hay even though it wasn't necessary. When the last horse had licked the final morsel of feed from its bucket, she went down the line and unhooked them one by one. Sloan had seemed happy with that boy. He was too old for her, but she had seemed happy with him. Clare decided to clean out the run-in shed. Once the snow melted it would be nothing but mud. It was hard going—the wheelbarrow stuck in the snow and almost tipped over several times. The horses watched her, sleepy eyed while they munched the abundant hay. It would keep them warm through the night. Back and forth Clare pushed the barrow, fifteen, twenty times. Her arms began to tremble. When the sheds could not be any cleaner, she brought three more bales of hay from the house, even though there was plenty on the ground, and spread them with the same care she had the first five. The water trough was half full, but Clare uncurled the stiff hose and dragged it behind her and filled it. Now her legs were trembling. While the tub filled, she stood still watching the horses, some of whom watched her as well, puzzled by this amount of attention. She sighed. I should be happy, she thought, that Sloan ain't sad.

But she was as far from happy as it seemed possible to get.

Looking back on it, John thought it must have been a divine hand that caused him to look up when he parked in his driveway. There in the wind and swirling snow his sister sat on the roof outside her bedroom. She threw a snowball at him and smiled. He eased out of the car. "Colleen," he said quietly, looking up at her. "Stay right there. Don't move, okay? I'll come up and get you. And then we'll go out for a treat, but don't move."

She threw another snowball and scooted toward the edge.

"Stop! I'll be right there, and we'll go get you a treat. But we won't go anywhere if you move another inch. Do you understand?"

Colleen nodded.

John ran upstairs and flung open her bedroom door. He leaned out the window in her room and reached his hand toward his sister. "Come on now," he said and leaned out farther, his stomach resting on the sill. He held onto the window frame with one hand and extended the other as far as he could. If I climb out there, he thought, she might move and then slide or lose her balance. She was inches from the edge. But if he waited for her to move toward him, she might slip. "Don't move, Colleen," he said. "I'm serious. I'm going to get you and then we will go anywhere you want. Stay right where you are." He crawled out the window onto the roof and inched slowly toward her. "Don't move, sweetie, okay? Stay very still and hold out your hand. That's it." He moved a little closer and grabbed her arm.

Inside, he dropped onto the bed, holding Colleen close to him. Her clothes and hair were wet, but he was shaking so badly he couldn't tell if she too trembled. "Are you cold, sweetie? You need a change of clothes. Here." He pulled a blanket around her. "Change your clothes, okay. I'll be right back." John shut the window, bounded down the stairs, and returned as Colleen was pulling a sweater over her head. "Good girl." He held the nails in his mouth while he hammered the window shut along the bottom, around the sides, even the top. Colleen watched him quietly. Eventually, John turned around. "You look fine," he said. He ran his hand over her hair. "Let's get you a towel." He took her hand and led her into the bathroom, where he began rubbing her head. "Finish up, now. Get it good and dry or you'll catch cold when we go out."

Downstairs the house held the stillness that comes with a snowstorm. John flung open the door to the parlor. "Jesus Christ, Mom, I just pulled Colleen off the roof."

Mrs. Avery's pale face went even whiter. There were remnants of her beauty left in the high, clearly cut cheek bones, the deep-set eyes and perfectly shaped jaw line, but she appeared more a ghost than human.

"I had no idea," she said to John's rigid face. "I…" she looked around as though she might find an answer somewhere in this shadowed room closed to the outside by drapes heavy with dust. She turned helplessly back to him and put her hand to her heart. "I had no idea."

"Christ." John looked at the wall over her head. After a moment, he said in a quieter voice, "What's she doing home from school anyway?"

"The office called and said she wasn't feeling well, and the nurse brought her home."

John heard his sister pelting down the stairs. He stepped into the hallway. She was half-way down, holding her hands over her head and leapt into her brother's arms.

"What are you doing home from school?" John stepped back with her sudden weight then hoisted her onto a hip. "Are you sick?"

Colleen shook her head.

John shifted the weight of the child, holding her with one forearm and touched his other wrist to her forehead. "No fever anyway." He was still shaky but holding his sister helped calm him. He was glad she was home. He would spend the afternoon with her, take her shopping or maybe to the movies. After the movie, they would get something to eat if she felt like eating. By then it should be six or seven and he could go to the Bistro. There was always someone at the Bistro, especially on Thursday, getting an early start on the weekend. He'd have some drinks, a late supper, a nightcap, and it would be time for bed. The hours spent. He bounced Colleen a little on his hip. "You want to go shopping or the movies?" Colleen looked at him solemnly, her eyes huge. "Is it shopping?" The girl shook her head. "The movies then."

"You shouldn't take her out if she's sick."

"She's not feverish. I'll bring her back if she acts sick. Look, I'm sorry I yelled at you, but you've got to watch her better. You know she's not scared of anything."

As soon as they entered the buttery smell of the theater, Colleen put two fingers in her mouth and smiled. She held onto his pant leg while John bought the biggest tub of popcorn possible, an orange drink, and a Coke, and when they chose their seats, he put the tub of popcorn in the girl's lap. She looked up at him and her eyes crinkled in pleasure.

"Go ahead. Dig in."

Colleen took a fist full, which she couldn't fit into her mouth. She laughed.

"You're spraying that popcorn all over the theater."

The movie was a typical Disney—the heroine with over developed breasts and ass, and the hero with Superman shoulders. John tried to concentrate, to follow the plot. He worried about how much popcorn his sister was eating, but soon after the film started, she touched him on the shoulder and handed him the tub. She sighed and scrunched farther down in the seat, her eyes following the figures on the screen and her hand resting on his arm.

She is a gift, John thought, a precious, precious gift that I will honor. I will not do anything to compromise myself, my family or her in anything I say or do. I will be grateful for this dear, beautiful, special child and not ask God for anything more. I will be nicer to her mother so she in turn will be able to show affection. I will take her home after the movie and fix dinner for her and our mother. I will sit down at the table and eat with them.

The film seemed to go on forever. You would think a cartoon would be reasonably short. John told himself it had to end soon. Considering children's attention spans, they were bound to become restless. He was getting a headache, but Colleen sat mesmerized, apparently content to stay for hours.

When at last they came out of the theater, the light had turned toward evening, and a sharp wind blew through the parking lot. John stopped at the McDonald's drive-through and bought his sister chicken nuggets and milk, which he handed to her over the seat. Her eyes were sleepy and after drinking some of the milk, Colleen laid her head against the car seat and slept. When they were home, he carried her upstairs, put her into her pajamas, and washed her hands and face. She watched him, not fully awake, her eyes dreamy.

"You thinking about the movie?" John tucked her into bed and kissed her forehead. Colleen nodded, smiled, and rolled onto her side. It was early to put her to bed, but maybe she had a touch of something after all. Probably the last thing she needed was a tub of buttered popcorn.

John considered changing his clothes, decided against it, and got back in the car. He turned on the engine, backed out of the driveway and onto the road. He did not turn left toward town; he did not drive to the Bistro. Instead, he took the road leading out of Coleton, the road into the country, the road that led to the Holler, and then passed it and on up into the mountains where it stopped in front of Clare Raffienne's house.

After taking care of the horses, Clare drove to the village two miles away, where she purchased three bags of carrots, three jumbo boxes of sweetened cereal, and a super-size jar of peanuts. Back at the farm, she filled two feed buckets with a mix of the three items, tied them together with baling twine to the back of the saddle after she had tacked up Lonesome then rode him up the mountain to where the forest began. She dumped the contents at the edge of the woods. The bear might or might not be out of hibernation, but if she was, she would be half blind, crabby, and hungry as hell.

There was nothing more outside that Clare could think to do. It was getting dark anyway. In the kitchen, she sank onto a chair to take off her boots. She realized she hadn't eaten all day. To eat would have meant to stop, and to stop would have meant to think. She was easing the second boot from her foot when lights appeared in the driveway, an engine shut off, and John Avery walked through the door. He took off his coat and tossed it on a chair in one motion, while Clare dropped her boot and stood. She didn't move when he approached her and bent his head to kiss her mouth. He put his arms around her and pulled her against him. He was trembling. She wrapped her arms around his waist as though to quiet him, but he could not stop shaking. At some point, they made it upstairs to Clare's bed, where they eventually laid limp and sweating in the cold. She pulled a ratty comforter over them, and they slept without saying a word. On waking, the young man had no idea what time it was or where he even was. Then, like a blow, the memory came to him and who it was that curled around him. Not two months into the job and he was in bed with a client. Throughout his ethics class and his internships, his professors and supervisors had droned on and on about boundaries and liabilities and he had barely listened. Someone like himself would never even come close to stepping over the line. Since adolescence, available girls had been a given, drawn to his black Irish good looks, but, not wanting to become one of those men who hurt rather than enhance other people's lives, he had never led any of them on. He made it clear he played the field with no strings attached and did not take advantage of anyone he saw as vulnerable. And now he had done the unforgivable—*the unethical.* He would quit his job, go into another line of work altogether. Something that didn't involve people. Like accounting. Christ. There were women in accounting too, but at least he would not be going to their homes. He sat on the edge of the bed, realizing his clothes were downstairs. It was so cold in this bedroom his nose was running, but he didn't want to take the blanket from Clare. Hesitating, with the edge of the comforter across his lap, his bare feet on the floor, John turned to look at her.

Without opening her eyes, she said, "Take the blanket. You're makin' the bed shake, with your shivering."

"I can't take your blanket."

"Well, I can't sleep with you rattling the bed like you are. Come on, let's make a fire." Clare rose and walked out of the room. John did not think it was possible to find her more beautiful than he had before, but he did.

He wrapped himself in the comforter and followed her into the kitchen where, sitting on the floor and still naked, she threw logs on the fire. He squatted, put his arms around her shoulders and drew the blanket over her, rested his head against her neck, but she shrugged him off gently. "People will wonder where you're at."

John placed the blanket around her. "I don't want to leave."

"You got to for now." Clare looked at him.

"I know." He stood, looked around the kitchen, and gathered his clothes. He stepped into his jeans and yanked them on, pulled on his socks, awkwardly stepped into his shoes, buttoned his shirt, and tightened and buckled his belt without saying a word.

"You comin' for a home visit this week?"

John nodded.

"Come after school. Bring your little sister. I'll give her a pony ride."

Why not, he thought.

Lost was lost.

Chapter Twelve

When Annie had lived on her farm, she had looked out her bedroom window every morning as soon as her eyes opened and the sky, the trees, tall enough to be part of the view from the second-story window, and the horizon behind them had given her at times outright joy and if not that, at least, hope. Now in this apartment, she kept her eyes closed as long as possible and when she finally had to acknowledge the hour, she looked at the ceiling and not at the window with its curtains drawn against the neighbors.

In her first apartment where she lived alone after law school, Annie had been sitting on the toilet thinking about what color towels she could buy that would make the bathroom less institutional when she heard the toilet flush. She had looked down between her legs at the water in the bowl and then back at the handle on the tank. She stared straight ahead and then out the window next to her shoulder. I can hear my neighbor's toilet flush, she thought. That means they can hear mine. Why hadn't someone warned her? How was it possible that in all her 32 years no one had mentioned that when you lived alone in an apartment you could hear other people going about their bodily functions? How did people stand it? How was it they could hear what a stranger was doing in the bathroom next door and know they would continue to hear it again and again throughout the day and possibly the night, and stand it? Living in the dorms or student housing at the university had been entirely different. There, even if you lived in your own space of loneliness, you did it in clusters. Clusters filled with the noise of roommates, friends, acquaintances and their chatter; or the sounds they made fixing meals and eating, knocking dirty dishes around in the sink, taking showers, opening and shutting doors, having parties and sex and playing music. You lived in a cocoon of background noise made by familiar people.

This morning in her apartment in Coleton, Annie had her head under the covers and her eyes shut when the phone rang. She reached to the floor for the receiver and pulled it under the sheet.

"It's such a beautiful day I decided to take it off," said Dr. Wittcomb. "But I know you wanted to meet and rather than cancel our appointment, I was thinking, if it's all right with you, why don't you come to my house?"

"Today? You mean instead of at your office?"

"Yes. Are you all right? You sound as though you are being strangled."

Annie pushed the blankets from her face. "I'm fine." She hesitated, trying to think of any reason why this might jeopardize Clare's case. Dr. Wittcomb's silence seemed to allow whatever Annie was mulling over as an understandable concern and one with which she could be patient.

Finally, Annie said, "All right."

"Do you know where I live?"

"No."

Dr. Wittcomb gave directions to a remote area half an hour's drive outside of town. She had to go over them three times. Annie hung up the phone, crawled out of bed, and tiptoed in bare feet to the window and pulled back the curtain. The world was gray with falling and fallen snow. It was the middle of April.

Dr. Wittcomb's house sat in the middle of a clearing surrounded by an old forest. Several large trees were left standing near the small cottage whose golden lights shone into a world made monochrome by the storm. Annie stepped out of the car and a wolf covered in snow trotted out of the woods, heading straight for her. She made a quick calculation and decided the animal would be on her before she could get the vehicle door open and safely closed, so she stood as still as she could manage with the wind snapping her hair and coat all around her. The door to the cottage opened and Dr. Wittcomb filled the space. The wolf came up to Annie, sniffed her crotch, turned, and bounded into the house.

"You found us," said Dr. Wittcomb.

Annie looked down at her boots, which were in three feet of snow. "Yes," she said, without enthusiasm.

"It's not easy. Many people get lost back here. Ms. Voight, you must have a good sense of direction." Annie noted the use of her maiden name. It would have taken some work, some forethought to have found that out. Dr. Wittcomb continued, "Come on in. I've just made a strawberry rhubarb pie." Inside, the smell of baking fruit, spices, and butter filled the house and the wolf lay stretched out, melting in front of the fireplace.

"Our bluebird snow," said the older woman. "I managed to find some fresh strawberries and rhubarb before this storm hit. A perfect day for pie, don't you think?" She placed two large pieces on plates. "Just throw your coat on that chair and we'll eat in front of the fire." She handed a plate to Annie and glided from the kitchen to a chair next to the wolf. "Please, come sit down and be comfortable." Annie sat across from the older woman.

Dr. Wittcomb looked at her pie, took a bite, then another and stared into space, considering. "I've made better, but not bad." Annie put a small amount on her fork, gingerly took a bite. The crust was light and crispy on the edges and the filling had just the right combination of sweet and sour. She was suddenly ravenous. The two women ate in silence until the pieces of pie were gone. Dr. Wittcomb put her plate on the floor. Chukchi, the wolf, raised her head, leaned forward, and licked away the red stains. Annie hesitated a moment then put her plate on top of Dr. Wittcomb's and Chukchi cleaned it in the same thorough way she had her owner's. Eventually, the young woman sat up straight, crossed and uncrossed her legs. "Dr. Wittcomb, I will be frank. I have read the DSS report on the Raffienne case, and yes, technically they have grounds for removing the child. Chronic truancy, some questionable hygiene… and that's weak, very weak… and the safety issue of a bear being practically a family pet. But you and I both know this is a very weak case. Much worse goes on in families and DSS turns a blind eye. Generally, it takes an act of Congress or a near death to get a child removed. Plus, I've done some research and no child has ever been removed from the Holler… Not ever. No one bothers with these people. So why Sloan? The fact that she is such an obvious exception troubles me."

"It troubles me too."

Annie hesitated. She realized, with a certain chagrin, she had come here for reassurance.

Dr. Wittcomb smiled at her. "Ms. Voight, how much do you know about the Graftons?"

"They've been foster care providers for almost five years."

"Yes. And as far as DSS is concerned, they walk on water. They take kids, specifically boys, that no one else will take. And somehow or other they manage them. The fire setters, the thieves, the sexually acting out, the chronic runaways. The kids who would hit you as soon as look at you."

"How do they do it?"

"Who knows. Maybe they put something in their food. And living way out in the middle of nowhere helps. Now they have a little girl. A little girl who really hasn't caused anyone any trouble except the school and believe me, the school doesn't care all that much when a kid from the Holler doesn't show up."

"So, what do you think is going on?"

"I don't know." It struck Dr. Wittcomb that she wasn't aware of John Avery visiting Sloan at the Grafton's. She sat still, thinking. How had she not been on top of this? In-home meant working primarily with the child not the biological parents. That policy, driven by Medicaid, made no sense in this case, or any other case really, but those were the rules. John Avery knew the rules or should, at least. Yet, as far as she could tell, now that she looked back on their conversations, Avery had spent most of the time with Clare.

"I don't know what's going on, but I agree with you, Ms. Voight, it is very strange. I will staff the case with Avery. I understand you made a visit to DSS."

Annie looked down. "Yes. It didn't go well."

"Never mind. You were within your rights and that director is an old dragon. A dragon and a bully. But I have a friend tucked away in a corner there. Keeps her head low, but she may have some information that could be helpful. I'll call her."

"How long has Clare been your client? I have a release. It's in my briefcase, ahh, in the car." Annie started to rise. Dr. Wittcomb waved her hand. "That's all right. Give it to me later. Clare only came to me just before the child was removed. And then only because she was court ordered. But I've known about her, her and her Pap, forever. That child doesn't belong in foster care. If there is any child that shouldn't be in foster care, it's this one."

Annie stopped breathing, an annoying response her body had to moments of panic. So far it had always started up again before she fainted. She had focused on divorce law in school, thinking that would be the bulk of her business here in this small town. That and some drug cases. Her knowledge of foster care law was scanty. When Marshall had handed her the file, she had been stunned to see Clare's name and even worse, the fact that she had lost her daughter.

Now she was in up to her elbows in a case that even the clinical director of the mental health clinic didn't understand. She glanced down at her boots, high heeled, sleek lawyer boots that were now stained by a gray line the snow had made.

Watching the young woman, Dr. Wittcomb decided not to reassure her. There was no point in acknowledging Ms. Voight's self-doubts. In her dark, perfect suit, she still looked like little more than a worn child. She walked Annie to her car. The snow had stopped, and the girl made a U-turn through the pristine snow on the yard and drove with care down the long driveway. Dr. Wittcomb watched her go and sighed. When had everyone gotten so young?

Chapter Thirteen

The Graftons lived even farther from Coleton than Clare, though not in the mountains, just straight out Route 301, on and on, to the edge of the county, the houses becoming fewer and fewer and the trees thicker and thicker until that was all he saw. At last, John spotted the sign, large white with poorly painted black letters, "Grafton Greenhouse." How in the world did they do business way out here?

The greenhouse sat very close to the road at the beginning of a long driveway. Inside, the air was damp and warm, at least twenty degrees hotter than outside. The place smelled of fertilizer, flowers, earth, and sweat. Several sullen boys were lifting sacks, carrying plants, and filling pots. Avery looked around for Sloan and finally saw her behind several robust ficus trees. She sat cross-legged on stacked bags of soil, putting together a posy. In a world of sticky, dirty work, Sloan looked immaculate, dressed in a white and blue polka dot dress, her red and gold head bent over the flowers in her hands. John said her name and when she looked at him, he saw Clare. But where the mother was dark and strong, her daughter, with her freckled white skin, luminous in the greenhouse light, looked as fragile as glass. Only her smudged green eyes seemed to have substance, and they watched him as though she were prey and he the predator. Ignoring everyone else, John walked toward her and extended his hand. "I'm John Avery."

Sloan didn't move. John dropped his hand and sat on the bags of soil next to her and arranged himself in a casual pose. "I know your mother, Sloan. She and I are working together so you can go home. I'm a counselor. I do what they call in-home therapy, and I will be coming to see you every week until you go home." As he talked, John watched a tall, bent man who looked to be in his sixties approach them. He stood up to shake the man's hand, which was dry with loose skin seeming to slide over the bones. The grasp, aggressively firm, took John by surprise.

"I'm Mr. Grafton of Grafton Greenhouse. May I help you?"

"Nice to meet you. I'm Mr. Avery from the County Mental Health Clinic. I'm Sloan's in-home therapist."

Mr. Grafton frowned. "Therapist? I don't understand."

"The clinic will be doing in-home therapy with Sloan. Didn't anyone tell you about this?" It was John who should have called the Graftons after Dr. Wittcomb had talked to him about the Medicaid regulations, but the thought hadn't occurred to him until just now. "I should have called, I suppose. To let you know I was coming. Though…" Another thought suddenly came to him. "I will be making unannounced visits as well."

"The Department of Social Services told us they would be doing that. Are you from the Department of Social Services?"

"No, I'm from the County's Mental Health Services Program. I do in-home therapy, which means I will be coming here. To see how Sloan is doing."

"She's doing fine."

"In-home is part of the reunification process. So, I will be coming here at least once a week."

Grafton looked at John closely with light, watery-blue eyes. "Now that's not a good idea," he said, finally. "Joan needs time to settle in. Get acclimated. She don't need all these people coming round disrupting her."

"Joan? No, her name is Sloan with an S."

"That's no name for a girl. And she don't need no therapy. Everything is going just fine, isn't it Joannie? We're doing just fine."

"In-home is part of the reunification process. Like I said. We work with everyone. Her mother, you, Sloan, and all the involved professionals."

"Do you have any identification?"

"Oh yes, of course. I should have had it clipped to my shirt. Sorry." John pulled a laminated badge out of his pocket, held it in front of Mr. Grafton's eyes, who looked at it and then at John.

"Do I have any say in this?"

"No." John startled himself with his tone. "It's up to DSS and ultimately the courts," he added more amiably.

"Will I get to say my piece?"

"Sure. Of course. You and I will be talking on a regular basis but now I need to see Sloan alone for a few minutes. If you don't mind."

"I don't see any reason you need to see her alone. She's just a little girl."

"It's part of the therapy. It's required."

The car was the only place John could think of that was totally private. When he opened the door, Sloan pitched herself inside, grabbing onto the steering wheel and the back of the seat, her knees getting caught up in her dress and her feet scrabbling on the floorboards. She wriggled and scooted behind the wheel, tugged at her clothes, yanked her skirt out from underneath her, and sat more-or-less properly covered by her dress in the bucket seat. John walked around and climbed in on the passenger side.

The girl's eyes fixed him with the same intensity as her mother had shown the first night he met her. "Are you takin' me home?"

"Not today. But your mother and I are working on it. So is your mother's lawyer. There are a lot of people who care about you and want to see you and your mother together again."

"Where's my mother?"

"She's at home doing what she needs to do to get you back. Hey, now. Don't cry. Don't get upset. Like I said, we are going to get you back to her as fast as we can."

"But where is she?"

"She's home, like I said. Waiting for you."

Sloan opened her mouth, but no sound came out. Her chest heaved but there was no sound. John took one of her hands and squeezed it. "Hey, stop now. Everything is going to be okay." Sloan began to gasp.

"Stop. Take a deep breath. Slowly. Like this. Nice and easy. In. Out. Slowly. There. Slowly, now. In and out. Okay, that's better. That's the way. We don't want you passing out." John patted the girl's shoulder. "You will be with your mother sooner than you can say Jack Rabbit." Feeling like an idiot, he closed his mouth.

"My mama's dead."

"What?"

"She would of come and got me if she wasn't dead."

"No. No." John started to pat her shoulder again then thought better of it. "She's not dead. She's fine. I promise you. Maybe I can arrange a visit. Please, stop crying. Sloan, I promise your mother is fine."

Sloan looked at him, tears standing on the edge of her lids, hanging there.

There was a long pause while they watched each other. "How is it here?" John said, eventually. "Is everything okay?"

The tears tipped and ran down her cheeks.

"There now. I know you're sad, but we are working to get you home as fast as possible." Christ, couldn't he think of anything else to say? "Listen, tell me what it's like here. What do you do? Do you go to the greenhouse every day? I bet you like the flowers. That bouquet was very pretty."

Sloan continued to cry silently. John opened the glove compartment, found a box of tissues, and handed them to her. The girl remained motionless, her eyes on her hands.

"Here you go. Take them. You're getting your dress wet." He took her fist and carefully opened her fingers and placed the tissue on her palm. Sloan didn't move. Finally, he reached in the glove compartment, took out four or five more tissues and wiped her cheeks, her chin, and lastly under her nose.

"Don't leave me here," Sloan said when he was done.

John sat back, leaned his head against the seat, and looked out the window at nothing in particular. "I have to. At least for now."

"Noooo…" Her voice was a high-pitched keen.

"Sloan, stop it now. It's going to be okay. We just have to do a few things before we bring you home. You'll be home with your mama before you know it."

"My mama's dead."

"I told you that's not true." He sat up and looked at Sloan. "Your mother is alive and doing what she needs to do to get you back. Try not to think those bad thoughts."

Sloan watched him, her eyes huge.

"Look, are they nice to you here? They don't… uh… do anything mean or anything, do they?"

Sloan stared at him.

"Do they hit you?"

"No." Her voice was low and dolorous. "Sometimes they pull my hair though. And they pinch my face."

"When?" John's mouth was suddenly dry.

"Every day." Sloan stared at him. Waiting. Testing the waters.

"They shouldn't do that," he said. "No one should pull your hair. Or pinch you."

"They do it to make me take my pills."

The pills. Yes. The pills. John wondered what exactly she was supposed to be taking. He should know, but he hadn't read the chart all that carefully. She was so thin it would be easy to overdose her. "Maybe you don't need them now. I'll find out."

A fist pounded on the window and John jumped as though a bomb had gone off. Mr. Grafton's bony face peered through the glass.

"You shouldn't be alone in the car with her."

John rolled the window down. "What?"

"I said you shouldn't be alone with her. It don't look proper."

"What on earth are you talking about?" John was pretty sure he knew what the man meant, but he wanted to be the one asking the questions.

"I'm just thinking of you and your professional reputation. I'll be taking Joan on up to the house now. It's our supper time."

As soon as Avery pulled out of the driveway and onto the road, he called Dr. Wittcomb. To his surprise, she answered on the second ring.

"I think I've messed up again," he said.

"Go on."

"Number one, I was rude to Mr. Grafton. Number two, Sloan reported that the Graftons pinch and pull her hair. To make her take her meds. She told me this while we were in the car. Then Mr. Grafton took her to the house for supper. I didn't know what to do so I sat in the car for a while trying to decide. It seemed to me that this might be a CPS issue, so I went to the house to talk to Sloan some more. Mr. Grafton answered the door and when I asked to speak to her, he said she was in bed. I said, 'at five o'clock?' He said she wasn't feeling well. I asked to come in, but he said no, the other children were eating their supper, and he didn't want to disturb them. I stood there in the doorway, and he didn't invite me in. So, I left."

"Were there any marks?"

"Marks?"

This kid is so green, thought Dr. Wittcomb. What did they teach in college these days, anyway? "Yes. Marks," she said. "On her face. Bruises from fingers or a thumb."

"I didn't see anything."

"Normally we would call CPS. We would tell the child that we were calling, and we would tell the foster parents. We would give them a choice. Do they want us to call while they are present, or do they want to call themselves? We try to keep from developing an adversarial relationship by giving them options. But we are mandated reporters. We must report any suspicion of child abuse. Having said that, I will now say this is not a normal case. Where are you now?"

There was nothing but a tunnel of trees lining the sides of the road with no distinguishing markers. The weather had turned warm again, the snow was melting, and John could see the new leaves budding on the branches. "I'm heading along route 301 back to the office."

Dr. Wittcomb considered. To tell Avery to go back now would do nothing to improve relationships with the Graftons. And making a CPS report would do nothing to improve relationships with the Department of Social Services. They wouldn't do an investigation on just the child's word anyway. Dr. Wittcomb decided to make an exception. "You can wait to call CPS until morning and make it hypothetical. Just ask if hearing a child report that someone pinches their face and pulls their hair is a CPS issue. They will ask you if there are any marks and when you say 'no', they will tell you it isn't."

"Should I talk to the Graftons about it? I mean they shouldn't be doing that, should they? Pinching her face?"

"Of course not. And, yes, discuss other ways to encourage the child to take her medicine. And talk to the psychiatrist. It probably won't help but try anyway. She doesn't need to be on meds at all, but he'll defer to the foster parents, who will say she is unmanageable. If he lowers the dose or stops prescribing, the foster parents won't be happy and then DSS won't be happy and that is a huge can of worms."

"Then why would I say anything to him?"

"Because it's the right thing to do. And John, you don't want to make enemies of the Graftons. Not if you want to work with them."

I'm in way over my head, he thought. In fact, you could say I've already gone under. "Should I apologize again?" he asked, knowing he wouldn't.

"No. Don't bother. And John, I have some news on this case that is concerning me."

The rush of adrenaline made John feel as though he was being stuck all over with pins.

"I have a friend; works for DSS. It seems the Graftons and the foster care people have worked a deal. The Graftons will open a group home. Take the 'throw-away kids,' the ones no one else will take. And they won't even charge that much money. On one condition. They get to have at least one girl."

"Is that legal?"

"It's perfectly legal to open a group home. All you have to do is meet certain basic conditions, go through some training, and get licensed. And you know who approves the license."

"The Department of Social Services."

"Correct. It has to go on to the state level but if the local DSS approves it, it's just a formality. And there is nothing in writing about the girl. Of course."

When she hung up, Dr. Wittcomb thought of the way Avery had looked this morning. Pale except for an edgy blush on each cheek and, whereas the young man generally carried himself with a James Dean languor, today he'd looked as though he might bolt out of his chair any second.

After he dropped off the state car, John placed the keys in the dropbox and the file in the file room. Without completing the day's progress notes, he drove to the Bistro. It was six o'clock daylight savings time, and the sun was still bright outside, but inside the lights were dim, making it difficult to distinguish people's faces. Yet, when he saw a girl with blonde hair standing at the bar, he felt as though he were coming from the dark into the light. He walked up to the space next to her, leaned his elbows on the highly varnished surface, tilted his face to hers and said, "Hey." It was Chrissy.

"Well, hello, Mr. in-home."

John turned away. "Don't be like that."

"You put us all to shame with your dedication."

"Don't be like that. And don't let's talk shop." He glanced over his shoulder. "Let's go sit over there. It's good to see you. What are you drinking?"

"Gin and tonic."

"A gin and tonic and a very dry vodka martini. How are you, Elliott?"

The bartender took Chrissy's empty glass and wiped away the moisture under it. "Can't complain. You?"

"Fine. Everything is fine." John carried the drinks to the table. He held his up. It was a lovely, large glass with three huge green Spanish olives. "Here's to in-home."

Chrissy touched her glass to his. "I thought we weren't going to talk shop."

"We're not." John looked at the girl's baby face. It must be hard to do family therapy with a face like that. He wondered if the fathers ever hit on her. Or even the teenage boys. "Where do you live, Chrissy? Do you still live with your mother and father?"

"No, I have an apartment. All by myself. Why? Do you want to come over?"

"Now you're being sarcastic."

"No, I'm not. You asked."

John took a long swallow. He tasted nothing but Grey Goose. Elliott always took care of him. He looked at the girl with her indigo eyes. Maybe it was because kids like her hadn't experienced tragedy. They remained innocent as babies. The vodka felt wonderful hitting his empty stomach. "So, Chrissy, how many cases do you have?"

"I thought we weren't talking shop."

"We're not."

"I have five. And they are all going badly."

It wasn't her fault. She was born with that face. And what did he know? She may have experienced plenty of tragedy. She was older than he was, had graduated three years ahead of him. From a good school. Up north. She may have had plenty of tragedy. And her cases were going badly. Not as bad as his, for sure. But they were going badly, and she seemed disappointed. "Let's have another," he said, "and we won't talk shop."

"I don't know. That's three for me. I have to drive home."

"No, you don't. I'll drive you home." John went to the bar and ordered another round. "You don't mind if we park a car in the back overnight, do you, Elliott?"

"Just park it next to the kitchen where you can't see it from the street."

"Right."

The second martini tasted as good as the first. Chrissy's disappointment was completely abolished by her third drink. The two did not talk any more shop, they talked nonsense and sarcasm, and she was coy and he was direct and then he was even more direct until they were in her apartment where they didn't talk at all until it was morning and they had to manage to converse enough to arrange their way back to the Bistro where Chrissy could pick up her car. It was Saturday.

Colleen was still in bed, but her eyes were open. She held one of her dolls crooked in her elbow, the head resting under her chin. Her hair was damp with sweat where the doll lay against her. She watched her brother come into the room. John sat on the edge of her bed. She smelled warm and organic, like yeast.

"Would you like to go with me this morning? To a horse farm? To see some horses and ponies?" Colleen put the doll on the pillow, slid out of bed, went to her dresser drawers, and took out a shirt and pair of pants. She looked over her shoulder at her brother, who nodded and rose. "Come downstairs as soon as you're dressed."

John pulled into the drive-thru at McDonald's and ordered two egg and cheese biscuits, hesitated, then said into the speaker, "No... wait a minute, make that four... and an orange juice." After paying, he handed a biscuit and juice over the seat to Colleen. She put the juice in a holder and unwrapped the paper, took the top half off the biscuit, looked at the sandwich, put the half- biscuit back, opened her mouth as wide as she could and filled it with food. She smiled around egg and cheese at John in the rearview mirror. He shook his head and smiled back. "Keep your mouth closed when you eat. You must be feeling okay this morning." Colleen bowed her head and ate carefully, spilling only a few crumbs in her lap. When she finished, she rested her head against the back of her car seat and stared out the window. She could be Snow White, John thought, asleep in her silence. When they turned off the road and entered Hozelroad Holler, Colleen sat up straight and leaned forward, one hand and her nose against the glass. She turned to look at her brother again in the rearview mirror, her eyes wide.

Ask, he thought. Ask me. Say *what* or *oh* or *look*. Something. Instead, Colleen laughed and returned to staring out the window until they were past the debris, and it was just dense trees and underbrush, and she leaned back once more, smiling faintly.

Clare was in the pasture throwing pads of hay around when they arrived. She reached to yank the twine from a new bale, separating a large chunk. She flung it, moving from the shoulders, her arm outstretched. John watched her for a moment then unbuckled his seat belt, climbed out of the car, opened the back door, unbuckled Colleen, and brushed the crumbs from her lap. He handed her a McDonald's napkin. "Wipe your mouth, please." He took her hand and led her to where Clare stood outside the gate. He held out the bag of food. "I've brought you breakfast."

Clare was watching Colleen. "This your little sister?"

"Of course." John put his free hand on the back of the little girl's head.

Clare stared, a crease forming between her eyebrows. Colleen smiled up at her and Clare looked away. Then back again.

"Colleen, this is Miss Clare. She owns the horses here."

Colleen nodded.

"Don't call me Miss Clare. Just Clare." She knelt so she was eye level with the little girl. "Would you like a pony ride?" Colleen's eyes shifted to the horses, whose heads were bent to the pads of hay. She looked back at Clare, who straightened. "Come on. I have a pony just the right size for you. You can put that food in the kitchen, John Avery."

When John came out of the house, his sister was sitting on the back of a blond, fat pony who looked like an illustration in a book. Colleen's feet stuck out from the round belly. Clare put her hand on the girl's thigh. "This is Butter. It's pretty obvious why we call him that. He has been here a long time and he is very nice. Do you like him?"

Colleen nodded.

"Good." Clare led them around the yard, down part of the driveway, back again, and around several trees. Colleen held a few strands of the bushy mane in her fingers and stared at the pointed ears. Eventually, Clare led them back into the pasture where she helped Colleen slide off, undid the halter, patted Butter on the rump, and guided the girl with her hand on the small of her back into the yard. "Okay, Avery. Let's go eat breakfast."

"Colleen's already eaten," said John. He eased into a chair next to his sister and watched Clare fill three glasses of water from the tap and place them on the table. She sat across from Colleen, watching her.

"I would think it would upset you," said John.

"What?"

"You know. Being around another little girl. It would be understandable."

"What would be? Understandable?"

"Having, you know, ah, lost your own daughter."

Clare turned her gaze on him. The angles in her face shifted. If she were a wolf, he thought, she'd pin her ears.

"Being around another little girl would only be a problem if I was never to get Sloan back. And that ain't the case. Is it?"

"No. No. Of course not."

John shut the door after buckling Colleen into her seat. He leaned against the Honda and did not make a move to open the door to the driver's seat. "I'll come back without her. So, we can talk business," he said to Clare.

"She's the most beautiful creature I ever seen."

"Others have said so. Yes."

"I think you should bring her back soon. She liked that pony."

John said nothing.

Clare stepped around him and opened the car door. She leaned in and said, "You want to come back here? Go for another ride on Butter?"

Colleen put two fingers in her mouth, smiled in a way that made her eyes crinkle, and nodded.

"Okay," John said to Clare. "Okay."

She straightened and leaned her body against the car in one easy motion. "You can come on back by yourself tonight," she said.

Chapter Fourteen

The girl sat at the table with her chin on her chest and her eyes closed while the boys, heads bent low, spooned and slurped cereal into their mouths. Nat picked up a strand of Sloan's hair and let it fall. It was still so wet, droplets of water splattered on her shoulder and lap.

"You ain't cheekin' your meds," he mumbled, then switched his empty bowl with hers.

Since it was Saturday, all the children went to the greenhouse right after they finished eating. Sloan slept on bags of seeds in the shade of the large Ficus trees while the boys worked. She lay curled on her side with one bare foot resting on top of the other, her knees bent, and an arm crossed over her chest, her hands in a prayer position under her cheek. The first hour, her sleep was deep and dreamless then her eyelids flickered as images formed in her mind. She whimpered. Toward noon, Nat came and tugged on her toe. Sloan sat up with the marks of her fingers on her cheek. Her mouth was dry and rotten tasting and her hair hung in a curtain around her face. Nat hopped up and sat beside her. "Better wake up. It's nearly time for lunch."

"I ain't hungry." In fact, she was starving.

"I ain't mad at you for not cheekin' your meds."

"All I think about is Mama." Sloan controlled her breathing in the way she had learned to do in order not to cry. Nat gathered her hair away from her face. "It's dry now," he said.

"We should run away today."

"It's too late. If we run away, we have to leave early in the morning. So we can get far before it's dark."

"Then we'll go tomorrow."

"Tomorrow's Sunday. You go to church."

On Sundays, Mrs. Grafton took Sloan to the Baptist church where the people sat in rows and talked all together and sometimes stood up and sang loud songs and then someone shouted at them from behind a tall box. At the gathering afterward, there were cookies and juice. The first time they went to church several women who looked a lot like Mrs. Grafton gathered round her and hugged her or patted her and said things like, "at last, she's so beautiful, so precious, your prayers are finally answered, we are so happy for you, what's her name? You must be thrilled!" Mrs. Grafton smiled for the first time that Sloan had ever seen, and her sallow cheeks even turned a little pink. She put her hand lightly on Sloan's head and said, "This is our new daughter, Joan." Then they all sat down at a long table and ate cookies and drank coffee, or in Sloan's case orange juice, and Mrs. Grafton smiled again and then again when they said goodbye to the other ladies. There was less hugging and patting each Sunday after that, but Mrs. Grafton continued to smile and occasionally she held Sloan's hand for no obvious reason, and she always asked if Sloan would like more cookies and juice and when Sloan said, "yes" she would reach across the table and hand her more. She didn't smile on the way home in the truck, however.

Sloan pried her hair away from Nathaniel. "We'll get up before church. Real early. Before everyone else. I'll make sandwiches to take with us."

"I'm not gonna jump from a second-story window."

Sloan looked at Nat. "Why would we have to jump out a window?" Anyway, hers was locked.

"We're going to have to plan this very carefully. We should probably go on a school day. Get away before the bus comes. I'll have to convince the others not to tell. I'll tell them we'll come back for them. That we'll go first to find your place and I'll come back to show them the way. Your mamma wouldn't mind if they stayed with her for a while, would she? If it meant she could have you back. But the first thing is we'll have to figure out the way."

"Why would we have to jump out the window?"

"It's that or walk through a locked door."

Sloan stared at him.

"What do you think those dead bolts are on the door for? Decoration?"

Sloan continued to stare.

"They've started lockin' us in at night, dummy. After everyone is supposed to be asleep. That's why I can't spend the night with you." He slid off the sacks of seeds and walked away, turning to wink just before Mr. Grafton appeared through the Ficus trees.

"Nathaniel, you stay away from that girl." The man took Sloan's hand. "It's time for lunch, Missy."

Mrs. Grafton put a platter of jelly sandwiches cut into triangles on the table. Hands from all around grabbed at them. Nat put three on Sloan's plate. She loved the soft, sweet food. "We could check the way this afternoon," she whispered.

Nat took five triangles for himself. "Maybe. Later."

Laremy, the smallest boy, reached for the last half sandwich, but a rangy, painfully fair-skinned redhead snatched it away. "No, you don't."

Sloan put her hand over the three on her plate while watching the boys. Nat poured water from the jug into her glass. "They won't take your food," he said. She ate all her lunch and drank two glasses of cold water, which tasted fine with the jelly bread. She looked up at Nat, who was holding off the other four boys with his stare.

Mrs. Grafton carried a tray of food into the dining room, where she and her husband would eat their lunch. They took all their meals in the dining room while the children ate in the kitchen. The room had been added onto the house two years ago and the paneled walls still smelled faintly of pine. Highly lacquered, the oak floor shone like a gymnasium. One small window on each side allowed the sun to stretch thin bars of light across the plain rectangular table where Mr. Grafton sat at the head, waiting. Sometimes he read the paper while he waited. Today he sat with his forearms resting on the veneered wood, his impatient fists facing each other. Mrs. Grafton closed the door with her hip and put the platter of cheeseburgers in front of him along with a plate of French fries, a bottle of ketchup, and a bowl of applesauce. She sat to the side and placed a helping of everything onto her husband's plate then bowed her head over the hands folded in her lap.

Mr. Grafton bowed his head over his own folded hands. "Dear Lord, we thank you for this food and all the bounty you bestow upon us. Amen."

"Dear Lord, help him. Amen."

Mr. Grafton turned his head slowly and deliberately toward his wife. "What did you say?"

"That girl don't need her hair washed every night." The woman kept her head lowered; her eyes focused on her hands.

"What exactly are you talking about?" The man's voice was mild, but Mrs. Grafton did not look up and the back of her stolid neck turned a mottled red. She said nothing.

"Mother, I'd like to know what you are talking about."

Mrs. Grafton shifted in her chair and looked at the window where a fly buzzed. "You don't need to be taking her into the bathroom every night to wash her hair, as you call it. That's what I mean." Her voice was barely louder than the aggressive whir of the fly's wings which, having registered the smell of food, flew to hover between the couple's plates. Mr. Grafton swatted it away, but the insect returned as soon as the man lowered his hand and it settled on the edge of the platter where one hamburger remained. The man scowled and drew back. "Can't you keep these pests out of the house? You used to be a better housekeeper than this. Now you let flies into the house and you can't keep that girl's hair proper, either. I expected more help from you. Someone has to see to her hygiene."

Mrs. Grafton spread her hand a few inches above her food, fending off the fly. "Hygiene? I keep her hygiene just fine. Ain't nothing wrong with her hygiene." The fly moved off a small way, hovered over the French fries then dove onto Mr. Grafton's plate. He swatted at it again. "I ask for your help, but you're never around when I need you."

"You don't need to be washing her at night when she's already gone to bed."

Mr. Grafton looked at his wife. "Mother, you know it's easier when she's had her medicine." He drew out the words, mimicking patience. "Otherwise, she'd fight like a wild cat. You know that. Now go get a fly swatter and get rid of this fly."

Mrs. Grafton looked at her husband then shifted her gaze back to her plate. "You ain't never tried during the day. I comb her hair. It's all right. She looks fine. Ain't nothing wrong with her hygiene." All this she said with her head down looking at the hamburger on her plate. Once she stopped talking, there was no sound except the buzzing of the fly. The woman waited a few moments before putting her hands on either side of the plate and starting to rise to open a window and shoo the pest outdoors. But with a motion fast as a snake, Mr. Grafton grabbed hold of his wife's wrist, held it against the table, and twisted the skin as far as it would go. "You drop it, hear me. You don't question me. When I say her hair ain't right, it ain't right." He dug his nails into her arm. "Now you go into that kitchen and get a fly swatter and kill this blasted fly. And bring Joan back here with you. From now on she will eat in here with us."

After the children had cleaned the kitchen, they all went back to the greenhouse as they did every Saturday to work for the rest of the afternoon. Except for Sloan. As usual she was sent to the house around three o'clock for a nap while the boys, who at that time of day were becoming increasingly cross and harder to control, continued laboring in the greenhouse though most of their time was spent ducking out of Grafton's sight, squirting each other with the hose, loafing in some shade or peeing on the potted plants.

"Slip outside," said Nat just before Sloan left, "and I'll be behind the shed, and we'll go find the way to your house."

"We'll get caught."

"No, we won't. Pretend to take a nap, just be sure that woman don't lock your door. She probably won't since it's just you in the house. And she likes you."

It was easy as pie to slip away, just like Nat said. Mrs. Grafton was in the dining room banging the vacuum cleaner around and Sloan simply walked out the front door to behind the shed where Nat half sat and half sprawled, his legs spread out before him. "Hey," he said and got to his feet.

Being on land that was more-or-less flat, these woods weren't familiar to Sloan at all. The trees around her home grew on mountains where steep climbs ended looking over valleys. Often streams were on the floors of these valleys, running clear enough to drink and see the fish in them and the way the sun hit their silver or bronze scales as they darted through the water. There was the forbidding height of Big Hill, which Sloan had never tackled, but next to that was her favorite, a modest climb on a horse and she and her mother often picnicked there, going up over the edge down to the clear creek below with its lime green grass on the shore.

Now, Sloan walked between these trees that looked all the same, touching their trunks as she did so, looking at the ground in the manner she imagined Indians finding their way might do, hiding as best she could the fact that she didn't yet know the way home. She was confident that eventually she would recognize something, and the direction would become clear to her, but in the meantime, she didn't want Nat to become discouraged. For a while he followed her without speaking, but it wasn't long before he said, "Do you have any idea where you're going?"

Sloan stopped. Ahead and to the right was a small break in the canopy of trees, which allowed the sunlight to change the color of the leaves and cast shadows on the forest floor in a pattern slightly different from the surrounding sameness. Sloan pointed and walked toward it as though it were a clue, which it wasn't, and Nat followed her. When they reached the sun-dappled spot, Sloan looked skyward and so did Nat and then she heard it: the distinct sound of moving water. "I found it!" she said and sped off toward the sound, unmindful of the brush scratching her bare legs. Nat watched the curved hardness of those little girl thighs. He noticed the knobby ankles and the way they disappeared into white sneakers as Sloan stomped her way through the brush. She had changed out of the sandals she wore in the greenhouse into sturdier footwear, which would be necessary for their journey. Sloan snatched at her shorts, caught on a bramble. Then she was out of sight and for an instant Nat thought he had lost her when she shouted, "It's here. I've found it." Sloan stood on the edge of a wide, shallow stream. "This is it. It's here. I knew I would find it."

"Find what?"

Sloan looked over her shoulder at him. "The water, dummy."

"So what?"

"This is the stream that leads to my house. If we follow it, it will take us there."

"You don't know that. It could be any old stream. There are thousands of streams. How do you know this goes to your house?"

"I can tell by lookin' at it," Sloan said. Nat picked up one of the flat stones along the bank and threw it, making it skip across the surface. Sloan hunkered down and dipped her fingers into the stream. It was so cold it stung. She straightened.

"Let's go."

"Go where?"

"To my house."

"We can't go now. We was just going to find the way, remember? It's too late to start now. We gotta wait and go in the morning."

"We've got lots of time. It doesn't get dark until late now."

Nat walked away from the stream to a grassy spot under a tree where he sat down and leaned against the trunk. "I said we ain't goin' today. Come here and sit on my lap."

"Fine then. I'll go my own self." Sloan started walking in the direction the water flowed.

"You better not go by yourself. Bears will get you."

"I told you I ain't afraid of bears."

"You oughta be. Come on back here. We'll go Monday. That's in two days. Or maybe Tuesday. Depends on how long it takes me to convince the other boys not to tell. But we'll go soon. Now come back here and sit on my lap."

The girl stopped. Water ran downhill. Maybe she should head in the other direction. Where the water was coming from. She didn't want to go without Nat, but now that she had a way to get home, she didn't want to wait. She turned around and started back with every intention of walking past the boy and following the stream as far as she could, but a rock sailed past her head and landed in the water, splashing her with icy cold. "Hey," she said.

"Aw come on. I'll go with you. Just not today. We'll go aways, to scout things out, and then we'll go back before supper. We don't want the Graftons getting suspicious. They might lock you in during the day too."

They followed the creek to where a large tree had fallen across it. The water was deep here, over Sloan's head and running fast. Holding her arms out straight for balance, she walked across the tree then turned and tottered back, placing one foot in front of the other as though on a tight rope. Nat took off his shoes and hopped up in front of her, nearly knocking her down. He put his arms around her and held her steady. When she had her balance back, he let her go and bounded across the tree to the other side, did something resembling a pirouette, and bounded back. He sat down and put his feet in the water. "Jesus," he said, but did not pull them out. Both he and Sloan watched the water whirling around his ankles. She sat beside him, but her feet didn't reach the creek. Something plopped into the water from the bank. Sloan recognized the sound immediately. Every spring and summer she brought turtles home from the nearby creek where she hunted them. She kept them in a paddle pool, feeding them flies and tomatoes until they died or winter came or they managed to climb out. She hitched along the tree on her bottom then dropped to the shore. "It's gone under the branches. Come on. Help me get it." The water came to just the soles of her shoes, and she was bent so low the tips of her hair dipped into it.

"You're crazy. Get out of the water."

"Why? You're already in it. Help me. It's right there. See. Under that branch. It's goin to dig itself into the mud. Hurry up!"

Nat pulled his numb feet out of the water and dropped beside Sloan, mud squishing between his toes. "Shit," he said.

"Quick. It's going to get away." Nat saw the turtle, its short legs pumping, as it tried to bury itself. He reached into the water and pulled it out. Hissing, the turtle snapped its head and feet into its shell. "There," Nat said. "You happy?" Sloan took the creature, which was smaller than the palm of her hand, and rubbed the black shining surface. She turned it over. "See those rings? It's only three years old." In the hierarchy of treasures, the newborn painted turtles were at the top. They were no bigger than a quarter and their shells were still soft and this time of year in the early spring you could find them along the banks easily. By July, or even June, they had learned to hide in the deeper water or bury themselves into the soft mud of the shoreline and Sloan was rarely able to bring the tiny creatures home once summer arrived. This three-year-old she held now had no value that could compare to the babies, but it was still the next in line. It was worth more than any frog, even the spring peepers that Sloan kept in a jar by her bed where they sang all night during their short season.

"How can you tell it's only three?"

"By these rings in each scale. Here, you can see," Sloan said, but Nat was looking at her and paying no attention to the turtle. She turned the little thing back onto its stomach, holding it lightly in her hand so that it couldn't jump free. "Let's go back now," she said.

"You ain't bringin' that thing."

"I am too."

"What are you going to do with it?"

"I'll put it in a bucket."

"The Grafton's ain't going to let you do that."

"Why not?"

"You ain't that dumb."

"I'll take care of it. It won't cause no trouble."

"They'll probably throw it in a pot and make turtle soup and make us eat it. Besides, we're leaving in a few days. Remember. It would be hard carrying that thing the whole way." He stepped closer to her. "You can catch another one when you get home. I'll help you. Promise. Here. I'll put it back."

Sloan turned her back to him. "No, I will." She bent over, put her hands into the frigid stream and opened them. The turtle began swimming immediately, diving down as fast as it could, its head straight out and its legs pumping.

Nat reached into the water for Sloan's hand. "Look what you done. Your sneakers are wet. You should have taken them off the way I did. You're gonna catch hell for sure. And look. You got scratches on your legs. Let's go wash the blood away."

"It's okay."

"You can't go back looking like that."

"I want to go back now."

"No, the Graftons will figure out where we was if you go back lookin' like that. Take your shoes off. They'll dry in five minutes in this sun."

"No. They're okay."

"Come on." He took her by the arm and led her away from the shore and pushed her to a sitting position on the grass and began untying the laces on her sneakers.

"I want to go now."

"This will only take a few minutes." Nat put his palm on the heel of her shoe and pulled off one then the other. He lined them up in the sun. "Come on now. Let's clean your legs." He walked her back to the water and cupped some in his hands and ran it down her thigh.

Sloan stepped backwards. "It's cold. Stop it."

"Hold still." He cupped more water and rubbed her leg again. He slid his hand onto the inside of her thigh and moved it up and down.

"Don't."

"Hold still."

"Don't. Please."

"I'm just trying to make sure we don't get caught." He put his hands on her shoulders and pushed her down on the ground then sat next to her. He reached into his pocket and pulled out sticks of red licorice. "Look what I brought for you. Bet you had no idea, did you." He handed her a stick. When Sloan put the end in her mouth he said, "See how good I am to you. Now! Who's your best friend?"

Sloan was pretty sure Nat wasn't her best friend and maybe not a friend at all. She had a feeling her mother wouldn't want her to take presents from him, but she couldn't think why. One thing she was becoming increasingly sure of though, was that it was time to leave this place and go back to the Grafton's. Or better yet, head for home on her own. She started to stand. Nat pulled her back down beside him then, putting his hand on the back of her neck, brought her face close to his and kissed her on the mouth. When she finally managed to struggle away, he laughed. "Yum," he said, "you taste real good." Sloan balled her hand into a fist and socked him on the jaw. Nat slapped her open-handed across the face, knocking her sideways. "What the hell's the matter with you?"

"You ain't supposed to kiss me."

"Sure I am. Ain't nothing wrong with friends kissing. Where'd you get that stupid idea."

"Not on the mouth, they ain't supposed to."

"Sure, they are. Especially when they get presents. Didn't your mama teach you any manners?" He looked closely at her face. "You'll be in big trouble if the Graftons see your face all messed up." He sat up and pulled off his shirt, went to the water's edge and soaked it. "Now keep this against your cheek, so it doesn't get all red."

Sloan held the cloth where he told her to and watched him checking her shoes.

"They're still wet."

"I want to go home."

"Well, you can't. Not yet." He pulled her hand away, inspected her cheek, and put the compress back. "You'll have to do this for a while," he said. Twice he dipped the shirt back in the creek to freshen it with the icy water before placing it against the side of her face again, taking her hand and telling her to keep it there until he said not to. The third time he inspected the skin closely, touching it here and there. Satisfied any remaining marks would be minimal, he shook the shirt out and hung it over the branch of a tree and returned to the little girl.

It bears saying that as brave and strong as she was, Sloan never stood a chance.

Chapter Fifteen

Annie wore her best dress-for-success outfit, an Armani charcoal gray suit she'd found for half price, black Italian leather pumps, and her hair in a tight chignon. Clare wore her savage look.

"I've gotten reports from Shahanna about your participation in the Parent Effectiveness Training Group," Dr. Wittcomb said.

Clare looked at her steadily.

"They aren't very good." Clare said nothing. "Shahanna says you started off by bringing up your past, saying you had had relations with most of the men in the group and in the following sessions you haven't said anything. She reports you stare at her."

"No one says anything that ain't trifling in that group. They tell jokes even. I don't know what purpose it's supposed to have, but it don't have any as far as I can see. There just ain't nothing worth talking about. No one takes this class seriously."

Dr. Wittcomb looked into the middle distance. She knew Clare was giving an accurate description of what went on in this group and other groups like it. Unfortunately, the courts insisted on it. It was concrete. Either the client went or they didn't, and either they participated or they didn't. This could be written into a report and presented to the court, giving clear yes or no answers. The fact that these groups were useless was beside the point. Dr Wittcomb turned to Annie. "It's the only measurement so far as to the progress Clare is making." She tweaked her fingers to imply quotes around the word progress.

Clare counted on her fingers. "I been to four sessions. That makes eight more to go. Eight weeks. That's too long. I know what happens in foster care. I want to go to court now."

Annie shifted in her chair. "What other signs of progress could they use?"

"A home visit. To see if there is evidence the bear is gone. And other things."

"The bear is gone," Clare said, her voice a little too loud.

"Unfortunately, we have to have evidence."

"That social worker can come out any time. The sooner the better," Clare said.

John straightened his back ever so slightly. "You have to have proof that the home is safe and a fit place for a child."

"It is fit."

Annie had placed her chair behind her friend so she could watch her without seeming to. Clare had gone still, and she watched Dr. Wittcomb as though reading her. Annie had always thought of her as the alpha wolf, but now she thought she was more like a fox or a cat. A big cat, not one of the small nervous domestic types. She pictured Bagheera in his cage learning the ways of man. She saw the black panther break that silly lock and return to the jungle, more terrible than ever for his new knowledge. She glanced around, searching for a clock and finding none, looked out the window to the parking lot below with the state cars, all white, lined up in a row. How had Clare Raffienne fetched up here in this bastion of bureaucracy, in this room with its diplomas on mustard walls, metal desk, stacks of folders, and stale air?

"Isn't there anything we can do?" John asked Dr Wittcomb.

"I'll talk to Marshall." The woman reached into her drawer and took out four Mounds bars and offered them around. Annie and John held up their palms politely, shaking their heads. She unwrapped hers and ate it, chewing slowly, giving herself time to think. "I'll talk to the old dragon at Social Services. She might set up a visit just because she's sure she can find cause not to return Sloan home. It will certainly be unannounced, so Clare, if you have anything that … um… needs tidying, I'd start right now. And that bear must go and you will need proof. I'm sorry about that, but it is what it is."

"If you get that social worker to come to inspect my house, it will pass, I swear. And that bear is already gone." Clare rose, reached over, and helped herself to a Mounds bar. John moved his chair back and stood next to her with one hand in his pants pocket, fiddling with his keys.

Annie noticed the expression on his face as he waited for Clare to make the next move. Well, she thought. Of course. How did I not see this coming? She looked at Dr. Wittcomb, who wore an innocent expression, but maybe not so much. Perhaps it was the director who was the fox.

Annie and Clare were stuffing bourbon and beer bottles between bales of hay when a state car that was not John Avery's pulled into the driveway. Jumping down from the hay, they brushed away the chaff on their heads and clothes then made for the kitchen where they sat and folded their hands on the table. Ms. Platt knocked twice then opened the door and came in. Clare looked at her without getting up. "Do come in," she said, and Annie kicked her under the table.

Ms. Platt looked at Annie. "We still don't have the matter of confidentiality cleared up. The child's, that is," she added without conviction.

"You may have physical custody, Ms. Platt, but her mother is still the legal guardian. She signs any legal documents. She signs the releases. In fact, you have to get her permission to talk to anyone about Sloan or to have any medical procedure or anything else that requires the legal guardian's signature." Annie had done her homework.

Ms. Platt looked relieved. "You may be right about that. I'll check with my supervisor. In the meantime, I don't think there will be a problem if you're here while I just look around." She turned to Clare. "May I?" She had a clipboard in her hand.

"Look away," said Clare, and Annie kicked her again. "Be nice," she mouthed.

Ms. Platt opened the woodstove, shut it, examined the metal chimney, wrote a few notes, ran the water in the sink, said, "The Health Department will have to check this. It comes from a well, I suppose."

"No, it comes from a spring. Didn't you see the spring house when you drove up?" It was, in fact, the oldest and most substantial building on the property, made of stone and mortar.

"That's even more questionable than a well. All kinds of contaminates can live in a spring house. You will have to put in a UV light, I'm sure."

Clare frowned. "What's that?

"UV light, when it shines on a source of water, kills the bacteria."

"How much is that going to cost to put in?"

"A few hundred, I suspect."

"Are you kidding me?"

"No." Ms. Platt made more notes on her clip board before walking into the living room. She looked around then stepped into the thin hall where she spotted the feed room. She took a deep breath.

"What is this?" She stepped into the room of hay and sacks of feed, swiveled her head from side to side, wrote on the clipboard, looked at Clare and said, "How long has this straw and grain been in here?"

"Hay."

Ms. Platt stared at her.

"It's hay, not straw."

"Well, hay then. How long has it been here?"

"It's always been here."

Don't look between the bales, Annie thought. Just don't look between the bales.

"This is very bad. I can't believe no one mentioned this to me. Surely you know what a fire hazard this is. It will have to go, all of it, before we can even think about reunification."

The shaky stairs, the missing windowpane in the upstairs hall, and the obvious lack of heat in the two bedrooms were added to the clipboard. Ms. Platt eased her backside onto a stair step, rested the clip board in her lap. "You know I have to put the hay in my report. There is just no way I can ignore it."

"I'll have it out by tomorrow."

"I might be able to ignore some of the other things." The social worker shifted her weight from haunch to haunch. "I mean, the stairs aren't that wobbly." She scratched out a line on her tablet. "But the window needs to be fixed. You could use duct-tape to close it off. And the bathroom is adequate. You don't have any heat upstairs, but if you leave the doors open that might be okay. But the hay must go. And I worry about the woodstove. It doesn't look well ventilated. It could also be a fire hazard. And, of course Environmental Health will have to check the water."

Back in the kitchen, she said, "You'll get a copy of my report in two weeks."

"Two weeks is too long." Clare leaned her hip against the door that led to the back yard.

"Marshall will want a report as well," said Annie. "We need it ASAP so we can comply as soon as possible."

Ms. Platt sighed at the mention of Marshall. She stood in the middle of the bare kitchen in her too tight dress and pale soft skin with sweat breaking out above her upper lip and when Annie asked her if she wanted a glass of water, crimson burst along her cheeks. She looked at Annie steadily, hesitated a beat before she said with surprising dignity, "No. Thank-you. Not until it's tested." She reached in her purse for her keys. "I'm going to move things along as fast as possible. I'll write up this report as soon as I get back to the office. Maybe Social Services can help with the cost of a UV light. They do sometimes if the income indicates it. If I leave now, I can catch Environmental Services before they're gone for the day and I'll ask. Can you give me an estimate of your income? I just need a verbal statement. We can firm it up with documentation later."

"You mean annually?"

"Yes. Or monthly would do."

"Well, it varies."

"Just an estimate."

Clare straightened, crossed her arms, and looked out the window.

"Oh, it'd be around five, six thousand."

"A month?"

Clare laughed. "God no. A year."

Ms. Platt's eyes went wide, and Annie saw shock in them as disbelief crossed her face. The social worker looked steadily at Clare. "How can you possibly live on that?"

"We own the house and land. And I garden."

Annie looked away.

"We will need some kind of verification, but that definitely qualifies." To Ms. Platt's credit, her eyes never wavered from Clare's, never strayed to the rusted sink, the one cupboard, the questionable woodstove or the floor sagging in the middle.

Annie rose and walked toward the door. "Clare may have underestimated a little. We will look for last year's tax returns. Excuse me," she said as she moved in front of Clare and placed her hand on the door handle. "Thank you for coming so quickly, Ms. Platt. We appreciate it and I know you will move things along as fast as possible."

"Of course." The social worker put her clipboard under her arm. "For the record, Ms. Raffienne, we want reunification as much as you do."

"The hell."

Annie opened the door, moving Clare slightly aside as she did so. "Thank you again. We will call you in a day or two."

Once Ms. Platt was safely in her car, Annie turned to Clare. "Work with me a little, won't you? It doesn't do any good to piss everyone off."

"She took Sloan away from me."

"She's just doing what she is told. She didn't take Sloan away. The administration did. The law did. The government."

"She was there. Right there in the same room."

"She was doing what she was told to do."

"Just following orders like any good little Nazi."

"Don't do that. It won't help."

"And mocking her by asking if she wanted to poison herself by drinking my water was helpful, I suppose."

Annie laughed. "A mistake. I admit it."

Clare stuffed her hands in her pockets and looked down at her boots. After a moment, she said, "Okay, okay." She glanced up. "But, Annie, there ain't no way I can find any tax returns."

Annie laughed again. "Of course you can't. Never mind. The water might pass and, anyway, we've got bigger fish to fry. Like that hay in the house."

They walked into the feed room and began throwing bales of hay from the top of the stack. The house shook as each fragrant, tightly wrapped bundle hit the floor. Halfway through, Annie stopped to catch her breath and wipe the sweat off her forehead with her shirt sleeve. "Where will you put this stuff?"

"I'll get one of them big blue tarps from Lowes."

"That's fine, as long as the rain only comes straight down."

"I'll get two." Clare kept throwing bales. She moved quickly and Annie jumped down. "You know that hay is going to get moldy," Annie said. "And then the horses are going to get sick, probably die, you know that. You know that mold can kill a horse in a day, we've seen it happen and then you won't have a livelihood. And just try getting Sloan back with no means of support." Clare stopped. "Do you think my low income will be a problem? She said I was below the poverty line."

"It won't be a problem if you show you can care for Sloan adequately. Which means a stream of income. So, we'll do this right. We'll build a shed."

"I ain't got that kind of money."

"I do."

"I can't let you do that."

"You helped me when I had no one. And you've taken care of Lonesome all these years. And still are."

Clare stopped throwing bales of hay. She stood still, her head touching the ceiling. "Well," she said, finally. "I guess."

At dawn the morning after Ms. Platt's visit, Clare drank her Coca Cola straight from the can. She drank with her head back and eyes closed. When her belly felt tight, she put the can back in the refrigerator and went outside. There was the sound of an SUV coming around the bend. Annie parked, stepped out, and stood next to it. She had on a t-shirt and blue jeans and Clare thought she looked like a scrawny kid.

Annie smiled.

"You think you're up to this?"

"Why wouldn't I be?"

They drove Clare's truck to the lumber mill Pap had always used.

"Clare Raffienne," Henry said and that was all. He was a short man, a square man, with wide shoulders and no waist. He helped the women load and secure seven four by sixes—three for the back of the shed, two for the sides, and two for the door frame—in the bed of the truck, which they then drove to Clare's and unloaded. They returned to the mill where, with Henry's help, they sorted through a large, untidy stack of two-by-fours, throwing the straightest ones into the truck bed. They made two trips with the back of the truck piled high, the boards strapped in with rope and bungee cords. After they unloaded the last board, Clare brought a sledgehammer, twine, and posthole digger from the house. They measured a twelve-by-twelve section of land close to the pasture and marked it with stakes and twine. Clare selected a corner, spread the poles of the posthole digger apart, and jabbed the metal blades into the ground. She pulled the poles together, raised her arms and lifted a cylindrical lump of dirt between the blades, making the beginnings of a hole. The two women took turns repeating this until they had made seven holes three feet deep, and the sun was straight over head.

A truck pulled into the driveway and parked behind Annie's SUV. Three men jumped out. They looked to be in their late teens, early twenties.

"Did you bring lunch?" said Clare.

The oldest one nodded. Black-haired, light-skinned, and raw-boned, they all had the look of men from the Holler.

"Annie, these are my cousins Otis, Gunner, and Tom."

None of the men looked at Annie but directed their eyes to a space above her. Clare sat on the piles of wood. "What did you bring us?"

"Thought you might like some fried chicken," said Otis, the oldest of the three. He produced two large buckets.

"Tom," Clare said to the youngest, "run inside and bring us some water."

Otis and Gunner sat on the boards as far away from Annie and Clare as possible. Otis put the buckets between them. Tom returned with a plastic pitcher and five glasses. He sat with the other men. Clare opened a bucket and took out two pieces of heavily breaded, crispy chicken, shiny with grease. "Yum," she said. She handed a piece to Annie. She hadn't seen her cousins in months, did not, in fact, hang out with them. But every one of them as babies had shared her bed, waking with their small bodies curled against her and the sheets wet with piss. When the venison or the wood for the stoves ran out or when whatever their parents had done was serious enough that the law might even go into the Holler looking for them, their families moved in with the Raffiennes. Pap claimed he would have turned them away, but her grandmother never would.

From time to time, Clare called in her markers. The cousins never turned her down. She didn't know if it was out of loyalty to Pap or because they thought of her as crazy, a woman alone, unnatural, a woman who in her wildness was rumored to have burned a man's house down to the ground. There was a chivalry for women like this, women touched by something beyond them, out of control.

Now, Annie, Clare, and the three men sat in the unseasonably warm spring sun eating chicken and biscuits. No one spoke. Clare ate five pieces of chicken and three biscuits, downed a glass of water in several long gulps, then stood up. The men dutifully groaned, wiped their hands on their jeans, gathered tools from the truck, laid them in the center of the twelve-by-twelve square, picked up a six-by-four and dropped it into a hole. They filled the hole in with dirt and rocks, tamping around it with a tamping bar. After all seven poles were in, they began hammering up the two by fours. They worked until dark. The shed was complete except for shingles on the roof.

Gunner leaned on the post hole digger. "Your friend there," he said, careful to keep his eyes off Annie, "she's stronger than she looks."

Annie smiled and looked away.

"She's bashful too," said Clare.

"She ain't like you then," Otis said to the air around Annie. "Nothin bashful about our Clare. Even so, she stays too much to yourself, you know. Women ain't meant to live alone. 'Course, it would be best if she got herself a man."

"I don't need a man except for one thing."

The men laughed, looked at each other, and shook their heads. "If you get them shingles, we'll be back tomorrow." Still careful not to look at Annie, Gunner said, "Nice to meet you, miss." Then nodding in Clare's direction, "Don't work her so hard she runs off now."

Back in the kitchen, Clare filled two glasses with bourbon and Coke and handed one to her friend. "So, tomorrow we get all the grain and hay out of the yard and into the shed. The guys will put on the shingles." She watched Annie over the top of her glass as she drank. "Of course, you don't need to help with that if you're busy. I can manage."

"No, I'm not busy." Annie looked at her hands, which were blistered along the fleshy ridge of the palm.

"I got something for that." Clare went into the feed room and returned with a roll of duct-tape. "Here, put this on them. It'll fix you right up."

"Are you serious?"

Clare ripped off a piece and, using her teeth, tore it into squares. She put one on her blister and held her palm out for Annie to inspect. "Leave it on for 48 hours and the blister will be completely gone." When Annie hesitated, Clare took her hand and placed a square of the gray tape on each raw spot then wrapped a single strip around the palm and sealed it off. She drank some bourbon while Annie gingerly touched the spots.

"Just trust me, Annie. It works, I swear. So, when do you think we can go to court?"

Her friend looked up from inspecting her hand. "Ms. Platt has to come back to check and see if the house is fit and we should get another report from Shahanna about your participation… a positive one."

"I can't wait no eight weeks until them classes is over."

"We're working on it. Normally, the courts won't even consider a case until the parenting classes are completed, but I think Marshall can speed things up. I'm hoping, anyway."

Clare sat heavily in a chair. She ran her fingers through her hair. Annie sat across from her. "I'll be here as soon as it gets light," she said. Clare nodded. The women drank in silence for several minutes. When her glass was empty, Annie rose. "I'd better not drink any more. I don't want to get arrested for drunk driving on the way home."

"No, you sure don't."

After Annie left, Clare poured herself another drink. She sat staring at the black window, tried to keep her mind empty. Even so, the images started again.

This time when she heard the motor there was no surprise in it. The car approached, stopped, a door shut, and John Avery walked into the kitchen without knocking. Clare shifted her gaze from the window, looked up at him with her slanted, feral eyes. He knelt, put his head in her lap, and wrapped his arms around her waist.

Annie arrived early the next day. When she walked into the kitchen, John was at the table. He looked up and smiled. Clare was making eggs and bacon. "Have breakfast with us," she said.

Annie sat down, and Clare filled a plate with scrambled eggs and four slices of bacon; poured a tumbler full of orange juice and put the breakfast in front of John. She did not look at Annie. She took some applesauce out of the refrigerator, put it in a bowl, and placed it in front of John. Then she made two smaller plates and put them on the table.

When Annie glanced at him, John was watching her to see if she realized the way it was. It wasn't an insolent or even impertinent expression and yet it let her know nothing was going to change. He was more beautiful than any of the others and he knew it without it ruining him. It just gave him a certain grace. He switched his gaze to Clare and smiled. "You're a good cook."

"I know."

John laughed. He had lovely hands, his thin wrist bent just so when he used his knife and fork.

"I make the best fried chicken and potato salad you'll ever eat." To Annie's amazement, Clare blushed.

"I can't wait." John laughed again. "When will you make them for me?"

"Soon. Maybe tonight."

John watched her across the table. Clare dropped her eyes.

She was well into it, that was for sure. She was more into it than Annie had ever seen her, and it was one hell of a situation.

"So," said John. "Dinner tonight?"

Clare laughed. "Yeah, maybe." She poured him more juice and looked at Annie steadily. Annie stood and took her plate to the sink, washed it, and put it into the drainer. Then she took the other two plates and washed those. John watched Clare across the table.

"I guess we should get to work," she said, but did not get up.

"Have you been to see Sloan?" Annie leaned against the counter. They both looked at her.

"Yes." John rose. "I've got to get to work too. The breakfast was great. Thanks, and, um, I'll see you later." He looked at Clare but didn't smile this time. She watched him until he was out of the house then turned to Annie.

"He saw her yesterday and don't look at me like that. He's a nice boy. I think he really cares about Sloan."

"I hope so."

"Don't get all high and mighty with me, Annie. He's a nice boy. He brings his little sister here. She'll be good for Sloan when she gets back. I like him. I like him a lot."

"I can't think of a worse person for you to like right now."

"No one's gonna find out. And he's sweet. You know how I am."

"Yes, I do."

"I'm not going to feel guilty. This is who I am."

"I don't think I've ever seen you blush before."

"Oh, give it a rest." Clare wasn't blushing now. She stood up. "Let's get that stuff into the shed and that social worker back out here."

Chapter Sixteen

Sloan had never seen so many mirrors. They were everywhere along the walls, from floor to ceiling, bouncing back bright light.

"I'm taking you to the beauty parlor," Mrs. Grafton had told her, "To get your hair fixed."

The girl had no idea what a beauty parlor was, but she imagined everyone in it would be beautiful. They were not. Two very fat women draped in voluminous black capes sat looking at themselves in the mirrors in front of them while smaller women fussed at the old ladies' short hair. A man, also wearing a cape, sat in another chair, while a younger man, hardly more than a boy, fluffed and snipped at the gray fuzz on the sides of the older man's head. Other women walked between the rows of chairs or worked next to them. They were thin, some had bright hair, pink, orange, or white, and this, along with the dazzling light that filled the room, made Sloan wonder if this were Disneyland or at least part of it. Mrs. Grafton held her hand in a firm grip and gave the name Joan Grafton to a young woman sitting behind a kiosk. The girl did not look up. She ran a black painted nail down a column in the book lying open in front of her then started down a second column where she stopped midway. "Yes, you're here. You'll be seeing Jill." She looked up, her expression bored and slightly irritated until she saw Sloan. "Well, don't you have pretty hair," she said. Her own hair, cut chin length, was as black as any Sloan had ever seen and looked as though it had been chewed by rats. Blue kohl outlined her eyes and her lips were an uncompromising red. Sloan wondered if she was supposed to be Minnie Mouse. She looked up at Mrs. Grafton, but the woman's face was immobile. It had been immobile all day. Even so, Sloan tugged at her hand as they followed one of the young slender women to a station. "Is she supposed to be Minnie Mouse?"

Mrs. Grafton frowned. "What?"

"That girl back there. Is she trying to look like Minnie Mouse? 'Cause she don't really."

"What on earth are you talking about?"

The young woman pushed a stool in front of Sloan. "Here sweetie. I'm Jill and I'll be doing your hair today. Just step on this and into the chair, that's right, hang on a sec and we'll get you situated just right." She pumped a lever close to the floor with her foot as Sloan watched herself slowly rise in front of the mirror, her eyes a green blaze of wonder. Jill swooshed a black cape into the air and around Sloan's shoulders, fastened it in the back then lifted her hair out from underneath, spreading it wide. "What's your name, sweetie?"

"It's Joan," said Mrs. Grafton.

The stylist opened her hands, palms facing toward Sloan's head then she ran them under and through the child's hair, letting it fall slowly between her fingers back into place. "Strawberry blond. You don't see that very often." She took a few strands between her first two fingers and thumb and examined the ends. "So, Joan, what are we doing today? Just snipping off these dry ends? An inch? Maybe an inch and a half?"

Sloan had stopped watching herself in the mirror and looked at Jill. "Are you supposed to be Cinderella?"

"What? Oh heavens. Do I look like Cinderella to you?"

Sloan nodded.

"Well, I guess I could." Jill leaned forward a little, examining her own reflection. "Blonde hair piled up on my head. Blue eye shadow. Too much blue eye shadow, maybe." She looked at Mrs. Grafton. "Nothing like kids to tell it to you straight." She smiled at Sloan. "And you must be a princess with your beautiful long, red and gold hair and your flowy black robe."

Sloan smiled back at her.

"So, an inch? Inch and a half?"

"Cut it all off," said Mrs. Grafton.

Jill frowned. "You mean like to her shoulders? Her hair is remarkably healthy. Have you ever had your hair cut before, sweetie?"

"My mama cuts it sometimes."

Jill held a section of hair about three inches from the end between her first two fingers. "How's this? This will really tidy it up."

Mrs. Grafton made a gesture of impatience. "I want it cut off. Like mine."

Jill hesitated. "I guess you want it cool for the summer. Of course, she could always wear it in a ponytail."

"I want it short like mine. Maybe shorter. So you don't have to comb it… almost. So you can wash it real quick. At the sink. Once a week. No bother."

"Does she brush her own hair?"

"No, she don't."

"Joan, if we take off three, four inches, will you brush your own hair? So your mama won't have to. You're a big girl now. You can do that, can't you?" Jill looked at Mrs. Grafton. "Does she swim in a public pool? I know they put so much chlorine in the water it can be terribly hard on hair. Make it coarse, hard to brush. Hers doesn't look that bad, but it could be smoother, easier to work with if you use conditioner. We have a really good one here."

"I swim in creeks."

"You swim in creeks. Aren't you lucky. No swimming pools for you, huh?"

Sloan shook her head and smiled.

"I don't want to use conditioner; I just want it short enough so's it's no trouble."

Jill looked at Mrs. Grafton. Finally, she picked up a brush and brushed out the girl's hair. It snapped and crackled, sending out sparks. Sloan ducked her head.

"It's okay. It's just dry in here." Jill put gel in her palm, rubbed her hands together, and ran them over the child's head. "There, that should be okay." She took several long clips out of a drawer, sectioned the hair up onto Sloan's head, borrowed more clips from the neighboring station to hold the long pieces out of the way, loosened a piece in the front, held it straight up and cut it off two inches from the scalp.

Sloan opened her mouth and howled at the same time she hurtled herself out of the chair, sending the scissors flying and scrambled, despite the flapping black cape, into the cubby hole under the shelf and hunkered there ready to smack anyone who tried to touch her.

Jill grabbed her scissors off the floor. "It's all right. It's all right. Happens all the time when kids come for their first cut. They're generally younger, that's all." She gave the scissors a quick look to assess any damage then placed them into the sink. She tried to smile reassuringly at Mrs. Grafton, but the woman was bent over, peering into the cubby. "You come out from under there this minute," she nearly shouted.

Sloan didn't move.

Jill squatted in front of the girl. "You know what we give princesses after we have made them even more beautiful than they were before. We give them a lollipop. You'd like a lollipop, wouldn't you? It's okay, Joan, just come out and we will make you more glamourous than you can ever imagine."

Sloan didn't move.

"What's your favorite flavor?"

Silence.

"Your mama here just wants you to be comfortable when it gets really hot. Lots of princesses have short hair."

"She ain't my mother."

"Well, I know sometimes we feel that way, but really, Mama does know best."

"She ain't my mother and my name ain't Joan and it ain't Grafton. It's Sloan Raffienne and I want to go home."

Jill looked at Mrs. Grafton, who stood straight and obdurate. "She's my foster child."

"Your foster child?"

"Yes."

"I wish we'd known that sooner. I'm going to have to get my supervisor."

Jill returned with a big, blond young man who looked like a Viking warrior.

"I'm Michael, the owner, and I understand that this…" He waved a hand toward the cubby hole. "…is not your daughter but a foster child."

"Yes."

Michael put his weight on one hip. "I'm afraid we won't be able to cut or do anything to her hair. I'm sorry, but those are state regulations. Unless you have a written and notarized document from her mother, we are not allowed to touch a foster child's hair. Do you have such a document? No. Well, I am sorry, but there is nothing we can do until you have one. It's a shame you made a wasted trip. We'd love to help you when you have this straightened out. Have a good rest of the day." Michael rolled his eyes at Jill before he turned his back on the scene and, surprisingly graceful for a big man, slipped away.

"I'm sorry. If we had known, we could have saved you from this." Jill bent over again. "Come on out… ah… sweetie. No one's going to cut your hair."

When they were on the street, Mrs. Grafton held Sloan's hand. Instead of heading to the car, she turned left and walked to the end of the block, made a right, turned, and went into the Dollar General. She maneuvered the girl through the cramped aisles toward the back of the store, where she took a Raggedy Ann doll off a shelf. It was classic with red yarn hair, shoe-button eyes, stitched mouth, and cloth body. She had seen it here last week when she had come in to get jars of peanut butter and grape jelly. Mrs. Grafton held the doll in front of Sloan. "I'm sorry," she said.

Sloan looked at it blankly. She had barely kept up with her foster mother, limply tripping over her own feet and when in the store bumping into merchandise spilling into the aisle.

"This is for you."

Sloan gave no indication she had heard or understood anything.

Mrs. Grafton looked into the girl's exhausted, pale face and gave the doll a slight shake. "This is for you. It's a present."

Sloan said nothing.

Mrs. Grafton took Sloan's arm, put it around the doll, and pressed it to her chest. When she took her hand away, Sloan let the doll drop. The woman picked it up and tried again. "This is a present for you. I am sorry I tried to cut your hair. I will never do it again. Promise." This time when she took her hand away, Sloan held onto Raggedy Ann.

"She looks like you, don't she? Same red hair and pretty eyes. I thought when I seen her, why that looks just like Sloan." She rested her hand ever so lightly on the top of the girl's head.

Sloan dropped her head, resting her cheek on the red yarn.

Mrs. Grafton's hand hovered in the air. "Don't you cry now. No need to cry. I just thought maybe you'd like a doll what looks like you. That's all. We can just pretend this never happened. No need to tell Mr. Grafton about the haircut. It would just make him mad. This will be our little secret. Okay?"

Chapter Seventeen

John decided that Sunday afternoon would be a good time to find out what family life was really like for the Grafton's band of children. The day was unseasonably warm for the end of April. He stopped the car next to the greenhouse. The gray plastic covering the top and sides of the structure looked dirty, and there was a triangle tear in the top over the door. The buds on the trees around the building were still just tiny bumps along dark limbs. A few scrub pines formed a copse several yards back from the building.

There was an astonishingly successful greenhouse out on route 336. It too was a fair drive from town but that didn't stop the wealthiest of Coleton driving out there and spending hundreds, thousands of dollars in the spring, all through the summer and well into the fall when they bought their bulbs for the next year. To have your plants, trees, and shrubs not come from Obelmyers was a sure sign that you weren't quite the right stuff. The truly elite had them do their landscaping. But who, John wondered, frequented Grafton's greenhouse? The ordinary people of Coleton bought their flora from Lowes or Walmart. Possibly there was a town farther down the road, but it would have to be awfully small because John hadn't heard of it. The spring sun on the plastic made it look even dirtier and the shapes inside were just a darker gray. John wondered again how the Graftons made a living out here and then it hit him. Of course. The foster children. He stepped on the gas and drove a little too quickly to the house. A white Dodge pickup with graying paint in places, dents along the sides, and the air of a humble, overworked, and aging horse, was parked in front. As he started to get out of the car, he noticed Sloan wearing a blue and white frock sitting in a tree and braiding a doll's hair. John was about to call to her when the tall, light brown boy came from around the house. He had an animal grace and though he didn't appear to hurry, covered the distance between him and the little girl in an easy, long-legged stride and reached for Sloan's foot just as she noticed him. She struggled to stand but was hampered by her hold on the doll. The boy grabbed her ankle and yanked her out of the tree, his arms sliding under her dress as he did so. He kissed her quickly on the mouth and then laughing, let her go.

John catapulted out of the car. "Hey!"

"That boy cannot be around Sloan," John said once they were in the house.

Mr. and Mrs. Grafton sat on the couch opposite him. The woman kept her eyes on the wall over his head and so far, had not said a word.

"We never let the boys play with Joan," Mr. Grafton said.

"I just saw that kid outside alone with Sloan and he was…" John glanced at the boy, who looked back steadily. "He pulled her out of a tree and put his hands under her dress. Then he kissed her. On the mouth. What's your name, anyway?"

"Nat."

"How old are you?"

"His name is Nathaniel and he's seventeen. And he couldn't possible have done what you said because these children are supervised at all times."

"I was just out there, and I know what I saw." John thought of Dr. Wittcomb and what he knew by now about staying on good terms with the parents and still he couldn't control the tone of his voice. He thought of Clare and what she would do if she were here. Of what she would do if she even found out about that boy. Of what with her face like knives, she would think of him here in this living room doing nothing. He took a deep breath. "Let's not quibble about your supervision. I'm sure you and Mrs. Grafton do a very good job, but no one is perfect, and Nathaniel was alone with Sloan, and he was holding her. Under her dress. And he kissed her."

Sloan sat in a straight chair next to him, her knees together and her head down. She hadn't looked up since they had arranged themselves in the living room.

"Missy, is that true? Did Nathaniel… touch you in a way he shouldn't?"

Sloan didn't raise her head.

"You shouldn't be alone with them boys, you know that. Why weren't you with Mother?"

The room was silent.

"Answer me, missy."

Sloan looked helplessly at John.

"I didn't touch her except to catch her when she fell out of the tree. She would have hurt herself if I hadn't grabbed her."

"That was not the way it happened. I was there."

"You must need glasses then."

What an unbelievable smart ass. "Now you listen—" Before he could say any more, Grafton interrupted. "And you, young lady, what were you doing up in a tree? You know you are not supposed to be in trees."

Sloan kept her eyes down and a had a death grip on the doll.

"Sloan," said John, struggling to keep his voice calm, "did that boy kiss you?"

Sloan shook her head no.

John sat back against the chair.

"I didn't do nothin' wrong, I swear." Nathaniel smiled at John.

John looked around the room, vaguely noticed the patterned wallpaper, the hall with the staircase leading to the bedrooms. He looked back to the Graftons sitting side-by-side and Sloan, her face wet, and Nat with his black ponytail and strong body. "I will have to call Child Protective Services. It's the rules. I know you don't want me to have to do that," he took a deep breath, "and neither do I. And this is not Sloan's fault. You mustn't blame Sloan."

"Now, there ain't no need to call anyone, Mr. Avery. That girl may have slipped outside when she wasn't supposed to and climbed a tree when she wasn't supposed to and fallen 'cause girls have no business in trees, but Mother will make sure nothing of the sort happens again." Grafton held his hand out to his wife. "Now, let's pray. Take Mr. Avery's hand there, Joanie; Nathaniel, you take Mother's."

John shot further back in his chair and pressed his hands into his lap. "I don't do that. I mean we… ah, don't get into religious matters. Not allowed. You can pray when I leave. Of course…" He glanced at the front door. "I want to talk to Sloan alone."

"You mean, Joan."

"We've already been over this. Her given name is Sloan."

"You take her out on the porch," said Mrs. Grafton, startling John.

The little girl sat on the swing hanging from the porch ceiling. She held onto the doll, crossed her ankles, and regarded John. There was no other furniture, so he sat on the top step, below her.

"Sloan," he said.

She nodded.

"I'm here to help you. But to do that, I need you to tell me the truth. Has that boy ever touched you where he shouldn't?"

Sloan lowered her eyes.

"Has he ever touched places that are private?"

Slowly Sloan shook her head.

She seemed older than when he'd first seen her, distant, ethereal… even fey. "Listen, Sloan," he said. "Stay away from that boy. Don't be alone with him. Okay? Can you promise me that? I'm going to talk to my supervisor about this. Maybe we can have that boy moved to another home."

Mrs. Grafton's voice carried. "You're gonna put us all in jail."

Sloan began to cry again.

Inside the car, John did not immediately turn on the engine. Christ. That boy was insolent as hell. He should be behind bars. And why would Sloan deny he kissed her? Maybe she was ashamed. She had no reason to be, but you didn't know with kids. If John reported this to Protective Services, who would believe him if the kids both denied it?

"My God, I hate this job," he said. He looked at himself in the rear-view mirror. "No, you don't," he told himself. "The truth is you love this job because without it you never would have met Clare. Let's get that straight and keep it straight."

Once John had driven away and the children were sent to their rooms, Grafton turned to his wife and said, "You call foster care today and have that boy removed."

"That ain't the deal."

Grafton stared into the distance, his mouth working. "Four ought to be enough."

"Nathaniel is worse than the four put together."

Grafton stared out the window, his mouth continuing to work then he stepped forward and grabbed his wife's upper arm and squeezed it as hard as he could. He bent his head close to hers. "You keep that son of a bitch away from Joan, you hear me? I don't ever want them alone together again." He let her go. "And call foster care anyway and see if they will take him away."

There was a twitch along John Avery's jaw. He has changed, thought Dr. Wittcomb. I should never have assigned him this case. I should have given it to one of the ones who are just putting in their time until they can find something else. Not Chrissy, though. Clare would push Chrissy right over the edge. One of the truly detached. Except Clare would probably have kicked them out of the house and not let them back in. Unlike John. Dr. Wittcomb frowned and reached in her drawer for two Mounds bars and handed one to Avery. "You could use a boost."

He accepted it and absentmindedly put it in his shirt pocket. "Thanks for seeing me so early. I really appreciate it. You see…"

Dr. Wittcomb waved a hand, indicating he should sit down.

John sat on the edge of the chair. "There is this boy. He's older than the rest. He pulled Sloan out of a tree and his hands went under her dress." He drew a deep breath.

"What was she doing in a tree?"

"Playing. You know. Kids climb trees. And this boy walks around the house and fast as a panther jumps and grabs her foot and then yanks her so she fell right against him."

"Could it have been an accident?"

"No. I'm sure it wasn't. You see, he kissed her. On the mouth. You should have seen the look on his face. Insolent as hell."

Dr. Wittcomb hove back against her chair. "Kissed her?" She stopped unwrapping the candy and placed it on her desk. "Go on."

"I took the kids into the house and told the Graftons what had happened, but Mr. Grafton had the strangest reaction. He was all over Sloan. Not the boy, who is the one he should have gone after. Kept insisting it couldn't have happened because the children are always supervised. Didn't say a word to that boy who looked about twenty-five and strong as a middle weight. And then, then he wanted to pray about it."

The woman raised an eyebrow. "Pray?"

"Yes, like in holding hands. They wanted me to hold hands with them. I said no, of course. And he insists on calling her Joan or Joanie even though I correct him. Says Sloan is a boy's name. Is that legal? Can we make him stop?"

"It would take forever and hopefully she'll be home by then. Did she say anything to you about what's going on? The little girl? You spoke to her alone, I'm sure."

"No, she didn't say a word, just sat as still as a terrified rabbit and she cried. When I confronted that boy in front of the Graftons, he denied it. And you know what? So did Sloan. Why would she do that? I know what I saw."

"It's not unusual. Kids feel ashamed, as though somehow it is their fault."

"How could it possibly be her fault?"

"It's not rational." Dr Wittcomb looked out the window. Spring was showing itself in the tiny buds on the trees and the dark pointed leaves poking through the ground, but she didn't really notice. She didn't really see anything, was only aware in an imageless part of herself of the inevitability of things and the knowledge of how little control she had. After a pause, she turned back to John. "You're right. We have to get her out of there. I'll call Marshall."

"Is there anything I should do?"

"Keep going out there. Unscheduled. That was a good move."

The clinician's eyes followed the boy as he left the office. She watched him walk down the hall and continued staring out her door after he had disappeared. Eventually, she reached for the phone, ready to ask Marshall for one last favor.

That afternoon, the case of Clare Raffienne versus the State of Pennsylvania was placed on the docket for the following Thursday morning at nine o'clock.

Chapter Eighteen

The night before court, Clare took her saddle, bridle, and brush box, and placed them in the new shed. She brought Lonesome out of the pasture, tied him to a ring nailed to an outside wall, and brushed him. She ran her hand along his top line, felt the leg tendons, his fetlocks, and knees. "What do you think? These old bones strong enough to take me up the mountain again?" She laid her head against his neck. She could have taken a younger horse, but she needed Lonesome for this ride.

Clare placed the saddle pad and saddle on the horse's back and cinched up the girth. Taking the dandy brush, she brushed the gelding along his forehead, around his eyes and then his muzzle, put the brush back in the box and tightened the cinch another notch. When she slid the bit into his mouth, Lonesome lowered his head so she could slip the bridle over his ears. Grabbing a hank of mane, she swung into the saddle. A breeze picked up and though clear, the evening turned cold.

They went straight up the mountain, the horse's haunches working hard, but his breathing remained steady so Clare kept to the straight climb. She rode the colts this way to muscle them up and had not minded passing the old places until tonight. Tonight, she minded, but it was nothing compared to her fear of tomorrow. Breaking away from the main path, she rode the horse between the trees. The moon came out and by its light, she made her way along the tree line. It was very cold. She looked down at the valley floor. Her own place halfway up was invisible, hidden by the woods, but Annie's old farm stood out clearly, the lights shining from the house and all the lampposts put up by the new owners.

Clare put a hand on her belly. Sloan had been conceived on that farm, on the bank next to the swimming hole. She had not loved the father, but when the nurse put the baby in her arms and she saw the red gold hair standing straight out and the skin as white as fine china, Clare had buried her face in the wrapped bundle and said, "Thank you, Jesus," though she was not one to turn to the Lord in any situation. Looking at the child, she knew exactly who the father was, a red-headed, well-built, nice boy from Coleton she never had to see again. Sloan belonged to Clare and Clare alone. Except now she belonged to the State of Pennsylvania.

Clare Raffienne versus the State of Pennsylvania.

She hadn't dressed warmly enough and was shaking. Even so, she rode the along edge of the mountain, her eyes on the ground. There were no footprints, but the food she had scattered was gone. That bear had been here all right. The light was fading so she dismounted and searched for prints on foot until it was too dark even for that. "Come on," she said and turned the horse around to start the trip home. Clare rocked miserably in the saddle as Lonesome picked his way. He stopped once, frozen, his ears intently forward. Clare peered in the same direction. Black and curved like a Lakota drawing, the she-bear moved among the trees and behind her the same silhouette, only smaller, followed.

She gave the gelding extra grain and threw several extra pads of hay into the pasture, then went inside and poured herself a Coke and bourbon. She forced herself to eat two peanut butter sandwiches before calling John. "You can come on over anytime now."

Later that night, Clare told him, "I don't want you comin' to the trial."

Even under the covers, John was trembling from the cold. "It's a good case, Clare. Annie says they had no business taking Sloan."

"I don't need you there watching me."

John rolled onto his back and pulled the blankets closer around them. Truthfully, he didn't want to be in court either. He didn't think he could stand watching her struggle. Her arrogance wouldn't be any help there. It was hard to imagine the whole unkempt, deathly pale, wild fact of her in front of the bench. What would the judge think? She might rule against her just by the look of her. He had to go. Almost all in-home therapists went to court with their clients. It was his job. He turned onto his side, draped his arm around her waist, and pulled her against him. "I'm going with you. I can't not be there and anyway, it's my job.

"The hell with your job. You'll just make me nervous."

"Clare."

"You want to help me don't add to what I got to deal with."

"Hey, I'm on your side, remember? You don't have to 'deal' with me."

"I already know you're on my side."

He desperately wanted a drink but didn't move because if he had one then Clare would have one and the last thing she needed was to go to court smelling like liquor. He whispered against her neck, "Just be yourself. Don't even try to be like them."

A ripple of irritation passed through her at the mere thought, then after a pause added, "I guess I shouldn't wear jeans though."

Annie stood along with Ms. Platt, the DSS lawyer, and Mr. and Mrs. Grafton in front of the judge's bench. She tried not to stare at the door at the other end of the room, behind the seats that lined up like church pews. Several people sat waiting for their cases to be called. Recently the format of juvenile court had changed. For the sake of the children, rather than use a witness chair, all involved parties now gathered around the bench, giving the procedure a misleadingly informal atmosphere.

"If your client isn't here in the next two minutes," said Judge Leatte, "we will not hear this case today."

"I understand, your Honor."

The door opened and Clare Raffienne walked into the courtroom. To Annie's horror, her friend was wearing a tailored blazer which looked similar to her own except it was obviously a man's. It was missing all but one button and she had paired it with a calico skirt, seemingly leftover from the sixties. It flowed down to the ankles of her cowboy boots. Her hair hung down her back in one thick braid. She looked like a cigar store Indian in drag. She hesitated.

"Ms. Raffienne?"

"Yes."

"You may approach the bench, and in the future, you may refer to me as Your Honor.

"Okay. Your Honor."

Annie closed her eyes.

Judge Leatte was a sharp featured, slender woman with a no-nonsense short haircut who had been hearing cases in this county for as long as anyone who appeared in a courtroom could remember. She stared at Clare. Then looked down at the papers in front of her. She read them with an air of bafflement then went back to the beginning and read through them again more slowly. She looked up and over her glasses at Ms. Platt. "Will you explain to me why you have put Sloan Raffienne in foster care."

"Your Honor, the decision was determined by the court on March 15."

"I know that, Ms. Platt. I can read. I also know that I was on vacation and the decision was made by a visiting judge. Now I want you to explain to *me* why this child is in foster care."

"Her living situation was dangerous, Your Honor."

"Clarify that Ms. Platt."

"Of course, Your Honor. The house the Raffiennes live in is unsafe. The mother has made a pet of a wild bear that is often around the house and her daughter, Sloan Raffienne, actually plays with her. The bear, I mean. Not the mother."

Judge Leatte raised an eyebrow.

"Also, the place is a fire hazard. Ms. Raffienne stores hay and grain in one of the rooms and heats with a woodstove. The place is old, made from wooden clapboards and could go up like a tinder box. Secondly, the child is often truant from school. When she does go, she is often unkempt and dirty."

"Ms. Platt, explain to me what you mean by truant and dirty. I am especially interested in what you mean by truant."

"She has many unexcused absences…"

Judge Leatte studied the documents and said without looking up, "Ms. Platt, how many times have you appeared in my courtroom?"

"I'm not sure, fifteen, twenty. I don't know, maybe more, let me think…"

"Never mind, Ms. Platt, that was a rhetorical question. The point I'm going for is I don't understand how you can hand me a report stating that the child in question missed 'several' days of school." Judge Leatte looked at Ms. Platt. "Several? What exactly does that mean?"

Ms. Platt began paging through the file she had brought with her. The judge waited. Eventually, the social worker said without looking up, "Yes, Your Honor, it does say several."

"Several is a meaningless term, Ms. Platt."

"Yes, your Honor."

"Ms. Raffienne, how many days has your daughter missed school?"

"I'm not sure, your Honor. But there was always a good reason. Besides, she already reads; she loves books. She can add and subtract too."

"Yes, well. The State of Pennsylvania has laws about children attending school, whether they can read or not." The judge's tone was neutral. Children from the Holler only went to school for the free food and if they dropped out before the legal age of sixteen, it was, by unspoken agreement, ignored by all professionals.

"All right Ms. Platt, now explain dirty to me."

Mr. Grafton put his hand on the bench. "Your Honor, perhaps I can help. Little Joan's hair was so matted when she come to us it took one whole afternoon to comb it out. We thought we might have to cut it off."

Judge Leatte looked at the hand as though it were a snake. "Mr. Tuttle, please inform your clients that they are not to speak unless I address them directly."

The lawyer nodded at Mr. Grafton, who returned his hand to the hat he held just below his belt.

The judge adjusted her glasses. "Did the child have lice?"

"No, Your Honor." Ms. Platt's cheeks were becoming mottled and there was moisture on her forehead and above her lip.

"Did the child ever have to go to the doctor due to poor hygiene?"

"It's entirely possible, Your Honor."

"I am not talking about possible. I am talking about facts. Are there any records stating this to be the case?"

"Not that I am aware of, Your Honor."

Judge Leatte looked down at the papers again then turned her attention to Annie. "Ms. Voight," she said, "it is nice to have you back in town. Say hello to your parents when you have the chance."

"Yes, Your Honor."

"I read in your letter that all the hay and feed have been removed from the house."

"Yes, Your Honor. I have included photos."

"I can see that, Ms. Voight. I also see your client has been attending parenting classes. How is that going?"

"She hasn't missed a class, Your Honor."

"The report from Ms. Soffee states at times her attitude is poor."

"My client is shy, your Honor. That can appear as uncooperative at times."

Judge Leatte again looked down at the papers. "I have a quote here that sounds anything but shy."

Annie said nothing. Judge Leatte looked at Clare for several moments. Finally, she said, "Ms. Raffienne, do you live up the mountain from Hozelroad Holler?"

"I do, your Honor."

"Didn't your grandfather sell horses?"

"Yes, Your Honor."

"I think he sold a pony to my granddaughter."

"He did, Your Honor. A brown pony with a white star."

"We still have that pony." The judge looked at Clare for several more seconds and at that moment, Annie had the impression that of all the people in this courtroom, these two women were the only ones that were well met. Judge Leatte straightened the papers in front of her and turned again to the social worker whose perspiration had spread to her armpits, where dark crescents were forming. "Ms. Platt, this may be the strangest case I've had brought before me and very possibly the flimsiest. The only issue of any substance is the question regarding the bear."

Annie was aware of Clare stirring next to her. She fought the impulse to take her hand.

"Ms. Raffienne, is that bear still around? Remember you're under oath."

"I ain't seen her, your Honor."

The judge leaned forward, crossed her arms, and said not unkindly, "Tell me about this bear. Is she some kind of pet?"

"No, she ain't, Your Honor."

"I have reports that she is often around your house. That when the Game Warden came out, you threatened to shoot him."

"Your Honor, I didn't know who he was. He come around with a gun. Some stranger comes around with a gun, of course I scared him off."

Judge Leatte kept her eyes on Clare. "A stranger in a uniform. A uniform with the label 'Game Warden' embroidered on it. A stranger who told you he was with Animal Control. It's in the report, Ms. Raffienne. I have his quotes. Shall I read them to you?"

"No, Your Honor."

"The court will need physical evidence that this bear has been removed from the area. Permanently."

"Physical evidence," said Clare.

The judge's demeanor did not change at the dropping of Your Honor, but nonetheless, Annie put in quickly, "Your Honor, we will contact Animal Control today. That bear will be gone by the end of the week."

"Once I have a document from them that the bear is secured and safely out of the area, the child Sloan Raffienne will be returned to the custody of her mother and the case of the State of Pennsylvania versus Clare Raffienne will be closed. And Ms. Platt. Don't waste the court's time further with issues like these others that you have listed here. If every dirty child was placed in foster care, the country would go bankrupt. And furthermore, many people live in old- fashioned clapboard houses. I happen to be one of them and though my house is not full of hay, it is full of enough dried up old antiques to set the town ablaze." She banged the gavel on the bench. The Graftons didn't move. They stood and stared at Judge Leatte until Ms. Platt put her hand on Mr. Grafton's arm and turned him around.

Outside, Annie watched the social worker get into a state car. "You know," she said, "I wouldn't want that job for anything. I actually feel sorry for that woman."

"Oh yeah?"

"We'll have Animal Control out there by the end of the week."

"And then what?"

"They will collect her."

"Collect her?"

"Yes, you know. With dart guns. To tranquilize her. Then they put her in a cage and move her far enough away that she can't find her way back."

Clare looked at Annie then away. "You've been watching too much TV."

John looked at the phone. He would not call again. He had already called three times. The first time the secretary had been very pleasant, the second time she had been neutral and the third time she had said, "No, Ms. Voight is still not back from court, and I assure you I will tell her you called as soon as she comes through the door."

Avery shut down the computer, locked his desk drawers, and was reaching for his suit jacket when Chrissy came into the office and sat down. She crossed her legs. After their night at the Bistro she had avoided him, for which he was grateful. Lately, however, she had started sitting next to him in staff meetings, chatting with him in the corridor and lingering in his office.

"I was wondering if you would like to go out for a drink tonight?" She bobbed her foot up and down.

John stared at the wall over her head. "I don't know. I've got a case going to court today. It's a custody matter. I may have to make a home visit tonight."

Chrissy watched him. "Custody case? That wouldn't be the Raffienne case, would it?"

John nodded.

Chrissy stopped bobbing her foot. "Be careful. These in-home cases. They can eat you up."

"I'm fine."

"Just be careful, John. That's all I'm saying." She stood to go then looked back at him. "By the way, I'm looking for another job. I can't do this much longer."

"Hey, don't run off. What are you talking about?" John sat on the edge of his desk.

Chrissy leaned against the door frame. "It's the hours, being on call 24/7, the driving. Just for starters. Then there are the families. My God, talk about the bottom of the barrel. They're hopeless."

"That's not true."

Chrissy sighed. "Really? I'm not making any headway."

"You are probably helping more than you think."

"Please. Don't patronize me." She sat back down. "So, how do you think it will turn out? This custody case?"

"I honestly don't know. The child shouldn't be in foster care in the first place. I think DSS has worked some deal with the Graftons. So does Dr. Wittcomb."

"They say she is a witch, you know."

"What?"

"That Raffienne woman. I went to school with her. Sort of. She was a grade ahead of me. Had quite the reputation. Would lay with anyone, so they said. And the boys loved her. Well, not love-love, but you know. She's not bad looking. But strange things happen to the men who get involved with that woman. Bad things. One guy died after she'd broken up with him. Got so drunk he passed out and froze to death in the VFW parking lot. Another lost his hand. No one knows the details, just that he landed in the hospital, nearly died, and when he got out, he'd lost the use of his hand. No one understood it, but there you are. There used to be this really fancy horse farm. Owned by outsiders. Mafia, most people think. Clare got involved with the manager. Was living with him, even. Then something went wrong, and the house burned to the ground. Boom. Just like that. It was arson, but the police couldn't prove it. Everyone knew, though, that it was Clare."

John stared at Chrissy, who stared back, her face as innocent as it had ever been.

"Clare's house, hut really, burned down shortly afterward, but it wasn't worth anything. And people from the Holler don't go to the law. So that was the end of it."

"I remember that horse farm. I think it was called Silver Storm. Something like that."

"That's right."

"I didn't know Clare was connected to it."

"How old are you, John?"

"Twenty-six."

Chrissy smiled. "You were just a little thing then. Playing with your Tonka trucks."

John reached for his jacket. "You know, I've changed my mind. I think a drink is just what we need."

"Now?"

"Why not?"

When he returned from lunch, the red message light on his phone was blinking. "I want to see you tonight. Bring Colleen. Please."

It was the "please" that bothered him.

When they arrived, Clare was pulling a golden roasting chicken from the oven. "My specialty," she said. He had expected her to be floating on air with relief, but instead she moved slowly and carefully, very much bound to the earth. There were three plates, three sets of silverware, and three glasses on the table. Clare smiled at Colleen and settled her in a chair. "I hope you like chicken," she said. Colleen nodded.

"Dark or white?"

Colleen pointed to a wing.

"She likes the wings," said John.

"Good choice. Would you like a drumstick to go along with the wing?"

Colleen nodded again. Clare fixed her a plate with the two wings and drumstick, mashed potatoes topped with a large pat of butter, peas, corn, and applesauce. She put a pan of gravy on the table and poured the girl a glass of milk. Colleen picked up a wing and looked at Clare shyly.

"Would you like gravy?"

Colleen nodded.

Clare poured gravy on the mashed potatoes and looked at Colleen, who pointed to the peas and corn.

"Good choice," she said and poured the gravy on the vegetables. She handed John the carving knife. "I'll let you serve yourself."

"What can I get you?"

"I like both."

John put a thigh and a slice of white meat on Clare's plate and the same on his own. She served them vegetables and poured gravy over everything on her plate. Colleen ate steadily and with concentration while Clare watched her. When they were finished, Clare made three pieces of jelly bread and poured the remaining gravy over them. Colleen looked at the food and then at Clare, who said, "Go ahead. Try it. You'll like it."

Colleen tried a small bite and smiled. She finished it all then picked up her plate and licked it. Clare laughed.

It had remained cold, and the windows were steamed over with the heat from the cooking. John put another log on the woodstove. Clare brought a chair and a child's book in from the living room and placed the chair close to the stove. She sat in it and Colleen climbed into her lap and looked at the pictures in the book, turning the pages slowly. Eventually, John said, "It's getting late. I'll take her home and come back."

"I wouldn't be any good to you tonight."

"Sloan will be back as soon as Animal Control takes that bear away. It's official. There is nothing DSS can do now."

"I know."

"What is it then?"

"I just want this to be over."

"It will be in just a few days."

"You think?"

They sat in silence, Clare and John watching the fire through the woodstove's open door and Colleen slowly turning the pages until her head drooped and John picked her up, carried her to the car and laid her, still asleep, in the back seat. He closed the door quietly and turned to face Clare, who had come with him. "It's not just about the sex, you know."

"I know. Don't be upset. I just need this to be over. I'll be okay once it's over."

John saw that she was shaking. He pulled her against him in a hug, but her body resisted, refusing comfort.

As it turned out, Animal Control would not have the bear out of the area by the end of the week. They would not have it out that week or the week after or the week after that. They were very busy, it being spring and all. Rabid animals coming out of hibernation, dogs running loose with no licenses, horses more dead than alive from starving through the winter. Also, they didn't have the means to tranquilize her or a cage big enough to put her in. Of course, they could always come out and shoot her. Clare listened to them telling her this then hung up the phone without saying goodbye.

That night at Clare's, Annie went into the house and called hello, but there was no answer. She stood at the bottom of the stairs and called Clare's name. There was only silence. Annie walked back outside. A halter hung from a lead rope tied to a ring on the shed and Lonesome wasn't anywhere in the pasture. She shaded her eyes with her hand and looked up the mountain. A pale horse walked slowly along the wood line. Horse and rider moved deliberately in and out of the trees just where the forest bordered the clearing. Annie sat on the woodpile to wait. Eventually, Clare and Lonesome descended, still at a walk. Two feed buckets were tied together with bailing twine slung over the back of the western saddle. They were empty.

Clare did not seem surprised to see her. She looped the reins over the fence rail, slid the buckets off the saddle, untied the bailing twine and put them back in the shed. "Come on in," she said.

"You leaving Lonesome tied here?"

"I'm going out again."

"Clare?"

"You talk to Animal Control?"

"Yes."

"What did they say?"

"They need to be the ones to take the pictures."

"I thought so."

They went into the kitchen. A thin bit of sunlight came through the window. It was getting toward evening and the kitchen, facing west, caught the slanting light. "You stay here," Clare told her. "I'll be right back." She went into the parlor and came back out immediately with the shotgun. She tied it to the saddle, gathered the reins, and swung up on the horse. "You don't mind my using Lonesome, do you? He's so steady."

"Let me come with you."

"That's not a good idea."

"I know. I'll be waiting right here though."

"I don't know when I'll be back."

"Doesn't matter." Annie sat on the woodpile as the horse made its way slowly up the mountain. The breeze moved through the leaves and the sky turned raspberry and then purple and gold as Clare and Lonesome disappeared in the trees. Annie thought it couldn't be a prettier night. It was too early for the birds to be mating, but still some sang, and even louder than the birds were the peepers calling to each other. She sat motionless and listened. When it came, the gun shot did not startle her as she had thought it would. A few seconds later, there was a second shot. Annie kept her eyes steady on the tree line. She waited for a third shot, but none came. Horse and rider burst clear, galloping full out, no more need for quiet reassurance. They came down the mountain as fast as Lonesome could scramble. Annie knew that wasn't good for the horse's legs, but she also knew it was the way Clare had to do it. They pulled up in front of the woodpile, with Lonesome's sides heaving and Clare's breathing hard and fast. She slid out of the saddle.

"I'll untack him," Annie said.

When she had finished rubbing the horse down and fed him some extra grain, Annie went inside. Clare sat wrapped in a blanket. "You can call Animal Control and have them come out and take a look," she said as soon as Annie walked through the door.

"Did it… um, I mean…."

"Clean shots. Both of them. I was at very close range."

"Oh, Clare."

"Just get Animal Control out here as fast as you can."

Annie stayed the night. The two women sat on the sofa drinking bourbon steadily, neither saying anything because there was nothing to be said, and when the liquor had slowed their minds enough and the images could be tolerated, even though only barely, they went to bed.

Chapter Nineteen

Mr. Grafton did not speak at all on the ride home. He aged ten years during that drive, his face going even grayer and the lines around his mouth turning into deep tracks. The Graftons said nothing to the children about having been in court. The man went into his bedroom, and they did not see him for two days. Mrs. Grafton came out of the bedroom only to fetch water and sometimes food, and she paid no attention to the children.

The lock remained on the refrigerator, but Nat picked and dismantled it and soon, except for jumbo-sized bottles of mustard and ketchup, all the food was gone. Since no one was making them do their chores, the boys sat in front of the TV, their faces devoid of expression as they stared at the flickering images in the room, which was darkened by the sheets they had taken off their beds and nailed to the window frames in order to keep any glare off the screen. Sloan stuck very close to Mrs. Grafton whenever she could and when she couldn't, hovered near one or all the other four boys, staying clear of Nat.

The first morning after everything changed, they all wandered down to the bus stop, their bellies full for a change, climbed on the bus as usual and went to school. The second morning they slept in, having stayed awake most of the night watching TV. After that, the Graftons spent a great deal of time away and when they were home, they were on the phone or shut either in the dining room or their bedroom. Occasionally, Mr. Grafton could be heard to raise his voice and once even Mrs. Grafton shouted, "I ain't willin' to go to jail."

On the third night the children were getting very hungry. What had been minor skirmishes over what channel to watch became fistfights and wrestling matches resulting in split and swollen lips, a black eye, and two broken ribs. Sloan went upstairs to her room and began packing. She took a pillowcase off one of the pillows and filled it with most of her clothes then filled the second one with her jacket, shoes, and socks. She wore jeans and a long-sleeved shirt and socks to bed. She pulled the covers up to her chin and tried to go to sleep. The television droned downstairs and one of the boys swore loudly, followed by a loud crash and something breaking. Probably a lamp. She pulled the pillow over her head, muffling the sounds. She wondered if one of the Graftons would bring her a pill since they hadn't in two nights. She thought she heard Mr. Grafton downstairs talking to the boys. She took the pillow away. It was him and he spoke with his usual authority. Sloan uncurled, got down from the bed, and hid the stuffed pillowcases under it. She pulled a pair of pajamas over her clothes, climbed back under the covers, and laid on her back and listened. Shortly after, the boys pounded up the stairs, all in a bunch, banging against the walls and swearing. One of them called out, "We're fucking starving!" They went into their bedroom and slammed the door. Mr. Grafton pounded up the stairs and said, "You boys have stolen all the food. I'll go into town tomorrow and buy groceries, but tonight I'm afraid you'll go to bed hungry. This is what comes from gluttony. That's what the lock was for. Because you boys ain't learned self-control and can't be trusted. Now stay in your room tonight and we'll have food for you in the morning. If you don't behave, I won't be able to go to the store and there won't be anything to eat." He shut the door and came into Sloan's room with her pill and a glass of water. He sat on the bed. "Here, little missy," he said. Sloan sat up, took the pill, cheeked it, sipped at the water, and laid back down. Mr. Grafton stroked her hair. "My little girl," he said. "My sweet, sweet little girl." Sloan could feel the pill dissolving against her cheek. "I gotta pee," she said.

"All right." The man took her hand and led her to the bathroom. He came through the door with her.

"Why, Joan," he said. "Why do you have clothes on under your pajamas?"

"I was cold."

"Well, you can't possibly be comfortable like that. Let me help you get them off."

"No." She pulled away from him. They stood staring at each other. She could taste the bitter pill. "You need to leave." To her surprise, the man nodded and said, "Okay, but I'll wait right here for you until you're done." He shut the door. Sloan spit what was left of the pill into the toilet and peed on it.

When she came out of the bathroom, Mr. Grafton tucked her into bed again. "Will you miss me?"

Sloan's heart jumped, and her mouth was instantly dry. "I ain't going nowhere."

The man ran his hand over her head. "My sweet girl."

Sloan felt sick.

"You will miss me, won't you? It's been bad here lately. Real bad. But things will be different. I promise."

John Avery put the photos on Dr. Wittcomb's desk. She looked at them then looked away.

"Clean shots," said John.

"Did animal control do it?"

"No, Clare did. Animal control just took the pictures."

"Dear God."

"Ms. Voight has already sent the originals of these photos to the court. And to DSS. Judge Leatte has ordered that the child be returned to her mother's custody immediately." John sat in a chair next to the desk. Dr. Wittcomb turned the photos face down. "This was never a case, you know. That bear wasn't likely to hurt that child. And if she was, no one in Coleton would normally care. How did this all happen?"

"I think you've answered that. One girl for a bunch of very hard to place boys. Boys who would normally be placed in very expensive residential care."

Dr. Wittcomb rubbed her eyes with her thumb and index finger. "I didn't think we bartered children in this country. I suppose DSS will bring the girl here to be returned to her mother."

"Actually, the Graftons are taking her to Clare's as we speak."

"What!"

"Yes, apparently the little girl ran away this morning. Took off through the woods. The Graftons found her with two pillowcases full of clothes. When they called DSS, Ms. Platt told them just to go ahead and take her to Clare's."

Dr. Wittcomb stared at him. Finally, she said, "Do you mean to tell me that the Graftons know where Clare Raffienne lives?"

"Apparently."

"And they are on their way to delivering Sloan to her right now?"

"Yes."

"Is anyone going with them? Like Ms. Platt? Or Ms. Voight?"

"Ms. Voight is going to meet them there. She's the one who called me to let me know what was going on. I don't know about Ms. Platt." John pulled car keys from his pant pocket. "I was on my way there myself."

Dr. Wittcomb hadn't been directly involved in a case in years. Hadn't wanted to be. This was such a mess. Sending the foster parents to the biological family's house. Had Ms. Platt lost her mind? Dr. Wittcomb reached into a desk drawer and pulled out a Mounds bar. She unwrapped it and offered half to John, who shook his head. He jingled his keys. "I'll get going," he said.

"I'm coming with you."

John became still, the keys silent.

"It's not you. You've done fine," she said. "It's DSS." She rose from her chair. "No telling what they're liable to do next."

"I guess we should clean," Clare said after she hung up the phone.

Clare washed while Annie dried the dishes, put them in the cupboard, and wiped the small countertop. When that was done, Clare stood in the middle of the kitchen looking lost. Annie handed her a broom. "I'll dust, you sweep."

They started upstairs in Clare's bedroom and worked their way through the house. By the time they were on the porch steps, the sun was high overhead. "Where the hell are they?" said Clare.

"They'll be here."

Clare sat on the woodpile. Annie sat next to her and the two of them stared down the driveway. "I need a drink," said Clare.

"That wouldn't be a good idea."

Clare put her elbows on her knees and her head in her hands. Then she sat up straight and returned to her vigil. She sat as still as a wild thing, willing her daughter's return. When they a vehicle rumbled up the road, Clare sprang to her feet, walked to where she could see and came back. "There's three comin'," she said. She sat down then stood up. She walked around in a circle and sat down, trembling.

The first vehicle to pull beside the house was a state car, the second was a truck with Grafton's Greenhouse painted on the side, and the third was another state car. Annie felt a sharp sense of relief at recognizing Dr. Wittcomb in the last vehicle.

John Avery was the first out, opening the door practically before the car stopped. Dr. Wittcomb hauled herself from behind the wheel and motioned for John to stay where he was. Clare stood. The truck door with Grafton's Greenhouse on it opened slowly, two bulging pillowcases dropped to the ground followed by Sloan who stood beside them holding onto a doll, her green eyes wary. Though there were no marks, her face looked bruised and tender and Dr. Wittcomb stepped forward with amazing speed and gently guided the child toward her mother. When they reached her, Clare folded over Sloan like a broken marionette and sank with her onto the woodpile. Sloan slumped against her mother, her head on her chest and her arms clutching the doll. Neither one of them made a sound. Dr. Wittcomb put her hand on Clare's shoulder for a moment then straightened and turned toward Ms. Platt, who remained safely in the car. "Open the door," she said. Ms. Platt did as she was told and ventured out, her high heels on the gravel causing her to stumble.

"Why are the foster parents here?"

"They brought Sloan."

"I can see that. My point is, it is extremely unorthodox to involve the foster parents in a return of custody. Even more than that to have them show up at the family's home."

"I just wanted to get her home as fast as possible."

"That doesn't mean you bring the foster parents along with you."

"They found her in the woods. I told them to bring her to the office and then we would bring her out here."

Mr. Grafton slid from the truck, holding his hat in his fingers, which were shaking. "Miss," he said, looking at Clare.

Dr. Wittcomb stepped between them, her hand raised, stopping him from coming closer.

"Mother," he said, and Mrs. Grafton came around from the other side of the truck and stood next to her husband. Sloan turned and looked at her.

"We will miss you," the woman said.

"Go on," the man told her. "Say it all."

"We hope she can visit us from time to time."

Dr. Wittcomb gave a loud sigh. "That is out of the question." She shot a look at Ms. Platt, who said, "That would be against the rules."

Mr. Grafton looked at his wife and when she didn't speak, he turned to the clinical director. "We have gotten fond of her, and she feels the same way about us."

"I'm sure you have grown fond, but it will be best for everyone if we make a clean break."

"My wife even got her a doll. That one she's got there. See how she's clutching it? You love that doll, don't you, Joanie."

"Joanie?" said Ms. Platt.

"That's his pet name for her. But I would have thought you knew that," John said, his voice ugly with disgust.

"That's enough now," said Dr. Wittcomb. "Go home, Mr. Grafton."

"Can we maybe meet her at Ms. Platt's office, then? Just for an hour or so?"

Ms. Platt took a careful step forward. "No, that would be inappropriate. Foster care isn't meant to be forever. The case is closed. If you think you need to debrief about this, you can come to my office and we'll talk, but Sloan will not be there."

"This just don't seem right. You never said we would have to give her back."

"I'm sure I told you the goal was reunification. The goal is always reunification. I'm sure we discussed this."

"No. Never. You just told us you had a girl for us."

"I'm sure I said more than that."

"No. You never. This just ain't right. You give us a child and we love her and take care of her and then you take her away."

Ms. Platt made her careful way along the gravel driveway to Mr. Grafton and put her hand on his arm. "You go on home now."

"But it ain't right. Mother, tell them. Tell them how close you and Joanie are."

Mrs. Grafton looked at the ground. "Let's just go home," she said to her shoes.

"Ain't no use us going home."

Ms. Platt gently guided the man toward his truck and opened the door for him. "Go on now. We will talk later."

Mr. Grafton turned to face his wife. "Mother," he said. "Say something. Like we talked about."

Mrs. Grafton turned away from her husband and walked around the front of the truck, opened the door, and climbed in. Grafton looked from Ms. Platt to his wife. "I can't believe this."

No one spoke, and finally he pulled himself into the truck, rolled down the window, and leaned out. "Don't you forget me now, missy," he said, his voice strange. Ms. Platt moved to block the man's view of the little girl. "Start your engine now, Mr. Grafton. Go on. Start it. Good. You can come to my office tomorrow morning, but now you have to leave. Now."

The truck jumped forward then settled as Grafton made a sloppy three-point turn before driving across the yard and bouncing down the driveway.

Ms. Platt turned to the group. "I'm sorry," she said vaguely. When no one answered her, she announced to the air, "The case of Pennsylvania versus Ms. Raffienne is officially closed." She walked to her car, ducked in, leaned out the window and said, "I'll have the paperwork to everyone in two weeks."

"All right," said Dr. Wittcomb.

The social worker rolled up her window, started her car, made a tidy three-point turn and was gone.

"Well," said Annie.

Clare rose, put her hands under Sloan's arms, and gently placed her feet on the ground. The child grabbed hold of her mother's shirt with one hand and tossed the doll on the woodpile with the other. Dr Wittcomb swayed forward a few steps. "Clare," she said. "Most children are in foster care for months, years even."

"Okay."

"Soon this will be just a memory." The doctor nearly winced at her words. Clare nodded.

"It's been what… only five weeks… and she's young. In a few years, this won't even be a blip on the radar screen."

"Are you trying to tell me something? Because if you are, I don't get it."

"No. Not really. Just that as hard as this has been for the both of you, it doesn't mean there will be lasting effects."

Clare looked at her impatiently. "I just want to take my child inside and pretend this never happened."

"Exactly. That's exactly right."

It was so dark when Dr. Wittcomb returned home she couldn't see the outlines of her cottage. The stars stood out in a black sky, but the new moon gave no light. Chuckchi touched her nose to the woman's hand as she made her way through the front door. Inside, Dr. Wittcomb went to the chair near the fireplace and sat down. She sat in the dark for some time and then rose with difficulty and turned on a light in the kitchen. Chuckchi remained next to the chair watching her owner. The doctor took the remaining half of a pizza from the refrigerator and put it in the oven. Then she poured herself a glass of red wine and sat back down. It was too warm for a fire. She drank the wine, which had an unusual, spicy taste. Eventually she touched the top of Chuckchi's head. The dog moved away, sighed, and put her head on her paws, blinked one eye then the other before she closed them. The timer on the stove went off and Dr. Wittcomb arranged the pizza on a platter, poured another glass of wine, and arranged herself on a stool at the kitchen counter. She ate and drank slowly until the food was gone. She threw a piece of crust to the dog, who, with great delicacy, held it between her paws and nibbled at it.

"This is not good," said Dr. Wittcomb. "Not good at all."

Chuckchi watched her.

This whole business had felt very wrong from the beginning. Perhaps it had been a mistake to reassure the mother. Perhaps she should have warned her instead. Against what? I've seen too much, thought Dr. Wittcomb. My view of things is skewed. She watched her dog and listened for the sounds of spring. She helped herself to a large piece of chocolate cake and poured the rest of the wine into her glass. When she finished the cake, Dr. Wittcomb washed her dishes, put them in the rack to dry, fixed a bowl of chicken and rice for the dog, watched her eat it then took her outside into the black night where the animal disappeared. Dr. Wittcomb eased herself onto the porch step to wait. It was always a question whether or not Chukchi would return. Dr. Wittcomb sat in the dark and thought about that other house alone in the woods. How had DSS even found Sloan? Probably through the school. Schools caused a great deal of trouble for marginal children though their intentions were good. Dr. Wittcomb wondered if good intentions absolved them from guilt. She felt Chukchi settle next to her. "I really should retire," she told the dog. Other than helping move the trial date along, she had been no use at all and now no one could help that little girl. It was done and could not be undone and there was no therapy that could erase the changes. She had no business thinking about who was guilty and who wasn't. She knew the dangers and she hadn't stopped it. If you wanted the truth about who was guilty, she should have thrown herself in front of that state car before she let the social worker drive Sloan away from her mother. Instead, she had been professional, had done the expected, had risked nothing, and played by the rules, and God only knew what had happened to that child. She had a feeling she'd find out soon enough. Dr. Wittcomb dropped her hand on Chukchi's head, who politely but firmly moved away. "Come on then," the woman said and hauled herself up by the porch rail. The two went inside and upstairs, where Dr. Wittcomb changed into a voluminous nightgown and settled herself under the covers of the bed. She read for a while but found she was absorbing nothing, so gave it up and lay awake in the dark for what seemed like a very long time.

Sloan no longer took the bus to school. Either Clare or Annie drove her in the mornings. Unlike John Avery, Annie often stayed the night at Clare's, sleeping in Sloan's room, empty now that the girl slept with her mother. In the afternoons, Clare brought her and Colleen home. This routine became a ritual, the waiting in the car as the children—half carrying, half dragging their book bags—straggled out of the building. Clare never took her eyes from the door until, emerging into the sunlight, there was the red gold hair. Sloan's eyes roved until they spotted her mother's truck and without smiling, she would pick up her pace, not running exactly but moving with determination and then jumping inside. Clare always had a snack, something sweet, waiting for her.

Two or three days a week Annie went to the school and ate lunch with this strange child. The first day she wore her lawyer's clothes and shoes and walked with purposeful strides into the principal's reception office.

"I'm here to have lunch with Sloan Raffienne. I'm on the list. Her mother—Clare—put me on the list."

An effeminate man with pretty eyes walked out of the principal's office. "Annie Voight," he said, "I heard you were back."

"Yes." Annie had gone to high school with Dick Rather. They had never been friends, but his parents knew hers and now she was grateful for that.

"And what brings you back to our lovely, though small town?"

"I'm working for Marshall Teage. I'm here to have lunch with Sloan Raffienne. I'll be doing this often. At her mother's request."

"That's rather unusual, isn't it?"

Annie said nothing.

"As long as we have documentation with her mother's approval. Of course, we want her to settle in and get back to normal, get back with her peer group as soon as possible, and lunching with her classmates is an important part of that. She's a bit standoffish from what I hear." Dick Rather had notions about the girl's mother, as did most people in Coleton his age, but he hadn't thought of her in years and now assumed that Annie's current busy-bodying was due to the fact that Clare's daughter had been in foster care. Those two, Annie and Clare, he recalled, had always had some sort of strange friendship. The last thing he wanted was any form of legal trouble, and the women were within their rights. His statement about a peer group had been perfunctory. He assumed the child's future was as dismal as her mother's.

Annie walked into the cafeteria, which smelled of grease, overcooked vegetables, and sweat, and joined Sloan in line. The child glanced at her briefly, selected a cheeseburger and a blue drink that looked like it belonged in the engine of a car. Annie sat opposite her at the end of a long table where there were no other children.

Sloan stared at her. "Why are you here?"

"Your mama asked me to come. And I wanted to."

"Are you my mother's friend?"

"Yes."

"Then how come you ain't been around until just a little bit ago?"

"I had to go away to school."

"Did you help Mama get me back?"

"A little. Mostly it was your mother."

Satisfied, Sloan smiled, and Annie blinked. She's her mother all over again, she thought. That same slow smile that takes you in, turns your bones to water, and gives nothing back.

John now visited Clare during the day when Sloan was in school and Annie at work. They would lay in a patch of sunlight on the grass. Sometimes when the weather was bad, they stretched out on the couch or inside the shed on a blanket covering the bales of hay. They even slept in the bed occasionally though Clare didn't like to. There was none of the breathtaking desperation that had once left them spent. Their love making was as easy and satisfying as drinking a glass of cold water when thirsty, sliding between cool sheets on a hot night or walking into a warm kitchen out of the winter's cold. They stretched and lengthened, shivered into pleasure.

Even though John saw his clients sporadically, when he did, he looked at them with such love and compassion that for a while they ceased to harm each other, briefly dropped their despair and opened themselves under his quiet gaze to the possibility of hope.

After having supper with Annie, Clare, and Sloan, John would sing on the drive home with Colleen in the back seat. He sang country songs, old and new, rock and roll songs, Johnny Cash, Elvis Presley, and modern rap. Immune, he sang songs of lost love. In communion, he sang songs of triumph. So huge was his joy he even sang patriotic songs. He sang softly and sometimes he roared. He didn't mind that he wasn't spending the night with Clare because he was thinking of how they would be the next day. And so he sang. He sang about the past. He sang about the present and he sang about the future. He sang and he sang and when he did, he smiled because he thought Clare and he were in love.

A week after her return, while Annie did the dishes, Sloan helped her mother throw the horses their nighttime flakes of hay. She walked behind Clare, swinging her arm wide as she arched the pads over the fence, one per horse, spaced around the pasture to avoid fights. When they were done, the girl climbed the wire and held onto the trunk of a tree for balance and looked toward the mountain. Clare held still. After some time, Sloan jumped down and crawled under the fence, grabbed one of the smaller horses by the mane and swung onto its back. She twisted the long hairs in and out of her fingers. "I ain't seen Sister," she said, keeping her eyes on the pony's neck. Clare rested her hand on a strand of barbed wire. She understood her daughter's attempt to appear casual. Finally, she said, "She must be off somewhere lookin' for a new boyfriend."

Sloan looked at her from under her brows.

Clare sighed and said simply, "She ain't comin back."

"How come?"

"She was shot."

"Who shot her?"

"I did."

Sloan lowered her eyes and continued stroking the pony. Clare thought she saw her daughter's eyelids redden. Other than that, the child did not indicate that she had heard.

"The law said it was the only way I could get you back. They thought the bear was a danger to you."

"So, you killed Sister to get me back?"

"Yeah."

"Why didn't you tell them she was our friend?"

"I tried. They wouldn't believe me."

"But she was our friend."

"I know."

"Why couldn't you make them believe it?"

"I tried."

"You could have kept trying."

"No. I had to do it quickly. I had to get you back quickly."

Cry, thought Clare. Cry so I can hold you and rock you and kiss the top of your head and make it better or at least okay. But the girl remained still and would not look at her. Then Sloan slid off the pony, patted its neck, ducked under the fence, and walked past Clare into the house. The woman imagined her child going straight backed through the kitchen without glancing at Annie, walking through the living room and on upstairs to their bedroom and flinging herself on the bed still wearing her clothes, which was exactly what Sloan did. When Clare found her, the girl pretended to be asleep, but she lay so lightly on the bed that she seemed to float there. She never mentioned Sister again.

The next morning, a mist floated among the trees and behind it the sun was so golden the new leaves spread themselves wide and pale green, absorbing and reflecting its light. Sloan's tossing had made it a night of sharp elbows, knees, and heels, and Clare rubbed at her shin where it was sore. The girl slipped into a less troubled sleep somewhere around four o'clock. Now, Clare propped herself up on an elbow and watched the lavender eyelids flutter in a dream. The air coming through the open window was cool and scented. Since Sloan's return, Clare had had to wash sheets frequently as the child often wet the bed, something she had not done since the age of three. Once they were washed, Clare hung them over the fence and woodpile to dry. At night she brought everything indoors and made the bed and it smelled of fresh air, horses, and bark. This was a rare dry morning, and Clare had to resist the urge to stretch out in the sheet's smooth freshness. The sun spread across the bed. She thought about the child sleeping safely next to her and how beautiful she was, how beautiful their life was now, how beautiful it was to hold Sloan both at night and in the mornings, how lovely it was to have Annie back, and John and Colleen, how marvelous it all was and that nothing lasted. If she ever doubted it, all she had to do was remember Pap. How easy it had been to kill him off. One minute he was doing what he had done all his adult life and the next he was lying on the ground dead as a door nail. The trick was knowing that it didn't last and not letting it ruin everything. Clare didn't know how to do that. She lay still in the spangled air that filled the room and decided a picnic might help. A daylong picnic. They would go up the mountain with the horses and camp next to one of the glades along a creek. There were many such places, but only one that interested Clare. She hadn't thought of it in years. Unc's place. The one-room hut that no one visited, and few ever passed. He was the wildest of them all, not in the way of getting drunk Saturday nights and driving at a murderous speed on the twisty turning road along Cat Creek, but in that he lived higher up the mountain than any of them and couldn't bear company. He was Gram's nephew. Some nights when Gram was sick of it all—the company, the noise, even of Pap—she would take young Clare to the place where she grew up. It was a two-room hut with no real kitchen, the last building before the peak. Back then Aunt Lottie lived there, and she would let Gram and Clare stay a night or two. Sometimes there would be a rap on the door and when Clare snatched it open, it would be Unc with a few squirrels, standing silently, careful not to look directly at her. He'd hand the carcasses to Clare and turn to leave without saying a word. The girl learned to stay put when she heard that soft knock and watched from behind a window as Unc put the squirrels carefully on the doorstep. He'd sit then, leaning against the house in a spot of sun until Gram came out to fetch the gift and hand the man some biscuits in a greasy paper bag. They'd exchange a few words before Gram would leave her nephew to doze for a while. Clare always stayed put and watched him sleep, her face pressed against the glass. She thought he was the most glamorous person she had ever known.

She wondered if he was there after all this time? If he was, he wouldn't like that many people high up the mountain near his home. They would go to the glade and stay clear of the cabin. Maybe, while the others were eating or playing in the water, she would slip off to see if he was still around. The thought of him stirred her stomach. Annie opened the door across the hall. Sloan rolled toward her mother, fixed her with a sea green, drowsy gaze. "Go back to sleep," Clare said then followed Annie down the stairs and into the kitchen.

Bent over, she rummaged through the refrigerator, straightened, and shut the door. "I have the stuff for potato salad. I'll make it while you go to the market and buy a couple chickens."

Annie stood with her hand on the coffee pot.

"Don't go all the way to Coleton. Use the little market down the road."

"What's going on?"

"A picnic. We'll ride up the mountain. I'll call John and he can bring Colleen."

Annie considered. It was a beautiful day. She had planned to catch up on some paperwork, but it could wait, and getting on a horse again, she realized, suited her just fine.

"Can you pick out a good chicken?" Clare put a sack of potatoes, celery, mayonnaise, and mustard on the table. She took out a bottle of cider vinegar from the cupboard and some salt.

Annie poured herself a cup of coffee. "Sure, I can."

"You have to be careful at Country Market. They get their chickens from the Blanchards. They're real good if they're fresh, but sometimes they sit there too long. Give 'em a good smell."

Annie had a picture of herself leaning into the meat counter sniffing the goods. "Anything else?"

"Apples, candy, whatever you think the kids would like that won't get smashed on the trip. And hurry. I want to get started as soon as possible."

Clare was taking the crisp, steaming chickens from the oven when Sloan walked into the kitchen. She gingerly broke off a wing and blew on it then gave it to Sloan, who closed her eyes as she took a bite.

Clare wrapped the hot chickens in aluminum foil and towels and put them in paper grocery bags and then dumped them into an empty feed sack, which still had bits of grain clinging to the sides. In another sack, she placed the plastic bags of potato salad, apples, Snickers, plastic knives and forks, paper plates, paper towels, two bottles of red wine, and boxes of Kool Aid that they would reconstitute with the water from the stream. She took them outside where Annie was tacking up Lonesome with Clare's old barrel racing saddle. He was the only horse sensible enough to carry the food. She secured the two feed sacks. John would ride him. Colleen would use Sloan's saddle on Butter and Annie would use Clare's on one of the training colts. Clare and her daughter would ride bareback.

After the sacks of food were secured, Annie caught her horse—a weedy, plain chestnut—and tied him to a tree. He seemed gentle enough and at least wasn't very big. She brushed him and spoke quietly to him as she ran her hand behind the brush. When she laid the saddle on his back he stood quietly, but he flinched and pinned his ears when she tightened the girth, so she did it slowly, one notch at a time until it was secure. He turned his ears backward but made no trouble. She was praising him and stroking his neck when John's car came up the driveway. Before it had come to a full stop, the back door opened and Colleen jumped out and scrambled under the fence, disappearing amongst the horses. John stuck his head out the window and yelled, "Colleen, come back here."

The screen door banged. Sloan ran down the steps, across the lawn and with the agility and speed of a weasel, slipped between the strands of barbed wire. "Wait for me," she called. The horses skittered and moved sideways, and Sloan took Colleen's hand. "I'll help you put the saddle on her," the older girl said and pulled her friend along to the shed where the saddles were kept. She took a small saddle off its wooden rack and carried it back to the fence and propped it against a tree then they both dipped back into the pasture, walked toward the chubby pony who stretched her nose toward Sloan's open palm. Sloan took hold of her mane with one hand and lifted Colleen onto the pony's back with the other. Clare brought the pony's bridle to her daughter who slipped the bit into Butter's mouth and the head stall over her ears and led Colleen out through the gate.

John walked up to Clare, who said, "Go ahead and help Colleen tighten up the girth."

He hesitated.

Clare bumped John with her shoulder to move him aside, checked Colleen's girth, and lifted her into the saddle. Sloan was already on her pony, a paint with one blue eye that made Annie nervous. She'd heard about these horses with bi-colored eyes. She watched him for a moment and nothing about him reassured her. Clare's mount was a tall bay, the best-looking horse of the bunch. John stood next to Lonesome, holding the reins.

"Put your left foot in the stirrup, grab the mane, and pull yourself into the saddle. It shouldn't be hard with your long legs."

John put his left foot in the stirrup and bounced up and down several times on the ball of his right foot. Then he stood still clutching a handful of Lonesome's mane.

"What?" said Clare.

"Won't it hurt if I pull on his mane?"

"No."

"Are you sure?"

"Horses don't have much feeling there."

John tugged a little. "Are you sure it won't hurt him?"

The women exchanged a look. "Yes," Clare said.

"But it would hurt if someone pulled my hair like that."

"It won't hurt him."

John stood still.

"John," said Annie, "there is actually a large body of research showing that horses have very few nerve endings along the crests of their necks. Almost none. Researchers have tested this by using pins. Thousands of pins. The horse looks like a veritable pin cushion and stands quietly eating its grain. Wannabe scientists have done their doctoral dissertations on just this sort of thing. The man who first discovered it is quite famous."

"Smart ass," John said into the horse's neck then grabbed a large handful of mane and bounded off the ground. He landed mostly on Lonesome's neck who grunted and sighed and looked back at Annie with his heartbreaking patience. John pushed himself into an upright position and sat in the saddle.

"Wagons ho," said Clare and nudged her horse into the lead. The big bay scooted sideways at the shadow of a tree, bucked and farted, his eyes huge and white rimmed. Clare sat as though nothing had happened, but when Annie's horse shied and jumped forward landing next to the bay, she lost her balance, falling backward. Clare grabbed her shirt and hauled her back into position.

"It's been a while," Annie said.

Once the party headed up the mountain, the big bay relaxed into the exertion of the climb though he still looked side-to-side, eyes big and ready to be spooked. The weedy chestnut settled into an unbalanced stumbling walk. Annie felt her heartbeat slow. Her legs lengthened and the muscles in her back relaxed, taking and absorbing the movement of her pony's haunches. It was wonderful to be riding again. The air grew crisp, and the shadow of a small bird flitted across the path, causing the bay to hop backwards. Annie watched Clare's seat automatically settle deeper, a reflex requiring no thought, the product of years in the saddle, her legs long and relaxed, persuading the horse back on track.

"Oh, shit," yelled John. "Sit down!"

The women looked back. Colleen was standing in the saddle, balancing herself with her reins. Sloan grabbed hold of her paint's mane to pull herself up so that she too was standing on her horse's back. The paint bolted hard sideways, knocking the girl astraddle then bucked, a mean, head low buck, hitting the ground hard with his front feet. Sloan slid to the side, only one leg across the horse's back and hanging onto the mane. The paint shot past Annie and Clare with Sloan hanging on and looking, thought Annie, like a red-headed Indian on the war path, riding across the high chaparral. The girl pulled herself back into position and yanked the horse to a halt. Colleen, who had dropped back into the saddle, laughed so hard she had to hold the saddle horn.

"I hate paints," said Clare.

"Why then, did you put your daughter on one?"

"Sloan can ride anything. You try that again, daughter, and you're walking. You go ride next to Colleen and make sure she keeps her fanny in the saddle."

"Are you sure this is a good idea? I've never ridden before," John called to Clare.

"Well, I know that."

"Neither has Colleen."

"I guess I know that too. Bring Lonesome on up here next to me."

Lonesome obediently stepped forward and came alongside the bay. "Annie, you bring up the rear. Watch the girls."

Watch the girls. From behind. There had been a time when no one rode with Clare Raffienne except Annie. A hawk whistled, and Annie looked up. According to Indian lore, birds of prey were messengers. If you saw one, it meant something was going to happen to you. Good or bad. Annie searched the sky and then saw it, a young one, small, with a brilliant red tail. She wanted to tell Clare, but her friend and John leaned their heads together, talking and laughing. Annie had seen an extraordinarily fat breasted robin as they left the farm and now there was the hawk. The girls, just ahead of her, demurely held hands. Sloan had to work to keep the long-legged paint, who jigged impatiently, next to Butter. Already she rode like her mother, absorbing the motion of the horse with her back.

The climb became steeper. The path narrowed, and John was forced to bring Lonesome behind the bay. In the shade, the air was bracing but in the sun the warmth welcomed. Annie noticed the roundness of Lonesome's back and the silver shine of his tail, and she knew there were very few people who would or could keep a horse his age in that kind of condition. The bay handled the rocks by lifting his knees high and prancing over them but Lonesome managed so intelligently and efficiently that he appeared effortless and the feed bags barely moved. In the distance, she heard water running over rocks. The cool air gave her an appetite, and she thought about those roasted hens, red wine, and Clare's potato salad. Eventually, Clare turned off the path leading the party through the deep shade of the forest which smelled of pine and damp earth and they rode in silence. The soft ground absorbed the sound of the horse's footfalls and then suddenly they were in an open glade, bright with sunlight and a fast-running stream. Its water blue and green close to the surface and along the bottom brown and gray rocks.

They dismounted, and Sloan tied the horses while Annie and Clare spread a blanket on the ground and unpacked the food. John filled a plastic jug from the stream. He came back shaking his hands. "That water is like ice." He added the Kool Aid to the jug and shook it until the water turned purple.

The children and the grown-ups sat in a circle around the food. John poured wine into plastic cups. "Cheers," he said raising his glass. The girls giggled and raised their cups of purple juice. "To Sloan," said Clare. "And everyone here."

"To friends," said Annie. Clare broke off a chicken leg and gave it to Colleen, who, her eyes on Sloan, grinned as she chewed the food. Sloan dropped potato salad onto the girl's plate. Colleen took a taste and opened her eyes wide then scooped more into her mouth. Sloan gave her another chicken leg. Clare twisted two thighs off the second bird and offered them to John. The chicken was still warm and juicy and fresh, and Annie thought it tasted faintly of oats and molasses. She served herself potato salad. It contained large chunks of celery, eggs, the right amount of mayonnaise and vinegar, and Annie thought that nowhere else did anyone make it this good. She drank the wine, which though modest had body without bitterness. John moved so that his side was against Clare's. "You're right, you do make the best chicken and potato salad ever," he said helping himself to more from Clare's plate.

She laughed. "And don't I know it." She took one of the thighs and held it to his lips and he opened his mouth and bit into it.

"Stop it," said Sloan.

Clare looked at her. "What?"

"Don't share food."

"We're just foolin' around."

"You look stupid."

Clare tossed her hair back. "Well, all right miss prissy pants, we'll eat like proper people." She smiled at Colleen who was staring at her, her mouth slightly open. "Though it's not near so much fun. Is it?"

Colleen shook her head, solemnly.

There was no path to Unc's place. For a moment Clare thought she might not find it, but she kept going and finally saw a spot in the woods where the sun broke through. She approached slowly. His hut had not changed much. There were more trees cut in front and it was more faded. He was sitting on one of the stumps. He looked up from frying fish over an open fire and then down as though it had been weeks, not years, since he had seen Clare. She sat cautiously on the woodpile. He looked so much older than she had ever imagined he could be. His hair, which he wore in a limp ponytail, had gone completely gray and there were deep creases on the sides of his mouth. His jacket and pants were ragged, and he had patched his boots with duct tape. Clare had never seen him in a regular house. He'd run away into the highest parts of these mountains when he was a teenager.

"How are you, Unc?"

He looked at her. His eyes were so brown they looked black. Though the skin around them was weathered with dark blotches and full of lines, she still thought they were the finest eyes she had ever seen. She settled more comfortably on the logs. "It's been a long time, hasn't it?"

Unc nodded, smiled, then flipped a fish.

"I brought some people up the mountain. They're all right. It's just for a picnic. It's kind of a special occasion. My daughter's been gone and now she's back."

Unc nodded.

"I had to shoot that bear. I don't know if you knew but there was a bear, a she-bear living around here. And her cub. DSS, the government, said the mother was dangerous 'cause Sloan and me raised her from a cub and sometimes she come around and Sloan loved her and fed her. She called her Sister cause I guess she was lonely. Anyway, I wouldn't let animal control kill her and run them off with my rifle, so they took Sloan. DSS, not animal control. I had to get her back, so I shot the bear and her cub. They wouldn't have given me Sloan back if I hadn't. Don't know if you noticed anything going on up here or not."

"Hard to miss something like that." Unc didn't raise his eyes from the fish browning up in the black and crusty iron skillet.

"Pap used to say it was always a mistake tryin' to tame a wild animal," Clare said.

"He was right." Unc took the skillet away from the fire. "You want some of these?"

"No thanks. Like I said we're having a picnic. We won't make a habit of coming up." They sat in silence for a while then Clare said, "Well, I guess I should be going. Hope we didn't bother you."

Unc shook his head. "You can come here anytime you want." He looked up at Clare. "I'd like to meet that daughter of yours. Bein' family and all."

Clare blinked. "I'll bring her, for sure."

After they had eaten, the girls took off their shoes and rolled up their pant legs and waded in the water. Annie laid on her back with her face toward the sun. She fell asleep with the thin mountain light warm on her skin. When she startled awake, Clare was gone. John sat watching Sloan and Colleen, who were trying to skip rocks across the creek. He turned and looked at Annie and smiled.

"Where is Clare?"

"She went for a walk."

Annie didn't say anything.

"She said she wanted to go alone."

Together they watched the children go deeper and deeper into the water. "Not too far," John called before turning to Annie. "You've known Clare a long time, right? People talk about her, you know. They say some pretty bizarre things. Like boys freezing to death because she dumped them, maiming some other guy and burning down people's houses and not even going to jail."

"What are you asking me?"

"Is it true? I mean it's like something out of a really bad movie."

Annie sat up. "Look John, this whole thing with you and Clare, you know I don't approve. If people found out the whole mess of it who knows how long Sloan might have stayed in foster care. But they didn't and even if they do now, it's your career not Sloan's life that's fucked."

"Well, thanks."

"What do you expect me to say? I tried to talk Clare out of it, but you know her... or you don't actually."

"I think I do."

"Then you go ahead and do what you're going to do. I sure as hell can't stop you. Or Clare. I wouldn't even try."

"You may have known Clare since you were kids, but you've been away a long time too."

"Yes, I have and maybe... well, who knows...."

Clare walked into the clearing. "What are you guys talking about?"

"Nothing," John and Annie said at the same time.

Clare flopped down on the blanket between them. "You worry too much," she said to Annie. "Can you hand me the wine, please?" She drank from the bottle, wiping her mouth with the back of her hand. Unc wants to see Sloan, she thought. Maybe I could bring Colleen with me. Unc would probably like the silent child. Maybe he could teach them both to fish. That would be nice. She called to the girls, "Come out of the water and sit here and dry off before we mount up."

The children stood dripping next to the adults, their legs rosy from the cold water.

"Do we have to leave now?" asked Sloan.

"Not yet, but I don't want you getting into the tack or on the horses when you're wet." Clare laid back on the ground, stretched full out, and closed her eyes.

"When are we going?"

"After my nap."

"I want to stay."

"I'll take a long nap."

"Can we go back in the water?"

"You don't want to be wet riding home. Annie, go ahead and give them a Snickers." She draped her arm over her eyes.

"I'll get it." Avery dug into the feed sack and found the candy. While the girls arranged themselves on the edge of the blanket, he laid next to Clare and let his thigh rest along hers.

"Hey." Sloan shoved the chocolate into her mouth, licked her fingers, sprawled on top of her mother, and pushed John's leg away with her foot.

"Get off, you're squashing my stomach." Clare tickled Sloan along the ribs and pushed the girl gently between her and Avery, but Sloan crawled right back and tickled her mother again, her knees on either side, her head bent so that her hair fell forward covering her face. Colleen, who had been watching the whole thing, came over and sat next to her brother, put a piece of candy in his mouth then dropped her head on his chest. Clare gave a husky laugh and pushed Sloan away again. "Stop tickling me. I give up. You win."

With the same weasel slipperiness Annie had seen earlier in the day, Sloan slid off her mother, pushed Colleen away with her foot, and suddenly had John between her legs, her bottom on his crotch. She rubbed herself against him in a rhythm that was unmistakable.

Clare exploded to her feet. She grabbed her daughter by her upper arms, held her at face level and said, "What the hell are you doing?" Sloan burst into tears.

"Tack up," said Clare.

In a cacophony of flying bags and blankets, spooking, squealing horses thrown bottles and frantic bridling and saddling, they managed to get themselves mounted and scrambled down the mountain. Clare, in front, her face a hatchet cleaving the air, led Sloan on her paint. Once they were back at the farm, she took Sloan inside immediately, leaving John and Annie to put the horses and equipment away, which they did without looking at each other or speaking. When they were done, John picked up Colleen, who had been tagging along behind him, and held her on his hip. "I'll call later tonight."

When it was time to put his sister to bed, Avery ran the water in the bath then went to stand outside the bathroom door. "You're old enough to bathe yourself now."

The girl looked up at him, her eyes dark.

"Look, Sloan bathes herself. She's not that much older than you and she has been doing it for years."

Colleen didn't move. Avery handed her a washcloth, towel, and nightie. "When you're done, I'll read you a bedtime story." He pushed her gently through the door, closed it, slid down the wall, and sat with his arms around his legs to wait. There was silence. It lasted so long he was wondering if he should go into the bathroom after all to see if she was all right then the door opened, and Colleen stood in front of him with her pink cheeks and her black hair curling around her face from the steam.

"Good for you." he said, "Now let's go read you that story."

This wasn't the night to read anything about sleeping girls being kissed awake by princes or any of that barely disguised sexualized fairytale slop. He instead chose The Jungle Book, the real one, the one written by Kipling, not the travesty produced by Disney, and stretched out next to his sister who had already climbed into bed. She held onto her doll and leaned against his shoulder. John allowed himself to get lost in the musical language of the book, no images in his mind except the mysterious jungle, the wolves, the beautiful black panther, and dimpled brown baby. His sister's head rested on his shoulder until he felt Colleen's weight change and she slipped onto her pillow, her eyes closed, her breath slow and even. He carefully straightened her out and smoothed the covers, pulling them under her chin. He placed the doll next to her on the bed. Then he stared down at his little sister and thought, *oh, hell. Oh, hell and damn.*

Chapter Twenty

Once John and Colleen were out of the house, Annie sat at the kitchen table to wait. It was growing dark when Clare came down the stairs and went into what was once the feed room. After a few minutes, Clare walked into the kitchen holding the shotgun against her leg, with the barrel cracked and pointing at the floor. She looked wrecked, her matted hair flattened against her head on one side, crimson crescents under her eyes.

"She's asleep," Clare said. "I don't think she'll wake up any time soon. You'll stay, won't you? Give her anything she wants if she wakes up."

"Wait. Where are you going? And what are you doing with that gun? What's going on? What did Sloan say?"

"I'll tell you later," Clare said quietly, looking down the barrels of the gun, one then the other. She walked toward the door.

Annie rose, nearly knocking over the chair. "Where are you going?"

Clare didn't answer. She strode out, letting the door slam behind her. Annie snatched it, flung it open, and once outside, grabbed Clare by the shirt before the other woman could open the truck door. "Where the hell are you going?" Annie said, panting.

"Get off." Clare put her free hand on Annie's chest, but Annie moved in closer and wrapped her arms around Clare's waist, clinging like a monkey. Clare reached behind and opened the truck door with Annie still holding on to her. She managed to twist, put her hands on Annie's shoulders and pushed.

Annie swatted at her. "Stop it. Tell me what's going on. Jesus. Just stop a minute, will you, and tell me what's going on."

Clare stepped backward until her thighs were against the driver's seat. She was still trying to push Annie away with her open hand in the middle of her friend's chest and when she couldn't, she grabbed hold of her and heaved them both inside with Annie awkwardly lying across her lap, hoping the gun wouldn't go off. Clare swung her legs inside and braced her feet against the floorboards, arched her back sharply, jouncing Annie against the steering wheel. But Annie took hold of the seat belt and held tight. She held on until finally Clare said, "Shit," and sat still. Annie slid backward out the door. "What the hell are you doing?"

"I'm not talking about this right now. Now step back from the truck."

Annie reached in and grabbed the keys off the dash and shoved them in her pocket. Clare, her face white and sharp, looked at Annie and said quietly, "I'll just hotwire it."

"Tell me what's going on."

"They… um, that boy and Grafton…"

"What?"

"Don't make me say it. Don't make me say that word. You know exactly what. Now move."

Annie put her hand on the top of the truck door for support. "We'll take them to court."

"Fuck court."

"We'll get them put in jail. We'll see that they pay. I swear."

Clare turned away, shoved her hair out of her eyes, and looked out the front window, though it was too dark to see anything.

"What about Sloan?" Annie asked. "She's going to need help—someone who knows how to deal with this kind of thing. We'll call Dr. Wittcomb in the morning. And Marshall. We'll go to the police and press charges."

Clare, still holding the gun, got out of the truck, forcing Annie to take a step back. "Fuck the law."

"The law got your daughter back."

"The law got her taken from me in the first place."

"Okay, that's true. But I wouldn't turn my back on it."

"I want to kill them."

"Who do you mean by them? Mr. Grafton? And who else?"

"One of the foster kids. An older boy." Clare looked like she might fall down.

"Do you want a drink?"

"No. What I want are them goddamn keys." When Annie didn't answer, Clare moved and lifted the hood of the truck. She held the shot gun under her arm.

"I'll call Marshall first thing tomorrow."

"Tomorrow's Sunday."

"He'll talk to me on Sunday." Annie slid into the driver's seat. Clare came around the side of the door, the gun butt at her shoulder with the barrels facing the ground. Annie put up her hands.

"Stop that. I'm serious," Clare said, her voice leaving no doubt of it.

"All right," Annie stepped out of the truck, put her hand on the barrel, and pushed it. "Okay, you're right, you can't rely on the law. And, no, justice is not fucking blind. It sees whether you're black or white, rich or poor, male or female, establishment or not. And believe me, you are not. And good old lady justice will notice this. You go off half-crazy and shoot someone, you'll get locked up so fast your head will spin. And don't think because Pap sold Judge Leatte a pony a long time ago that she will be able to do anything to save you. Or would if she could. This whole case has stunk from the beginning. You're right. The law should never have taken Sloan in the first place. But it did. And it will take her again if you give them half a chance. They will lock you up and throw away the key. And they will take your daughter for good and forever and probably give her back to the Graftons." Annie was breathing hard. "You want that? Huh? Is that what you want? Because that is what you'll get." She stood there panting.

Clare was quiet for a long time before she walked into the house and sat at the kitchen table. Annie sat across from her. "I'll call Marshall tomorrow." She could not keep her voice from shaking. "And we'll call Dr. Wittcomb first thing Monday."

"How can a therapist fix this? There ain't no fixing it."

"How was Sloan before she fell asleep?"

Clare shrugged. "She seemed to be relieved to have told me. Listen, I don't want to talk about this. If I talk about it, I'll go crazy. You stay here with me but don't ask any questions. Just stay with me." She handed Annie the gun across the table. "Keep it. Lock it in your car... no, that won't work, just stay with me but don't talk about it now."

"Of course."

Clare sat back against the chair. Eventually, she said "I want to kill them. I really do."

"I know you do. You know," Annie continued, her voice returning to normal. "In prison, there is a hierarchy. Child molesters don't live very long. Even hardened criminals: murderers, rapists, serial killers hate pedophiles."

"Seriously?"

"Yeah. And their deaths are really ugly."

"How do you know this?"

"It's common knowledge among lawyers, anyone in the law enforcement field."

"What about the guards?"

"The guards help out. They provide the opportunity."

Clare said nothing, just stared at Annie who, after a while, rose and went to the cupboard, took out the bottle of bourbon and put it on the table. Clare unscrewed the top, raised the bottle to her lips and drank long and deep, shivering as the liquor went down. Then she handed it to Annie, who took a few sips. The women passed the bottle back and forth several times until Annie took a deep breath and asked, "Do you want to talk about it?"

Clare stared her squarely in the eyes. "Do you remember when we first met? Those boys had you deep in the woods and were going to... well, you know."

"Of course, I remember. You saved me."

Clare snapped her gaze away, turned her profile to her friend. "Well, I didn't save Sloan."

"You did everything you could. Don't blame yourself." Annie reached out to touch Clare's shoulder, but she pulled away.

"Don't say things like that to me. We know each other too well to talk like that. If I would have done things differently this never would have happened."

"Okay."

"Sloan told me everything. But I don't want to talk about it. Don't ask no questions."

"Of course not, but let me help. Let Marshall and me put them in jail."

Clare hesitated, looked at Annie, and said, "Tell me why you didn't come back sooner."

Annie leaned back in her chair. "I had to see what was out there."

"And?"

"There's nothing much."

Clare too leaned back. "You know, as horrible as this is, I can stand it 'cause Sloan is here with me. I can't lose her again. I couldn't stand that. I'd have to kill someone."

"You won't. Lose her again, I mean. I swear. You just have to follow the law."

Clare took another long drink, watching Annie over the bottle. "Your timin' was actually perfect. With Pap gone, I couldn't have stood this alone."

"I'm sorry, Clare. I'm sorry I stayed away and I'm sorry I didn't stay in touch and I'm sorry about Pap and I'm sick about this mess with Sloan. You and Pap were my family. You still are. You not only saved me from those hateful boys, you saved me from my hateful parents."

Clare shook her head and almost laughed. "Your mom is mean as cat shit all right." She rose and ran her hand through her hair. She looked gaunt and exhausted. "I'm gonna go check on Sloan. Why don't you spend the night?"

"Of course I will."

Chapter Twenty-One

Dr. Wittcomb brought Chukchi with her to Clare's house. The weather had turned again, bringing a bitter wind. Annie had told her that the only way Clare would see her was at her home. The doctor knocked on the door. There was no sound from inside. She knocked again and pulled her long coat around her and tried to pat her hair back into its bun.

Annie Voigt opened the door and motioned her in. Clare sat at the table with Sloan in her lap and her head against her mother's chest. Clare had her arms around her.

"May I?" Dr. Wittcomb motioned toward a chair and eased into it. "I'm sorry," she said. "I so wish I could have found a way to stop this from happening."

"I guess we all do." Annie sat between the two women.

Dr. Wittcomb's bosom rose and fell. She looked out the window, then back at Clare. "Look," she said, "pressing charges is the right thing to do. For Sloan's sake. It tells her we take this seriously."

Sloan lifted her head from her mother's chest and looked at the clinician.

"It also, hopefully, will put the perpetrators behind bars."

"Hopefully?" Clare raised an eyebrow.

"These cases are very hard to prove."

Clare, her face all hollow, looked at Annie. "Just how hard?"

"Very," Dr. Wittcomb said. "To start, the first thing the defense attorney or judge or jury is going to say is that someone, probably her mother or her attorney or her therapist, put ideas in Sloan's head."

"Why would they think that?"

"Children can be easily led."

"Why would I want to put such an idea in my daughter's head?"

"To get even. Because you're mad. Because you want to appear to be the injured party. Because you're looking for financial compensation. Any number of reasons. Because you're unstable."

Annie looked down at the table.

"Unstable," Clare said.

"Yes, they will say that."

"Annie?"

Annie nodded.

Clare sat back, crossed her legs, shifting Sloan's weight. "So, tell me again why we are going to the law? Oh, I remember now. So, I don't shoot someone."

Sloan looked up at her mother.

"That is the sort of the thing you don't want to say in front of your daughter," Dr. Wittcomb said gently.

Annie ran her hand over the table. "Look, I'm sorry. I should have had more information. I admit it. When I came back here, I thought I'd be working on divorces. The occasional teenager selling drugs. Slip and falls. I didn't know I'd be getting into foster care or child abuse cases. Fortunately, this isn't Marshall's first rodeo. He's handled a few of these cases, and I run everything by him, met with him yesterday even though it was Sunday. And I'm reading everything there is on this kind of case." She shrugged, looking at Clare. "As fast as I can. All the recent briefs and older, similar cases in the books in Marshall's very well-stocked library. But if you want a different lawyer, I would totally understand."

"I thought Marshall was supposed to be the best lawyer in town."

"He is. And most attorneys shy away from these cases. It's up to you, of course, but I wouldn't change lawyers," said Dr. Wittcomb.

Clare looked at her daughter. "I don't see making her go over it again, if it's not going to put anyone in jail."

"We won't make her do anything she doesn't want to do. It's a fine line," said Annie.

Car doors slammed outside, followed by a firm knock on the door. The police had arrived. They walked into the kitchen without waiting for an invitation. The man, Detective Guire, was blond, intensely muscled, and good looking. The woman, Detective James, was blonde as well, but it was obvious the color wasn't natural and her features were sharp, her skin worn. Annie was surprised at how professional they both looked in their dark, well-fitting suits. After they introduced themselves, James leaned down in front of Sloan and looked into her eyes. "May Detective Guire and I talk to you for a while?"

Sloan looked at her mother, who nodded a curt assent.

The girl slid off her mother's lap. "I guess."

"Where do you want to talk? In the living room or your bedroom?"

"Downstairs."

"Okay. We'll just go in this other room for a while." When the detectives took Sloan with them out of sight and hearing, Annie offered to make coffee. She put out three mugs, asked Dr. Wittcomb if she wanted milk or sugar. The woman said "yes" and Annie added generous amounts of both then poured milk into her own mug and bourbon into Clare's.

"Do you mind if I take some notes?" asked Dr. Wittcomb.

While she did this, Annie washed and dried the dishes, scrubbed the counter, swept the floor, and rearranged some dishes in the cupboards. Clare sat in silence and sipped her coffee.

When the detectives finally returned to the kitchen, the man stood straight, a hand inside his pant pocket. James sat at the table. Sloan climbed quickly into her mother's lap and leaned back.

Dr. Wittcomb rose to her feet. "Do you need to talk to the adults?"

"Yes, ma'am," said Guire. The clinician held out her hand toward Sloan. "I have a dog that looks like a wolf in my truck. Would you like to see her?" The girl's eyes widened. She slid from Clare's lap, took Dr. Wittcomb's hand, and out they went.

Clare watched them go. Annie motioned to a chair and Detective Guire sat in it stiffly. "The case against Mr. Grafton is very thin," he said. "Sloan remembers being held under water, arms or restraints around her, and pain between her legs. In the morning her hair would be wet. This all happened at night, however, after she was given her medicine. So, it's very flimsy. It could easily have been dreams. The good news is she is consistent."

"What part does the water play in it?" asked Annie.

"Sex offenders often have specific rituals. It could be water is some way for Grafton to get aroused. Or clean up evidence."

"Pain?" said Clare. "Pain?"

"I'm sorry, ma'am."

Annie looked down at the table again then turned to the detective. "Okay. So, honestly speaking, what do you think are the chances of a conviction?"

"Like I said, very slim."

Clare's eyebrows drew together, blackbird's wings over feral eyes.

Annie worked at keeping her expression bland. Even the detectives were completely still. The room seemed to hold its breath while Clare turned this new information around in her mind. She looked out the window as though to check out Sloan then turned back to the detectives. "So. Slim to none."

"We definitely have a case against the boy, Nat Washington, though," said Detective James, who sat down beside Clare in a rush, and Annie saw that it was an offering. There was a terrible quietness to her friend. James leaned toward her. "I don't think it was dreams. I believe your daughter. It's just that it could have been dreams. That's what the defense will say, and we have no solid evidence that it wasn't."

"My daughter said it wasn't."

"That's just not going to be good enough, ma'am," Detective Guire said.

"Stop calling me that."

"But you have enough evidence against the boy?" Annie asked quickly.

"Yes. Sloan was fully awake during the alleged incidents. She describes what happened clearly and her story stays consistent. She doesn't get confused over the details."

Clare looked away.

"We can have her examined to see if there is physical evidence."

"What?" Clare snapped her attention back to the detective.

"An exam. By people who are trained in this sort of thing."

"What kind of exam?"

"It's done by expert nurses."

"What kind of expert?"

"Gynecology," said Annie. The two detectives looked at each other.

"You mean like her privates?" Clare stared at one detective then the other.

Both nodded and simultaneously said, "Yes ma'am."

"I think my daughter has been 'examined' quite enough."

"It could help with a conviction." The man left off the ma'am, but it hovered in the air.

Annie stood. "Let me talk with my client. We'll call you this afternoon. Can you leave a card?"

"Yes, ma'am," said Detective Guire. He reached into his shirt pocket and handed one to her. "But the sooner we can have her examined, the better. It's too late for fluids, but there could still be bruising."

"No one is touching my daughter like that again." Clare took the card from Annie and ripped it in half.

"We don't need to have an examination," Detective James said quickly. "They are not that conclusive anyway." She gave Guire a hard look, her eyes tired, then she turned back to Clare. "If Sloan stays as consistent as she was with us, it's still a good case against the boy. And we have the interview taped, of course."

"But that's just against the boy."

"The lack of supervision, the locks on the doors… we might be able to take the Grafton's license. They wouldn't have any more foster kids."

"Jesus," said Clare.

The women didn't speak for several minutes after the detectives left. Annie realized she was holding her breath and exhaled slowly, trying to watch Clare without being obvious. She had no idea what to say or what kind of advice she should give. She felt lost and sick and extremely incompetent and wished Marshall were here. The silence became painful, yet all Annie could think of were platitudes. She decided to get herself a drink and started to stand when

Sloan banged the door open. "The lady's dog looks just like a wolf but she's really gentle and she touched noses with the horses, and she wasn't afraid at all, not at all, and she liked the horses and they like her, and can we have a dog just like her, please, mama, please?"

"I know the breeder," Dr. Wittcomb said. "She generally has a litter of pups in the spring. It's possible you could have a puppy in a few weeks."

Without a moment's hesitation, Clare said, "Yes."

Annie understood she would have said yes to anything Sloan wanted at that point and for a moment, a brief moment, the women smiled along with the girl at the thought of a young thing, brave and innocent, coming into their lives.

That evening when John came to the farm, he did not bring Colleen. He tapped on the kitchen door, opened it a slit, and poked his head into the room. Annie and Clare were sitting in front of the woodstove.

"Where is Sloan?" he asked.

Clare had looked up the minute she heard the rap at the door. "Upstairs asleep."

"May I come in?"

"I think I'll go on to bed too," Annie said, rising from her chair.

"Sit down. Stay here in front of the fire. John and I will go outside. I could use some fresh air."

Clare leaned her hip against John's car, her face ghost white in the light coming from the kitchen window. "Sloan was asking about Colleen. I thought you might bring her."

"I think we should talk first."

"Okay."

"I can't ever be alone with Sloan."

"No."

They watched each other.

"So, you understand. I don't think it would be good for her. I know it wouldn't be good for me. The risk."

"You were never alone with her anyway. She was always with Colleen."

"Well, yes."

Clare straightened away from the car. When she spoke, her voice was low and sure. "If you think for one minute Sloan would hurt Colleen, you can get in your car and leave right now and never come back."

"I don't think that. It's just that, well, Sloan has been… hurt."

Clare held John's gaze so firmly he felt he would stand there forever if she didn't release him. She said quietly, "You was about to say damaged, wasn't you?"

"No. Clare. No. Just hurt. Badly hurt." He edged a tiny bit closer to her. "She probably will need therapy."

"Therapy don't help anybody."

"I don't know. Dr. Wittcomb knows a thing or two. She's better than the rest."

"I ain't taking Sloan back to that place."

"Maybe she would come here."

"She already has. She is going to help Sloan get a puppy."

"A puppy." John grinned. "What a good idea. Who thought of it?"

"Sloan."

"Good for her. It should really help. Take her mind off the other stuff."

"Yeah."

They looked at each other for a moment and John's smile faded. "Did the police come?"

"Yeah."

"What did they say? Will you go to court?"

"No."

"Seriously? You mean they don't think they have a case? I mean… Christ." He shook his head.

"Apparently no one believes the kids in this kind of thing so there ain't no point. They might get the boy, but no chance against Grafton."

"And why not Grafton?"

"It happened at night. After her meds. It could be just dreams."

John took hold of Clare's wrist, turned it so her hand was palm up, and rubbed his finger along the tender inside. "Look, I know you just want to forget this whole thing but think of the other children those two might hurt."

"The Graftons will probably lose their license," Clare said, her voice distant.

"That's it? What about all those other kids out there? Like Sunday school kids, kids in the park, friends' kids?"

"I can't do nothin' about it. Besides, I can only think about Sloan right now. And I ain't putting her through what they would do to her to prove their case."

"Like what?"

"I don't want to talk about it. Look, Sloan needs to go back to being normal. Just being a kid who lives at home with her mama. And has a friend come over to play. She needs Colleen more than ever. She needs that more than therapy. And she needs to be around a man, a good man, one that won't—hurt her." Clare's voice broke.

John reached out and drew her against him, his arms around her. "Sure, she does," he said.

Chapter Twenty-Two

The house was quiet. Annie listened for a few seconds, looked out the window at the dawn sky, then sat up and swung her feet out of bed. The floor felt like ice. She went down the stairs on tiptoes, tread softly across the dark kitchen, and touched the woodstove. It was cold. The Mr. Coffee she had given to Clare so she didn't have to drink the greasy percolator coffee was empty and cold as well. She looked at her watch. Sloan should be getting ready for school by now. Annie put a filter, water, and coffee in the machine and turned it on. She placed a box of Fruit Loops, a carton of milk, a bowl and spoon, and a glass of orange juice on the table and went back upstairs and slowly opened Clare's bedroom door. Her friend was stretched out on her back, arms at her side, staring at the ceiling as though she were in a coffin.

"Shouldn't Sloan be getting ready for school?" Annie said.

The child rolled from her side onto her back, flung a languid arm across her mother and slowly opened her eyes.

"Let's go downstairs," said Annie. "Get some breakfast."

"Can Colleen come over and play?"

"No," said Annie carefully, "she'll be in school."

Sloan sat up. "I guess I should go to school too." She wiggled from under the covers and headed down the stairs.

"You can't keep her with you all the time. I know you want to, but you can't."

Clare rose slowly and pulled on her jeans. She picked a sweater off the floor, stepped around Annie, and followed her daughter. In the kitchen, she poured coffee and sat morosely at the table. Sloan was already nearly finished with her bowl of cereal. When Annie started piling wood in the stove, Clare left the coffee and took the logs from her. "Let me do that. You done with your breakfast, Sloan?"

"Can I have toast?"

"Get dressed and you can have toast when you come down."

Sloan jumped off the chair and ran upstairs. Clare continued with the logs. She spoke into the stove. "I can't stand the thought of her being away from me."

"Nothing will happen to her in school. She's safe there."

"I got someone comin' to look at that big bay this afternoon just when school lets out. Going to pay me three thousand dollars. I can't afford to turn that down."

"I'll pick her up."

Clare found the box of long matches and began scraping one against the side. "She don't need to go to school." Clare kept scraping the match until it lit and then she reached it toward the kindling. Her hand shook and it was not from drinking. Annie almost wished it were. If, all those years ago, Clare hadn't lifted her onto the back of a pony and away from those boys high in the mountains behind the Holler, Annie too would be a victim. And if it hadn't been for Clare, she wouldn't have made it through that terrible summer after she had left her husband and was trying to make it back here in Pennsylvania. It was having Clare near, buying horses cheap, selling them for enough to buy food, managing. Just barely. But making it. No question in her mind she wouldn't. Stuffing her money in her jeans pocket, dependent on no one, happy just the way things were. Laughing and falling asleep as soon as her head hit the pillow. Watching this had given Annie the courage to keep going. And now her friend's hand shook.

Even so, the fire took. Clare shut the iron door.

"Where's my toast?" Sloan stood in the doorway dressed in jeans that came above her ankles, no socks, sneakers, and a sweater inside out and backwards.

"I'll make your toast right now," Annie said quickly. "Clare, finish your coffee. I'll put Sloan's lunch together and you can make sure she has all her books."

"Lots of butter," Sloan said.

"Please," Clare automatically corrected.

"Please," said Sloan. Annie put large chunks of butter on the hot toast. Sloan licked her fingers and wiped her chin as she ate. "Can Colleen come over after school?"

Clare focused on her daughter, who was shoving the last butter-slick piece of bread in her mouth. She watched her as she might watch someone she didn't know. She looked at her, taking in every bit of her, the color of her skin, the clothes, the cheeks puffed out with food, her slippery fingers.

"So," Clare said, "you ready for school?"

Sloan nodded.

"Okay, I'll take you. Annie will pick you up and get Colleen. I'll be here waiting for you."

There was no shade on the side of the school where Annie stood as close to the door as she could without getting smacked in the face when it opened. The day had turned brilliant, and the sun made her squint. Damp spots grew under her arms and between her shoulder blades.

The door opened, and a group of children straggled out to be greeted off-handedly by parents. They came out in small groups, the door slamming behind them then a slight pause before it opened again for more children. If she is not in the next group, I'll go inside, thought Annie. But if she went inside, she might miss her, and Sloan would be in the open with no one to protect her. A matronly figure organized the youngsters and hustled them to the proper cars. She called out names, corralling those kids whose parents had not yet arrived into a ragged group. Annie was about to speak to her when the door opened and Sloan appeared, her book bag hoisted over one shoulder, her eyes scanning the parking lot. Annie tapped her on the shoulder and the girl glanced at her before turning her focus back to the parking lot and Annie's SUV. She headed resolutely for the parking lot and left Annie to follow behind. Once settled in the car, Annie rummaged in her purse for the Snickers Clare had repeatedly told her to have ready for her daughter as soon as she was safely next to Annie.

"How was school?"

"I like my new teacher."

"That's good. That's very good. What do you like about her?"

"He's fair."

"He?"

"Yeah."

"What do you mean he's fair?"

"He's just fair, that's all."

"How does he show he's fair? Does he treat you differently than the other children?"

"No." Sloan looked at her quizzically.

"Well, I just wondered if he was… um, okay with you."

But Sloan had lost interest in the conversation and concentrated on her candy bar. She licked her fingers as the chocolate melted onto them and then wiped them onto her shirt. When she finished, she leaned her head against the back of the seat, rolled it to face Annie, and gave her a chocolatey smile.

The next day, Clare eased the cinch tight hole by hole on a training colt as she talked to Annie. "When we had that picnic up the mountain that horrible day, I went to visit someone." She tucked the extra leather on the strap into a slot on the side of the saddle, laid her arm over the seat and looked at Annie. "Have I ever told you about Unc… Gram's nephew? He's wild. I mean way more than Pap or me. He started living up the mountain by hisself when he was a teenager… not sure exactly how old but young. He's stayed up there all his life. Hasn't even been inside a house. At least I never heard that he has. I hadn't seen him in years before that day. He said I should come back and I want to. Him being kin and all. I just need to talk to family. You understand?"

"Sure."

"I got cousins in the Holler. You met them. Some of them. But they've been on welfare all their lives. Made fun of Pap 'cause he earned a living. We've always been different. Unc is the same as us in a way. Anyway, I just feel like I want to talk to him. I'll be back in time to pick up the girls from school."

"That's not necessary. I'll go get them," said Annie.

"No, you already drove all the way out here, don't want to make you drive back."

"I brought us pizza for lunch."

"It will keep till dinner. Hey… do you mind if I take half of it to Unc? I don't even know if he's ever had pizza. It might be a nice treat for him. I'll pick up another one in town. The girls would love it for supper."

"Sure. It's in the car."

"Hold the reins for me. I'll wrap it up." Clare came out of the house holding a paper grocery bag and took the reins from Annie, who stood with the colt next to the back steps. "I'll be back by three, promise. Even if I can't find him."

"I can get the girls, Clare."

"You drove all the way out here. I don't want to make you drive back into town."

I drove out here to see you, Annie thought, but said nothing. Watching Clare leave, she remembered the days when, young and arrogant, in warm weather or cold, they rode into the mountains together. Just the two of them. They would ride to the top and look down at the valley as though they owned it and the mountain too and everything was just fine.

It was too late in the season to still be fishing, but there was no sign of Unc. Perhaps he was hunting, but it was too late in the day for that too. Clare called his name. No answer. She dismounted and sat on a stump. She could wait an hour before she needed to return home. After a minute, she stood and looked inside the cabin. The floor and walls were made of wood planks. There was a cot with a dirty comforter, a table with a kerosene lantern on it, a woodstove, and a chair. That was it. Clare returned to the stump. She looked into the trees and the thick underbrush. I should go home, she thought, but then she saw Unc coming down a narrow path. He had a towel over his shoulder and carried a fishing pole and fishing basket made of twigs, like the one Pap used to use. His gray hair was loose and fluttering and with the pole that could be a staff, he looked like a wizard. "Hey," he said.

"Hope you don't mind. I just came for a short visit."

"Glad you're here. Just in time for lunch." He dropped the basket next to her. "Go on, look. Three beauties."

"Actually, I brought you a pizza. Have you ever had one? I think you'll like it."

"Course, I've had one. I'm not a Neanderthal."

How? wondered Clare. Did he go into town after all? Or did someone bring it to him? A woman, perhaps. Or a friend. Did he have friends?

"I'll save that for supper. It'll keep. I want to fix these fish while they're fresh." Unc took them out of the basket. They were gutted, hanging from a line through their gills.

"They're beautiful." Clare watched while he arranged the logs and made a fire and when the iron skillet was hot, he placed the fish in it in a neat row. Immediately she could smell the clean, sharp fragrance from their freshness. "It's late in the day to be fishin, ain't it?"

Unc gave the towel a small flick. "After I caught them, I cleaned myself up for company."

"How did you know I was coming?"

"I didn't. Just kidding you."

Neither of them spoke as the fish cooked. When Unc pulled the skillet off the fire and placed it on a log between them, Clare said, "I can't stay long. I got to go get Sloan from school."

Unc nodded.

"Something awful happened to her when she was in foster care."

Unc looked up from delicately pulling the meat away from the trout's spine. He waited.

"Something so bad you can't even begin to imagine it."

"Maybe I can." He watched her quietly from under his brows.

"There was a boy. And the foster father. An old man."

"I run away when I was fifteen, swore to myself they would never touch me like that again. No man would. I never went back. My paw looked for me, but I could always hear him comin'. Him and his brother. They never found me. Not till I was big enough. They never come back after that."

Clare looked at Unc for a long time before she spoke. "Did Gram know?"

"Dunno. She was already married to your Pap when I left. Had been for years. Anyway, she never said nothin'."

"I've talked to the police. They said they can't prove anything about the man. Maybe the boy, but nothing for sure. Pap says you should never let the government into your life. If you do, you'll never get them out."

"If I'd asked for help, I'd of been put into foster care. I'd have ended up in jail for sure. So, I'd say your Pap was right."

The next afternoon, after Clare had brought Colleen and Sloan home from school, she said to Annie, "Can you watch the girls for me? I think I'll go into town for a while."

"Sure." Annie blew on her coffee.

"I mean really watch them."

"I know."

"They'll wanna go out to play. They'll want to ride."

"Okay."

"You have to go out with them. Stay outside with them."

"I know. What is it? You know I'll watch them. Anyway, nothing's going to happen here."

"Huh." Clare appeared more wrecked than ever, dark hollows under her eyes and cheeks, sickly pale skin, hair uncombed and greasy. She looked like she might throw up.

"Are you okay?"

"Of course I'm not."

"Are you eating? Taking care of yourself?"

"Yes, I'm eating. I cook every day. Dinner. Lunch. Breakfast."

"I'll do the cooking if you want me to."

"I like to cook," Clare said crossly. She reached into her pocket and brought out the keys to her truck. "Just stay with them. Okay? I won't be long."

Annie resisted the temptation to ask her where she was going.

The day had started out with blue skies and bright sunshine. It was spring, the time for planting, and Clare was surprised the greenhouse was empty. The door at one end was partly open and from where she was parked, Clare could see no one was inside. The grass was tall and shabby, uncared for, but a truck stood in the driveway and a garden tractor in the yard. Both Annie and John had told her that when men had done what this one had, they always did it again. Many, many times with many, many children. The boy maybe not. But the man, for sure. Clare watched the house. From her distance, the windows looked black. She watched for a while and then opened the truck's door. She stepped out and stood still, waiting for some movement, for a door to open, for someone to come outside. When no one did, she walked over to the greenhouse and through the slightly ajar door and looked around. A few plants appeared healthy, but most were wilted, dead, or dying. It was warm and dry inside and there was a sharp odor that Clare couldn't identify. Sacks of seeds were stacked in one corner with tall Ficus trees around them. The leaves were abundant but had gone yellow. The details. The cops had said Sloan was good with the details. Well, here they were. Details. Like Ficus trees big enough to hide behind. Clare picked up a fallen leaf, yellow with curled edges that had once made a lush cover. She began to sweat. She looked around one more time and left the greenhouse and climbed back in her truck. She started the engine and drove up the driveway, parking right in front of the porch. She took an elastic band from the dash, secured her hair at the base of her neck, and got out of the truck. After putting the keys in her pocket, she walked up the stairs and looked through a window. Nobody was in the front room, but she heard a man's voice call, "You there, what do you think you are doing?" He came out of a room off the kitchen and walked toward the front of the house. The man looked out the window at her. Clare moved from the window and tried the door handle. It wasn't locked and she opened it. Mr. Grafton looked past her for Sloan. She stepped through the door, put her hand, fingertips only, on his chest and pushed him gently. He took an automatic step backward. Clare gathered his shirt into her fist and at the same time took her knife from her pocket, touched the tip just above his Adam's apple. She lifted his chin and drew a shallow, delicate, crimson line. "You ever come near my daughter again, I'll kill you," she said. Before Grafton could respond, they heard feet pounding down the stairs. Nathanial skidded into the room and stopped. Clare looked at him, lowered her knife, wiped it on her jeans. She motioned Nat to come forward. Shoulders swaying, he did. He stopped right in front of her and stared into her eyes. She picked up a strand of his long hair, let it run through her fingers, wrapped a curl around and around, then cut off a lock just above his ear. She smiled at him, showing her white teeth. The boy glanced at Mr. Grafton, who had not yet wiped the blood from under his chin. Before the boy could turn back to her, Clare had the knife tip under his jaw then slid it from one side to the other, the blood following in a delicate line behind it. "Oops. I guess I slipped." She grabbed a large hunk of hair in a fist and yanked his head backwards, his Adam's apple sharp against his skin. They both stayed so still they could have been a sculpture until Clare shuddered, pushed the kid backward, returned her knife to her pocket, and whirled out the door. When he heard the truck start, Nat went to the window, memorized the license plate number. "She's just attempted murder," he said.

The girls played follow-the-leader around the house on their ponies. They rode bareback. Annie made herself comfortable on the woodpile where she nearly dozed while the children trotted figure eights, bouncing dustily until Clare arrived home. Annie stood up. Clare slammed the truck door, her eyes following the girls briefly. Annie walked over and glanced into the truck bed. No grain. No hay. Clare had not been to the feed store. There were no groceries in the cab. She had not gone food shopping.

A few heavy raindrops hit the truck.

"Let's put them ponies into the field," Clare said.

It didn't take long; they led the ponies through the gate to the pasture, slipped the bridles off, gave the animals a pat on the rump as they trotted off then headed toward the house. The girls skipped up the porch stairs. At the door, Colleen turned toward the pasture, waved her hand, and said, "Bye Butter."

Annie stopped.

"Don't say nothing," Clare said.

"What?"

"Don't make a big deal out of it,"

Inside the girls sat at the kitchen table. "Well," Clare said, hand on hip, "do you want PB and J or bologna sandwiches? I'm not cookin' tonight."

"Bologna," said Sloan. "No. PB and J. No, I mean bologna."

Clare waited a beat. Her cheeks flamed, and she looked distracted, barely focused on what was going on in the room.

"Me too," said Colleen.

"And for you? Annie, what will you have?"

"Clare?"

"What?" Her black brows came together.

"Ah, bologna is fine."

"One or two."

"Clare?"

Clare stared at Annie.

"One."

Clare put mayonnaise on ten pieces of bread. She lined them in two rows on the small counter. She took the bologna out of the refrigerator and put one slice on each of the five pieces, mustard on top of that, and covered them with the other five bread slices. "Stop fidgeting," she said to Annie.

"I'm not."

"Yes, you are. Here, eat your sandwich." She handed it to Annie. She put two sandwiches on paper towels and placed them in front of the girls, brought her two to the table.

Annie passed glasses of water all around. Clare ate her food absently, staring at nothing. The children ate in silence, absorbed by their supper. When she was done with her sandwich, Sloan asked for cookies.

"Me too," Colleen said. Clare went to the cupboard, took out a box of Oreos, and put them on the table. When the girls had finished, she told them to go upstairs and play. She listened to hear them close the bedroom door. "Don't make a big deal out of this."

"But it is a big deal."

"If you fuss about it, you could ruin it. I don't care what any therapist might say. I know when you're training a horse, if you make a big hoo-ha every time they do something right, you turn them into a nervous wreck."

"You don't think we should reward her at all?"

"Finally talking is reward enough. Believe me. If you fuss over her, you'll confuse her."

"We should at least call John."

"He'll be out here any minute."

"I wonder if we should call Dr. Wittcomb."

"We'll tell John. You don't need to call no one else." Clare stood, put her glass in the sink, and turned around and leaned back with her palms against the counter. "I almost killed someone today."

"Of course you did." Annie went to the refrigerator and retrieved two beers, handed one to Clare, then took a long deep swallow of hers. "Let's see now. Colleen says her first words today and you almost murder someone. Just another day in paradise."

"I'm serious."

"Okay."

"Two people, actually. That man and that boy. I went to their house and I cut them with my knife." She waved her hand in the air at the look on Annie's face. "It was only a scratch, but I wanted to cut that man's throat. I really did. And I had that boy's head pulled back and it would have been sooo easy to jab that knife right through his jugular. I could almost feel the blood running all over my hand, all warm and wet, the life running out of him." She shook her head. "God, you have no idea how much I wanted to do it."

"But you didn't."

"No." Clare shrugged. "Obviously."

"I'm glad," Annie said carefully.

Clare picked up the dish rag; put it down. "I'm done with the police. We ain't pressing charges. I'll kill those motherfuckers if they come near her again. And I'd enjoy it."

"Did you really cut them?"

"I told you I did."

Annie knew better than to go into the legalities of what Clare had done. The Graftons wouldn't dare contact the authorities anyway. And no one would listen to the boy.

Chapter Twenty-Three

"She said, 'bye Butter' and 'me too?'" John sat on the edge of the couch in the living room with Clare across from him in the rocking chair. She stared out the window at the dark. Annie was in the kitchen making blueberry pie.

"She really spoke? She said those words out loud?"

Clare turned to him. "Crystal clear."

From upstairs they heard, "I want a gun," then from Sloan, "You're an Indian. Indians don't have guns."

"I'm going upstairs to see her," John said.

"You go on up if you want, but if you get all over her about this, it could ruin it. I ain't no psychologist, but I think you should just let nature take its course."

"Dr. Wittcomb said it would happen this way. One day she would start talking just like she had been doing it for years. I'd given up, though. I mean, she's almost six."

Clare watched him.

"I can't believe it. Can't get my head around it. I can't even imagine what my mother will do. She'll go nuts. Talk about getting all over her. I have to tell her, of course." He rubbed his hands down his thighs, frowning. "I wonder if she'll even talk at home."

Clare leaned her head back, looked up at the ceiling. John studied her throat, the V of her flannel shirt where it was unbuttoned, her pale skin against the dark mass of hair curling on her shoulder. Colleen had chosen to talk here, at Clare's house, with Clare, to Clare. He wasn't surprised. Not a bit.

She lifted her head and straightened her back. "Listen. Why don't you let Colleen stay here tonight? Maybe for a while. Those girls are good for each other."

John rolled his head, touched his cheek to his shoulder for a brief moment and said without looking at Clare, "I'd have to stay too. I wouldn't want her waking up in a strange bed and me not be here."

"Sure. You can sleep on the couch. And tomorrow we'll go get that puppy. They'd love that."

With a practiced hand, John pulled the covers under Colleen's chin and Clare, fussing with the sheets, tucked them around her daughter. "Are you sure you'll be all right? Annie can sleep here and you can sleep with me," she said to Sloan.

Sloan pushed her mother's hand away emphatically. "I want to sleep with Colleen, Mama." Annie stood awkwardly at the end of the bed.

Sometime in the early morning hours, Clare startled and sat straight up in bed. She hung there for a moment before bending over and covering her face in her hands. Annie could feel her trembling. She put her hand on a thin shoulder and pulled Clare back down. Clare rolled onto her side and Annie wrapped her arm around her waist and drew her close in an effort to stop the shaking. "Hush," she whispered against the damp, tangled hair. "It will be all right."

John settled his head into the pillow and pulled the quilt around him then, cramped, he stretched, putting his calves on the arm of the couch, his feet in the air, but it was too cold, so he pulled his knees back up under the blanket and curled into a ball. How had he ended up here trying to sleep on a couch in this battered old house with his sister upstairs spending the night and apparently preferring this place to anywhere else? She had spoken her very first words today, but he hadn't heard them. When they were eating blueberry pie, he asked how her day had been. She looked up blankly and Clare cut her eyes at him. What was he going to tell his mother? He was sure she would want her daughter brought home where she belonged. He could see her mounting frenzy. Her questions would silence the child as he had already done. He rolled onto his back and stared at the ceiling. He'd think of something. He fell asleep just before the light slid into the living room, casting bars across the floor, only to wake moments later as Clare slid under the blanket and encircled him with both arms and legs, her entire body pressed against him to lend him her warmth. "We'll have to find you another blanket," she said before getting up and going into the kitchen, where John followed her. She squatted in front of the woodstove, stacking a fire.

"I don't think I'll stay the night again."

Clare looked up at him.

"We'll see how Colleen is when she gets up."

Annie appeared in the kitchen doorway along with both girls. Colleen was rubbing the sleep out of her eyes and holding Sloan's hand. "What's for breakfast?" she said.

John closed his eyes, looked down at his sister, and let out his breath slowly. "Um. Well. How about eggs and bacon?"

Colleen didn't speak on the drive to her mother's. She said not a word as they went up the porch steps to the house, John holding her hand. "Are you glad to be home?" he dared to ask.

The girl looked up and smiled at him.

Don't rush, he reminded himself. She needs to do this at her own pace. When Dr. Wittcomb first diagnosed Colleen, she had said it was a matter of control. So, let her set the pace. Don't ask her to speak, don't act surprised when she does. Let her take her own precious time.

He ventured into the parlor, still holding Colleen's hand. "Mom?"

His mother looked up at him with her vague, sweet smile. "Yes, dear?"

John sat in one of the heavily cushioned chairs. The room smelled faintly of urine. "I just wanted to check on you. See how you're doing."

"I'm fine."

He pulled Colleen onto his lap. "I have something I want to tell you. But first you have to promise you will stay calm."

"All right." Mrs. Avery smiled again.

"Mom. Colleen spoke yesterday. She said her first words."

The smile faded from his mother's face. God, her son thought, she had been so beautiful once.

"She spoke?"

"Yes."

"What did she say?" Her voice was choked, as though the words had gathered there and were stuck.

"She said 'goodbye.'"

"Goodbye? Who did she say goodbye to? Where was she when she said goodbye? How do you know this, John?" Mrs. Avery's tone rose.

"She was at one of her little friend's houses. Playing after school. I was there to pick her up."

"Why are just telling me this now? If she talked yesterday."

"She wanted to spend the night, and I let her. I wanted her here with me when I told you. That's why I waited."

Mrs. Avery left the couch and knelt in front of her son and daughter. She took Colleen's hands. "Oh, my darling. I knew you could do it. Speak to me. Say 'hi' to your mama." She pulled the girl off John's lap and encircled her in her arms. "My sweet, sweet girl. Talk to your mama," she said into Colleen's hair.

"Mom...," said John.

"I want to hear your voice. I want to hear you say mama. My heavens. 'Goodbye.' What a terrible thing to say as your first word. I want to hear you say mama."

"Mom. Dr. Wittcomb has said we must not rush this. If we try to force her, she will just retreat again. Let her take her time. You have to calm down."

"Of course. I just want to hear her say mama. Just once. That's all. Just say mama, Colleen. Maamaa. It's not hard. It's real easy. It should have been your first word. It's so easy. Little babies say it." Mrs. Avery was still holding her daughter tightly.

"Mom, let her go. Stop trying to force her."

Mrs. Avery loosened her grip, and Colleen spun away and crawled back into her brother's lap.

"Go sit down on the couch, Mom. I want to talk to you about Colleen's treatment plan. There. That's better." John straightened his back. "Since she spoke to a child her age, we think it's best that she spend time with her. It will help her socialize and encourage her to keep talking."

"Who's we?"

"Dr. Wittcomb. It won't be for long. A week or two. And, of course, I'll bring her here to visit you every day. Or every other day. It won't be long at all before she is jabbering away at you."

Mrs. Avery asked why a few more times and John continued to lie, but it was surprisingly easy to convince his mother to do as she was told, and this made him sad. Not sad enough to tell the truth, but sad enough to wonder what had happened to this woman, how had she become so damaged. He had an image of a beautiful, vibrant, black-haired girl, and now here she sat, thin, pale, and ghost-like. He placed Colleen gently on her feet and sat next to his mother on the couch. He wrapped his arm around her shoulder and kissed her temple. "I love you, Mom. And Colleen loves you. Very much. It won't be long before things will be all right again." His mother nodded and smiled, and he kissed her again, this time on the forehead before leaving to take his sister back to Clare's.

Chapter Twenty-Four

Eventually the Graftons established a modicum of order in their household. With the child they called Joan gone, they separated the boys into the two bedrooms upstairs and put new sturdier locks on the doors and windows. It took Nathaniel three days to get out. He could have managed it sooner, but he didn't want to leave evidence. After everyone was in bed, he dropped from the window to the porch roof, eased himself onto one of the pillars, and slid to the ground. He picked the lock to the front door then the one to on the refrigerator, helped himself to bread, cheese, and milk, then tiptoed across the living room and listened at the Grafton's bedroom door. When he finished listening, he retraced his steps, relocked the front door, shimmied up the column to the porch roof, and let himself into the bedroom. He repeated this for a week. Occasionally while eavesdropping he heard the Graftons say Joan's name, but he could never make out the words surrounding it. He heard Mrs. Grafton's dull monotone drone and Mr. Grafton's spikes of anger or distress, but they were for the most part indecipherable, though once he heard Mrs. Grafton say very distinctly, "You've lost your mind." Another night Mr. Grafton said, "I have relatives in Ohio," to which Mrs. Grafton replied, "Dear God." None of this told him where Joan lived or where she went to school.

During the Graftons' many trips to town, he rifled through the desk where all the mail was kept, trying to find a clue as to the girl's whereabouts.

The dog breeder lived on the other side of Coleton in a single-wide with a tacked-on porch. Magic, the mother Husky, lived on the porch with her six puppies. There were many other dogs chained or caged in various shelters outside: overturned metal barrels, packing crates, lean-tos made of plywood. Five of the puppies had blue eyes, one had brown and there were three males and three females. Five came running when the breeder opened the door, and they jumped all over Sloan and Colleen, who squealed with delight. The sixth pup greeted everyone by putting her front paws on their knees then sat among her squirming siblings and looked steadily at the assembled group, occasionally wagging her small sickle tail. With their black masks, they all looked like small raccoons. The breeder stood behind Clare and the others, chattering about how most people wanted a Siberian Husky with blue eyes, but she herself preferred the brown eyes, finding them warmer in appearance. "Is the one with the brown eyes male or female?" Clare asked.

"Female."

Annie noticed that the pup's black almond eyes were very much like Clare's.

"We'll take that one," said Clare.

"Mom," Sloan protested.

"What? Don't you like her? Male dogs pee on everything, especially hay bales, and I like them brown eyes. And she seems quieter than the others."

Sloan knelt, patted the pup's head, and looked thoughtfully into the dark almond eyes. "Kind of like a bear's," she said.

The transactions were made and when everyone was settled in John's car, Clare plucked the puppy off Sloan's lap.

"You two will mangle her to death by the time we get home. You need to quiet down and give her a chance to adjust." She settled the pup on her lap where she sat up front next to John.

"What will we call her?" asked Sloan.

'How about Magic, like her mother?" Annie suggested.

"You can't use the same name twice," said Sloan. "It's bad luck."

Annie looked at the girl, looked away, and said carefully, "What about

Crystal? As in crystal ball."

"Too girlie girlie."

"Okay, what about Voodoo then?"

"Voodoo. That's weird."

"How about Black."

"Black," said Sloan. "That's dumb. She ain't even black, she's gray."

"How about Obeah," said Clare from the front.

"Obeah? What's Obeah?"

"It means magic."

"But I never heard that word before."

"It's French."

"What do you think, Colleen? Do you like the name Obeah?"

"O-be-ah," she said.

The girls burst into laughter and began saying the name every way possible; accents on the first, second, last syllables, going up the scale and down, deep and husky, in whispers and in high lilting songs.

John drove carefully, keeping his stinging eyes on the road. He took the turns with care, controlling his breathing. His sister's voice sounded like any five-yea- old's, as though she had been speaking since she was two. Clare was right. Colleen must stay on the farm with her and Sloan. His leg, as he accelerated, trembled. They drove into the dusk, the girls giggling, the adults silent. John felt Clare leave, gone to wherever it was she went and the longing grew in him, fiercer than ever, but there was something else too. Uncertainty.

Clare found an old chicken cage in the feed shed. She put a ragged horse blanket in it and took it up to the bedroom. She allowed the girls to play with Obeah outside for about ten minutes then carried the puppy upstairs and settled her into her crate. Annie, Sloan, Colleen, and John followed her. The girls hung over the crate. "Goodnight, sweet puppy," said Sloan and right after her Colleen said the same thing.

$\mathcal{D}$r. Wittcomb's office was lit by the evening light coming through the three windows. She kept the lights off as long as possible, finding the shadows soothing and easier on both herself and her clients. She watched the boys as the social worker went over the reasons they were here. Dr. Wittcomb had seen these types far too often. The bi-racial boy was beautiful enough to break many hearts and would always be trouble. Had Clare decided to take him to court, he might be locked up by now, but she had not, and he was loose in the world.

"There have been multiple thefts from numerous homes and breaking and enterings," Ms. Platt said.

"Are we sure these boys are the perpetrators?"

"The police found a BOSE stereo, reported stolen, in their bedroom. The amount of money stolen totals over twelve hundred dollars. That's a felony."

"How do we know it was one or all of these boys who stole the money?"

"Nathaniel was reported buying cigarettes, food, and even liquor. The liquor he bought was from a store thirty miles from his foster home. The owner reports he showed an ID indicating he was twenty-one. He was suspicious, but the ID looked legitimate, so he sold him the bourbon, but he did take down the license plate of the truck Nathanial was driving. It belongs to the Graftons."

"Has anyone pressed charges?"

"The boys deny everything. The Graftons say the radio belongs to them."

"And the money?"

"The Graftons say they pay the boys to work in the greenhouse."

Nat smiled.

"And the car, Ms. Platt, how do the Graftons explain the car?"

"They don't exactly. They said something about letting the boys use it for farm use."

Nat looked away, still smiling.

"And there is something else." Red splotches appeared on Miss Platt's cheeks. "The same vehicle was reported outside Sloan's school. She doesn't take the bus and leaves by the pick-up door, the one where parents come for their children. The teacher in charge of dispersing the children has been doing this for years and knows the cars, and she didn't recognize the white truck. She didn't think it was important until she noticed the same truck parked next to the playground a few days later."

Dr. Wittcomb reached into her drawer for a Mounds bar and paused when she realized the rudeness of eating it in front of the others. She dropped it back into the drawer and looked out the window. The grass was a bright green and daffodils, with their garish yellow heads, lined the walkway to the building. Perhaps the warm weather was here to stay. She thought about Chukchi and how she wouldn't like it, then she thought about the puppy Clare had bought for the girls. Those little girls. "May I speak to you alone, Ms. Platt?"

"These boys are considered a flight risk."

"I realize that. I will alert the secretary to keep an eye on them and if any or all of them leave, she will call the police." The red-headed boy made a noise of disgust and Nathanial laughed.

Dr. Wittcomb rose from her chair and waved her hand at the boys, motioning them to follow her. Nat rolled his eyes and smirked at the others. The waiting area was empty except for a man talking to himself and a woman sitting very straight, holding her purse in her lap.

"Sit there against the wall."

The boys sat in the wooden chairs and stared back at her. Dr. Wittcomb went to the patient sign-in window and said, "Keep your eyes on these boys, and if they move out of those chairs, page me and call 911. No. Call 911 first then page me."

The receptionist, a tiny young woman, looked at Dr. Wittcomb and moistened her lips. "911?" she said. She glanced at the boys and Nat blew her a kiss.

"Just call 911 and page me if they move out of those chairs. I will only be a minute or two."

Dr. Wittcomb flowed quickly down the hall and settled at her desk. "What are your plans, Ms. Platt? Nat Washington must not be allowed to run loose."

"No. Apparently all the boys are locked in their bedroom at night. This isn't allowed, of course, but in this case perhaps it is a good thing."

"Ms. Platt, these boys have been driving around the county robbing homes, buying liquor, and Nat has been stalking Sloan Raffienne. I think, somehow, they have figured their way around locks and the trivial matter of keys. Now I realize the hands of justice move slowly, but that boy must not be allowed to be free. I want to know what your department plans to do about this."

"Believe me, my supervisor agrees with you. The four other boys are going to the Haven in two days. The Haven won't take Nat, so he will be at the Grafton's until we can place him in a residential facility. We've put out feelers all over the country. Including Lexon, Alabama."

"Lexon?"

"Yes."

Lexon, Alabama was the most expensive facility in the country. The institution could eat up a county's or even a state's entire yearly budget for child placement in a matter of months. Technically it was a residential treatment facility, but the professionals who knew of it did not think of it in this way. Visitation was not encouraged, and when a social services or juvenile justice worker did venture to its secluded location, they saw only a very small part of the cinder-block compound. The employees they met were cordial and the few children they saw were clean, healthy, and well behaved. No one was allowed past the visitor's center. The average length of residency was two years and eight months. The recidivism rate was extremely low, due to the fact that most of the children aged out. For children with special needs this happened at age twenty-one.

Dr. Wittcomb looked at Ms. Platt anew. "Has this been approved by the inter-agency coalition?"

"Yes. We called an emergency meeting."

"And the paperwork has been sent?" Lexon, Alabama never turned away a referral. There wasn't a delinquent in the United States they couldn't handle. How they managed this no one seemed interested in finding out, but if the referral was made, it was a done deal. Dr. Wittcomb couldn't remember the last time the coalition had agreed to spend the kind of money it took to send a child there.

The blotches on Ms. Platt's face were fading. "Yes. Lexon hopes to have an available bed in two to three weeks."

"In the meantime, the boy supposedly stays locked in his bedroom?"

"We can only hope."

Dr. Wittcomb nearly smiled. "And I would hope the entire helping profession could do more than that. Still. You have certainly done your part and I thank you, Ms. Platt."

Lexon, Alabama. Who would have thought? "If you ever want to change jobs, let me know," Dr. Wittcomb said, handing the other woman a Mounds bar.

Every day from 10:15 to 11:00, Clare and John, or Clare and Annie, parked along the street where they had a clear view of the playground during Sloan's recess. Dr. Wittcomb was often there as well. Sloan was now her client. Clare had signed the requisite paperwork, an assessment and treatment plan had been worked up, a case number assigned, and an official record created except Sloan never came to the office. Instead, Dr. Wittcomb made school visits where she glided along the halls, sat in the back of Sloan's classroom, slipped out the back door to wander in the woods, making sure no one lurked there. Often, she merely sat on a bench near the playground and observed. Even though Clare had been explicit that Dr. Wittcomb's role was only to watch over and protect, the clinician couldn't help but notice that Sloan was rarely part of any group, that she hung, instead, on the periphery. It was hard to tell if this was due to her choice or exclusion. Either way it worried the woman as much as the fact that Clare sat poised in a vehicle with a knife in her pocket.

Fortunately, it was two weeks rather than three when a bed opened up for Nat Washington. Annie felt as though a war had ended. First was the burst of relief then the return of nerves and vigilance. You told yourself that things were okay now, that it was over, you could get on with your life and be normal, but the body didn't believe you. Shell shock, she thought. Battle fatigue. Or the now official diagnosis. Post-Traumatic Stress Disorder. Well, it had been traumatic all right. Annie couldn't think about the time Sloan was in foster care because of the images that formed, images so horrible they made her feel sick even before they were fully formed. How, she wondered, did Clare stand it. If Annie had been the one with the knife against that man and that boy's throats, she was pretty sure she would have used it for more than a scratch. When she told Clare this, her friend waved her hand in the air. "Don't talk about it. But listen," she said. "There ain't no point in you keepin' an apartment in town. You're here more than there. You should move into the feed room now that it's empty." When Annie demurred, Clare said, "It would be a comfort to me." And that, of course, was that.

They took a weekend and moved the metal frame, box springs and mattress, a substantial high boy Annie's father had given her for college, and a battered cedar chest her mother no longer wanted, into her new bedroom. Annie pushed the bed against a wall that she would use as a headboard. The chest she put at the foot of the bed and the high boy on the opposite wall. There was no closet, so she left most of her clothes in boxes lined up on the floor. It was a big room and when Annie settled in for the night, she felt its sparseness. The tree frogs filled the air with their lusty cries, but around their noise was silence. She would not hear her neighbor's toilet flush. She stretched out her feet to the corners of the bed, shivered as her muscles let go and rolled over. A figure stood in the doorway.

"Clare?"

"I tried to snuggle in with the girls, but the little fiends kicked me out. Literally."

Annie pushed the covers back from the side of the bed. "Come lie here then. Are you cold?"

Clare stretched out on her back. "No, I ain't cold. It's just I wake up scared sometimes."

"I know, so do I." Neither spoke for a few moments then Annie said, "Would it help if John spent the night?"

"The girls can't deal with that now."

"He could leave early before they wake up."

"Suppose one of them gets up at night and comes in my room for something. No. It wouldn't work."

"Are you in love with him, Clare?"

"Yeah, I guess so. I know I never felt this way before. Christ, can you believe it? A damn social worker."

"He's not a social worker. He's a therapist."

"Same difference. I just can't believe that, after all this time, at my age, I meet someone that doesn't bore me after three weeks."

"Do you think it could be because he helped you get Sloan back?"

Clare snorted. "He didn't help much. It was you and Dr. Wittcomb." Clare pulled her knees up, settled the blanket around them. "What about you Annie? You think you'll ever have another man in your life?"

"I've gone out to dinner with Marshall a few times."

"Marshall Teige. Well, well, well. The perfect match. Do you love him?"

Annie laughed. "No. But I like him. He's bright, funny, good company. And he doesn't rush things."

"Nothin' like your ex though?"

"I'll never feel that way again. No. That can happen only once. Thank God."

"I used to envy you. Your loyalty."

"A lot of good it did me." Annie propped herself up on an elbow. "You're not saying you feel that way about John, are you?"

"Maybe. I just know I'm edgy until he gets here in the morning."

Annie shook her head and settled back into the bed. "If I believed in God, I'd say he had a very dark sense of humor. John's lucky he kept his job. I guess the danger is over now. No one can prove anything. But imagine, Clare Raffienne falling for a suit."

"He wears a sports coat, not a suit."

"You know what I mean. You just never know, do you. You have no control over whom you fall in love with."

"Who said that?"

"I did. Just now."

Clare laughed. Then she rolled so she could look at Annie. "I worry about Sloan, though. How can she ever have a man in her life after what happened?"

"She'll be fine. She's only eight."

"So. People don't forget. Even kids."

"She'll be fine because of how much you love her, and you'll take care of her."

Clare said nothing, and Annie listened to the frogs and to her friend's breathing knowing she was still awake, but she couldn't help herself. The sounds faded, and her own breathing changed, became deeper, and she slid into sleep. When she woke the next morning, Clare was stoking the fire and a pot of oatmeal bubbled on the stove.

If the girls were there, Clare never left the mountain. No one did recess detail anymore, but Annie and Clare continued driving Colleen and Sloan to and from school. After school the girls played with the puppy, teaching her to fetch and to sit and lie down, though she proved to be remarkably stubborn and only listened when she had a mind to, keeping the girls trying over and over to succeed. When the girls weren't playing with Obeah, they rode their ponies in the pasture or around the house. Clare wouldn't let them leave the property without her.

For the first time in her life, Clare didn't ride the training colts every day.

She fed and cleaned up after them as always, but when she was finished, she spent a great deal of time in the kitchen cooking. Roast chicken, of course, spaghetti and meat sauce, meatloaf, potato and cheese casserole, pies, cakes, rolls and biscuits. Clare hated going to the schools to pick up the girls, much preferred it when Annie brought them home. She timed it so that the minute they burst through the door she would have a pie just cool enough to eat or a cake or cookies waiting on the table. Dinners became bigger and bigger with fruit salad, potatoes laden with butter and or sour cream, green bean casserole, rolls, slaw, pickles, applesauce and always dessert accompanied by ice cream. As the days became longer, the five of them would ride into the woods in the evenings, Annie, Clare, and John, keeping the girls between them. Annie knew this wasn't necessary, but even she felt better for it.

John's clients didn't like being scheduled before noon, so he went to Clare's in the mornings then left for work in the afternoons and returned around six. He always stayed to tuck his sister into bed and sometimes until after the girls were asleep. He would sit on the couch with Clare curled against him, his arm around her shoulders. Annie tucked herself on the other side, knees drawn, her head on the arm rest. There was no cable this far up and Clare, refusing to pay for satellite, had put a tall, handmade pterodactyl of an antennae on the roof that barely produced a picture. Still, the three of them watched the furry images and dozed. Annie was always the first to fall asleep, and Clare would tap her lightly with her foot so she could go across the hall to bed where she could be more comfortable.

Chapter Twenty-Six

More and more, Clare rode one of the training colts to Unc's cabin. He would look up from what he was doing: baiting a hook, cleaning his gun, fixing a meal, or just leaning against his cabin, resting in the sun, then he would look away and continue his activity, though his face softened enough to let her know she was welcome. She would halter the horse to a tree, undo the saddlebags filled with food she had brought him, and take them to her uncle, who opened them with slow delight. He ate a few bites of what was there before offering her a cup of coffee. She watched his large, square hands as he did these things. He had shaved off his beard and smelled of wood smoke, pine, the mountains and sweat. He always offered to share what she brought and sometimes he had fish, squirrels, or rabbit on the fire, and they shared this as well.

If he wasn't in the cabin, Clare went to the spot in the creek where the fish were still biting.

Today she found him fly fishing. She watched as he brought the rod back then straightened his arm, flicked his wrist, and sent the line arcing toward the water where it kissed the surface. He stood in the water to his thighs. He didn't get a bite, so he repeated the beautiful motion, flicking the lure onto a different part of the stream where the shadows lay dark and opaque.

After watching him for a while, Clare called out, "Hey! Where did you get that fine reel and rod? You didn't make those."

"Shhh, you'll scare the fish."

"Sorry."

Unc reeled in his line and secured the hook on the cork handle. "It's too late in the day anyway."

"Where did you get that set up?"

"I got friends." He waded out of the water and stood beside her, the cloth of his pants clinging to his thighs and calves, dripping water on his bare feet.

"Do you ever go into town?"

"No, but my friends do. I trade them fresh fish or meat for things I need."

Unc handed Clare his rod, sat on the ground and put on his shoes then they started walking toward the cabin. "How often do you come down to see your friends?" Clare asked, holding the rod carefully upright.

"Three, maybe four times a month."

"Really?"

"You sound surprised."

"I guess I am."

"Doesn't fit in with your wild man image?"

Clare laughed. "I guess not. Next thing you know, you'll tell me you got a girlfriend."

"I do."

"You gotta be kidding me."

"Maybe I should take offense at this line of questioning." Unc didn't look at Clare, but he smiled, the skin around his eyes crinkling.

"How long have you had this girlfriend?"

"A while."

"Like years?"

"Yeah."

Clare was silent for a time then asked, "Does she cook for you? Does she bring you food or do you both sit around the campfire eating fish?"

"Hey. What's this about? I'm not allowed to have a girlfriend?"

"Of course you are. I just thought you would have told me, that's all."

"Why would I tell you?"

"Oh, never mind. I mean, why haven't you moved in with her? I assume she has a house… of some sort. In the Holler."

"I like it better here."

"And she doesn't?"

"I guess not." They had reached Unc's cabin. He picked up the saddle bags and looked inside. "Ahh, fried chicken. You do do fried chicken good." He offered a drumstick to Clare, who took it and said, "Better than what's-her-name?"

"Let's not do this."

Clare sat down. "Why don't you come to my house for dinner sometime? The girls would love it."

"I might. How's your little girl doin'?"

"They put that son-of-a-bitch boy in prison. We don't talk about it. Any of it. He was caught hanging out by her school. I should have killed him. Anyway, he's locked up now. I don't think Sloan even knew he was there. The old man is still loose, I guess, but he's just an old man."

They sat in silence eating the chicken until Clare stood up and stretched. "I better go. The girls will be home from school, and I like to be there. You come and eat with us sometime."

"Okay. Thanks for the food. And Clare, you don't need to worry about your girl. She'll be fine with you lookin' out for her."

"I guess."

$$Chapter\ Twenty\ Seven$$

Spring settled in for good and the days felt as though they would be warm and sun-filled forever. Toward the middle of June, Unc caught four big Brownies, the last of the season. Their scales shone dark and rich, and they were fat from good feeding, ready to settle into the deep water away from the heat of the summer.

"They are magnificent," Clare said.

Unc nodded. "Let's eat them now." He whacked their heads against a rock and Clare watched the light leave their eyes. She picked them up and felt the weight pull on her arm. Unc took the fish from her, and they took them back to his cooking pit in front of the cabin. He stacked the dry wood under the grate, lit it, let it reach a blazing heat while he gutted the fish, leaving the heads and tails on. He waited until the fire had died to just the right temperature and placed only two on the grate, they were that big. Their skin crackled as soon as they hit the iron, the edges turned golden and then deep brown. Unc forked them and flipped them over. They ate these two, crunching on the crisped skin. The flesh was just the right firmness and tasted of the stream and the wood smoke from the fire. Delicately, they picked it from the bones. They ate while Unc cooked the last two, keeping his eye on them, careful to turn them at the right moment. The second batch was as good as the first and Clare wished she had brought cold beer to go with them. She would remember next time, though with the season being over it was doubtful Unc would find any more fish like these. Perhaps a rabbit or two. Clare didn't much like squirrel. But a well-cooked rabbit could be fine. She licked her fingers. Unc took the bones, heads, tails, and guts deep into the woods so the bears would not come too close to the cabin. The training colt grew restless, pulling at the rope and pawing the ground. The horse dropped his haunches and pulled hard, his neck outstretched, as he tried to break free. Clare patted his neck. She could leave now, Unc wouldn't mind, but she wanted to see him again to thank him for the fish. And so it was she did not ride into the clearing around her house until after Annie had brought Sloan and Colleen home.

The two girls were in the back seat so they could chatter and giggle together as they rode home from school. Colleen couldn't stay with them forever, Annie knew that, was surprised she had been here this long, but the situation certainly seemed to be working. She observed them in the rearview mirror. No one would guess they were different from any other children.

The first thing the girls did when they arrived at Clare's was run through the doorway and up the stairs to get Obeah out of her crate. Clare kept her there when she was busy with a colt and couldn't keep an eye on her. Huskies were famous for running off, though so far Obeah had found what was going on around the house interesting enough to stick around.

Not seeing her with the horses, Annie called for Clare. When she received no answer, she called again in the house. It was clear she wasn't there either. This was a good sign. It was a fine day and Annie felt the relief of things swinging back to normal. The girls let the puppy out to pee and came right back in for their after-school snack. Annie put pie and milk on the table and sat with them, Obeah on her lap. She was a well-behaved puppy in her own way. It had been a good idea to get her. She swept the crumbs from the table into her hand and the pup nibbled them politely from her fingertips. When the children were finished, they went outside with Obeah. After putting the dishes in the sink, Annie followed them looking toward the mountain, but did not see Clare. She might have stopped at Unc's. Annie suspected she did that more and more. It was a beautiful day. The redbud and white dogwood had bloomed and shone through delicate, pale green leaves. She scanned the yard and then the horse pasture. Butter was there nibbling at new shoots of grass, but Annie saw no sign of the girls or Obeah. She called their names and heard only birdsong and a horse stomping at a fly. She looked at the mountain again but did not see Clare. She walked around the house and saw Sloan throwing a stick for Obeah to chase. The pup ran after it and brought it back. When she threw it again, Obeah didn't even turn to look at it, continued instead gazing at the girl waiting for her to do something interesting.

"Fetch," said Sloan. The pup wagged its tail and stayed put.

Sloan clapped her hands and began to run around the yard. Obeah promptly ran after her, short puppy legs going as fast as they could. Colleen followed behind her. The three ran in figure eights, circles, and snakes. Annie sat on the stairs to the front porch, elbows on her knees, chin in her hands. The sun warmed her, lured her into serenity, gave her a feeling of sleepy optimism. Watching the coltish girl, she decided Sloan would be all right, different but okay. She was tough like her mother and would grow up willful, uncivilized maybe, but fine. The trio continued their dizzying game. Annie noticed the puppy beginning to pant. She was about to tell Sloan to stop and give Obeah some water when she heard the phone ring. "Stay in the yard," she yelled and ran inside. It was a man calling to ask if Clare would train his two-year-old stallion. Annie told him that she didn't think Clare took stallions, but he insisted that his was gentle as a lamb, wouldn't hurt a fly. They all said that. Annie said she would relay the message, but she didn't think Clare would do it. Still, the man continued, telling her he would put a newborn baby on the horse's back, he was that kind and smart, smarter than any horse he had known. Annie rolled her eyes. She wanted to be rude to the man, but it was Clare's business and who knew, she might decide to take on a stallion after all.

Outside, Obeah suddenly burst forward and charged across the driveway and into the woods at a dead run, digging in with her haunches, her back paws landing in front of the tracks made by her front feet and her sickle tail held high.

"Wait!" Colleen called.

Sloan sprang after her, darting in and out of the familiar trees until suddenly there was no sign of the dog. She ran back to the driveway. "Have you seen Obeah?"

Colleen shook her head.

"You sure she didn't run back here?"

"Maybe."

"Listen, I'll look for her in these woods and you look out here."

The girls split up and called, "Obeah, Obeeaaah." Colleen stayed near the driveway, but Sloan, taller, stronger, and used to navigating these woods, went in deeper and then deeper still. There was no sign of Obeah, but the puppy couldn't have gotten far. She was too little.

Chapter Twenty-Eight

*M*r. Grafton traded the white Dodge Ram for a blue Ford with a plywood makeshift cover over the bed, painted to match. He had bartered for it with a man from church. They didn't fill out any papers or even change the registration. It was a transaction among friends, no need to involve the government or pay unnecessary taxes. Mr. Grafton paid the other man $1,000 in addition to the Dodge to sweeten the deal. When he drove the blue truck home and his wife saw it, she went into the house and didn't speak to him for the rest of the night.

The next morning, he started piling what he considered the bare necessities into the covered bed. In order to have at least some of the items she cared about, Mrs. Grafton helped. When they had piled what they could of their belongings into the back, they headed west.

"This ain't the way to Ohio," said Mrs. Grafton.

"Yes, it is. I'm taking a shortcut."

"What kind of shortcut?"

"You hush. I'm the one who's driving." Mr. Grafton turned right onto the road that at its beginning looked so innocent. He drove purposely on as the ruts and rocks grew bigger. He continued past the Holler and shifted gears to handle the steep climb into the mountains.

"You're crazy." Mrs. Grafton stared straight ahead.

"I just want to see our little Joanie one more time."

"It's because of your little Joanie that we have to leave our home."

"She ain't got nothin' to do with it."

Mrs. Grafton turned her head and looked out the side window. "The hell she ain't."

They bounced along the rough road, the makeshift top groaning. Mr. Grafton down shifted again, and the truck crawled forward. When they came to Clare's driveway, he pulled in and then backed up and turned the vehicle around. "I'll just walk up to the house," he said.

"You mean sneak," his wife answered. He was about to tell her to shut up when a puppy with a raccoon's face came out from the woods, followed by a tiny version of Snow White. The old man slid out of the truck quick and vicious as a weasel despite his stiffening bones. Teetering, he took hold of the handle and called to the dog. She stood still, wagging her tail uncertainly. He bent over, hands on his knees, panting slightly. "Here puppy, puppy," he called, his voice high, lilting and obscene. The pup did not move. He took a quick step forward and snatched her up.

"Hey," Colleen said.

Grafton put the dog in the truck and slammed the door. "What a beautiful puppy," he said in the same coaxing voice. "Is she yours?"

Colleen put her fingers in her mouth and nodded, then took them out, wet with saliva and said, "Give her back."

"I will, I will, of course, I will. I just want to see her for a moment. Why don't you come here and tell me about her?"

Colleen shook her head, her eyes locked on the old man's.

"Now that's not very nice. What's her name?"

Colleen said nothing.

"Oh, come on, be a good girl and tell me about your puppy. She's so pretty. Almost as pretty as you."

Colleen began to back up.

"Hey," Grafton said, all trace of coaxing gone from his voice, "if you want your puppy back, you better come here and get her." He put a hand on the door handle again, the other swept toward the child, palm up, fingers open in invitation. Colleen stepped forward slowly.

"There's a good girl. Come get your beautiful dog." His arm remained in the air. Colleen stopped just out of reach, but then Obeah yelped, and the girl's eye shifted away from the man to the truck window. Grafton jumped into movement, shortening the distance between them, grabbed Colleen by the arm, pulled her off her feet and threw her in the truck. He snatched Obeah with the same sly speed and tossed her onto the road hard enough that she cried out and rose limping. Colleen's eyes grew wide with disbelief. She opened her mouth in an O but no sound came out. Then she made a fist and socked Grafton on the jaw as he tried to start the truck. He took one hand off the wheel, and with his fingers spread, covered Colleen's face, and shoved her backward into his wife's lap who, with movement born of memory, took hold of her and held on. Grafton shoved the truck in gear, stepped on the gas with such force that the vehicle jumped forward and stalled.

"Shit." Grafton forced himself to breathe deeply and keep from stomping on the gas petal. He turned the key, the truck started and, with the makeshift covering swaying and groaning, bounced down the rough road much faster than he had ascended. He did not see Sloan standing at the edge of the driveway, stock-still, watching the back of the truck disappear.

Colleen struggled, arms and legs thrashing.

"Give her those pills in the glove compartment," Grafton said.

His wife hesitated then shook her head. So, he had been planning this all along. He had planned to kidnap a child, maybe not this child, but a pretty little girl to keep as his own. It had gone this far. She thought of jumping out of the truck. She put her hand on the door handle.

"Don't you dare. You get them pills like I said. Do it. Do what I said *now.*"

Mrs. Grafton reached for the glove compartment, opened it, took out the bottle of pills.

"Here, give it to me. Hang on to the child. I'll get the lid." He drove one handed, put the pill bottle in his mouth and tried to twist it open. The top didn't move. He tried again with no luck. "Damn it." He put the bottle in his lap and struck Colleen in the face. "You be still. Here, Mother, you open it." Mrs. Grafton took the bottle from her husband and with practiced skill opened it, tears rolling down her cheeks. Colleen opened her mouth in that unearthly silent cry and Mrs. Grafton popped in a pill.

"Give her four more."

Colleen spit and choked.

"Do it."

Mrs. Grafton pinched the child's cheeks, preventing her from spitting, and shoved in four more.

"Now wash it down with that soda."

So, he had worked it all out. Every detail. She looked at the soda can then at her husband.

"Don't look at me. Get the can and wash them pills down." Grafton reached over and grabbed a hunk of his wife's hair and slammed her head against the window.

After she had poured Pepsi down Colleen's throat, held her mouth shut and worked the muscles under her throat, forcing the child to swallow, Mrs. Grafton stared straight ahead, her arms and legs wrapped around the girl.

"Stop crying, Mother. We are going to be fine."

But she knew nothing would be fine again. They were kidnapping a child. Mrs. Grafton again considered jumping out of the truck, but they were bouncing over the rocks and ruts, her head hitting the roof and the top sounding like it might come off and then they were going even faster past the Holler where strange people lived then out onto the real road. Grafton tore down it and his wife gave up. She knew.

After she hung up the phone, Annie walked out the front door, shut it behind her, turned around and stopped. Damn. She had told those girls to stay in the yard. She moved around the side of the house, expecting to find them and Obeah in the pasture even though they had been strictly forbidden to take the puppy in there with the horses for fear she might be kicked or stepped on. There was no one there. Annie turned around intending to walk down the driveway when Sloan came running around the corner breathing hard, holding the puppy in her arms.

"They'—ve take—en Colleen." She put Obeah on the ground, bent over panting, trying to catch her breath.

"What did you say?" Annie felt herself go empty, her insides plummeting headfirst.

"The Graftons. They just took Colleen."

"That's impossible."

"I ain't lyin', it's true!"

Annie walked around the corner and looked down the road. "There is no one there."

"I said they done took her away."

"How?"

"In a big blue truck with a blue top on it."

"That's not what they drive. They drive a plain old white pick-up."

"Not now. It's a big blue truck with a cover."

"But that would be kidnapping." Annie found it hard to breathe. "I, um, I told you to stay in the yard."

"Obeah disappeared and we was looking for her."

"You went all the way to the road."

"Colleen got there first, I seen her in the truck fightin' with him."

"How could you possibly see that?"

"I got there just in time." Sloan was still panting. Annie grabbed her by the shoulders and shook her. "Now you listen here, this is *not* funny."

Sloan yanked free. "I want my mother."

Annie dropped to her knees, said in a soothing voice, "I'm sorry, Sloan. I'm just frightened."

"I want my mother," the girl said again.

The horses began to whinny in the pasture. Sloan darted around Annie as her mother rode into the clearing. She ran to her and when Clare reined in the horse, Sloan rested her hand on its shoulder and looked up at her. "The Grafton's done took Colleen," she said.

Clare did not move. Annie started to approach her then stopped.

"When," Clare said in a voice so calm she could have been asking when they had fed the puppy, or the horses last.

"Just a while ago."

"You think we could catch up to them?"

"They was goin' fast."

Clare dismounted, held the reins out to Annie without looking at her. She got down on her knees and took Sloan's hands in hers and looked up into her face. "Tell me exactly what happened."

"Obeah ran into the woods and wouldn't come when we called. So I took one side and Colleen took the other and we went looking for her."

"You separated then. Could you see Colleen?"

"No… I was in the woods and she wasn't."

"Then what happened."

"I looked and I called, but I couldn't find Obeah."

"Did you hear Colleen?"

"No." Sloan hesitated. "She was too far away."

"How far did you go?"

"Colleen must have gone down to the road."

"And you?"

"I was still in the woods and then I heard Obeah cry."

Clare waited.

"I run toward the sound as fast as I could, duckin trees and through brush and there was Obeah and the big blue truck." Sloan took her hands from her mother's and picked up the puppy, who had raced up to her.

"Now tell me about the truck."

"It had a top on it that looked funny—like it didn't belong there."

"And inside, what was going on inside?"

"Mr. and Mrs Grafton was fighting with Colleen. Mr. Grafton put his hand on her face and shoved her into Mrs. Grafton's lap. Mrs. Grafton held on to her, but Colleen was still fighting so Mr. Grafton hit her."

Annie closed her eyes.

"Then what?"

"They drove away."

They heard a vehicle coming up the driveway and Clare looked up, hope lighting her face until John's vehicle turned the bend. He stepped out of the car smiling, his arms lifted wide. "What a fine, fine day!" he called.

For the life of her Annie couldn't speak, stood motionless holding the training colt's reins. Sloan turned to John and said bluntly, "The Grafton's done stole your sister."

John looked from Clare to Annie and back to Sloan. "What?" he said.

"The Grafton's done kidnapped your sister."

John looked at Clare, who nodded.

He stared at her.

"Did you see a blue truck with a blue cap pass you by?"

"No." John regarded Sloan, thinking it was possible the child was playing a nasty joke on them. "Are you sure you actually saw this? This is preposterous. It's kidnapping; it's a felony." He turned to Clare. "She must be mistaken. This isn't the wild west or Romania. Gypsies stealing children, for God's sake. Colleen's got to be around here somewhere."

Clare rose slowly to her feet, nodded, took Sloan's hand, and turned toward the house.

"Right," said John. "You look through the house. I'll check outside."

"Annie, would you untack the horse and come inside, please?" Clare's voice was low, gentle, matter of fact, and Annie, doing as she was told, walked in a trance of fear.

Inside, Clare sank into one of the kitchen chairs. She drew Sloan, who was holding Obeah, onto her lap and the three sat and waited and watched the door for Annie. Sloan leaned the back of her head against her mother. It only took a minute for Annie to untack the horse since she merely threw the saddle and bridle on the ground, opened the gate, and let the horse loose. When she came into the kitchen, Clare said, "Call 911. You know what to say and they will listen to you." She ran her hand over her face and leaned heavily against the back of the chair.

A squad car arrived. The two detectives who had been there previously stepped out. They walked up the back steps, the heavily muscled Detective Guire in front. He turned to James and pointed to a soft spot on the wooden stairs. "Watch your step," he said. She ignored him and they came into the kitchen and stood stiffly. Sloan and Obeah nestled closer to Clare.

"Mrs. Raffienne," said Guire, nodding slightly. He retrieved a notebook from his shirt pocket. "Can you tell me what happened?" he said to no one in particular.

"The Grafton's done took my friend."

"You mean your foster parents."

Detective James looked at Guire and then looked away.

"May I?" he said, indicating a chair. He didn't wait for an answer, pulled out two chairs, one for himself and one for James.

"Hi, Sloan," he said. "Do you remember me?"

Sloan leaned closer against her mother and nodded.

John burst through the door.

"Cops," he said. His pants were torn at the knee and covered with bristles and thorns. His hands bled from several small scratches, and he had bits and pieces of things in his hair. Guire looked at him briefly and then away. "Sloan?" he said. "Can you tell me what happened?

The girl repeated what she had told her mother.

"That is consistent with what she said earlier," said Annie. "Look, have you put out an Amber alert?"

"Excuse me," said John, coming around the table to face the troopers. "I'm Colleen's brother."

Guire nodded. "What can you tell us?"

"She's not anywhere around here. Oh, God."

"Take it easy, sir. We are on this. We will find her."

Clare frowned. If they believed Sloan, they wouldn't be so sure.

Annie pulled a chair close to Guire. "Have you put out an Amber alert? Notified the FBI?"

"There is a protocol to follow. Most likely she is lost in the woods. We have a dog on the way."

"Just how long do you plan to wait before you put out an alert?"

The detective looked into Annie's eyes for a beat. "Let me get some more information so we know what to look for. Sir… can you describe your sister?"

"She has black hair, blue eyes…." He stopped, shook his head. "I mean, she is beautiful. Everyone says so…." his voice trailed off. The detectives took notes.

"How old is she?"

"Six."

"How tall is she, would you say?"

John held his hand around his hip.

"Any distinguishing marks?"

"Um, she has very white skin, delicate, like I said… beautiful."

Guire kept his eyes on John. "Is there anything else you can tell us about your sister?"

"Um, well… she doesn't talk very much."

The detective made some notes on his pad.

"Look." Annie leaned in closer to him. "I asked you a question. Just how long do you plan to wait before calling the FBI?"

"We are following protocol ma'am."

"I know all about protocol, damn it. I'm a lawyer." In fact, Annie wasn't sure she remembered exactly what the proper procedure was. Not having thought she would be dealing with a kidnapping here in sleepy Coleton, the details of such a thing had slid to the back of her mind. Now, she was feeling like she might go mad if someone didn't do something soon.

John straightened. "I'm not from around here, you know. I live in Coleton. With my sister. I have a master's degree in psychology, and I work at the mental health clinic. We are not from around here… these woods, I mean." He waved his hand in the general direction of the door. He looked around the kitchen. "We don't live in this house."

"I'm not sure what point you are trying to make," said Guire.

"We treat all cases the same. According to protocol." Detective James's voice was weary. She looked at Sloan. "Sweetie. Is there anything else you can remember?"

"You mean like the license plate number?"

Everyone looked at her. "You have the license number," Guire said, carefully.

"XYX6546."

He wrote the number down. "Can you repeat that for me?" he said.

"XYX6546."

"You are absolutely sure that is the number?"

"Yup, I got a good memory."

"Excuse me." James rose and walked briskly out the door. No one remaining in the kitchen spoke. There was no clock to tick, but Annie could feel time pass, the slow drag of seconds moving into the future. She looked at Clare and saw that she had gone to a place she had never seen her go before. Ever. She felt sick again and swallowed several times, which stopped her stomach heaving, but nothing could stop the sickening spread of knowing and the fear that came with it.

Detective James returned. "That number isn't registered to the Graftons. It belongs to a Mr. Crenshaw," she said. "I called him, but there was no answer."

Guire raised an eyebrow then turned back to Sloan. "What makes you so sure it was the Graftons in that blue truck?"

"Cause I seen them. I know it was them."

Chapter Twenty-Nine

*A*nnie drove carefully, exaggerating all the required movements: slowing down for stop signs, turning on her directional, braking or picking up speed as expected. Unable to sit and wait any longer while the cops decided what to do, she'd whispered to Clare she would be back and slipped out of the house. She would go to the Graftons' house herself. If they were there, then obviously Sloan had been mistaken and Colleen was lost in the woods somewhere. If they weren't… well, she would see what she could see.

Why had she answered that damn phone, anyway? It was just some man asking about bringing his stallion to Clare to train. The last thing they needed was some stallion breaking through fences to get to the mares. Men and their stupid macho needs. Stop that, she told herself. This is your fault. If you had been outside with the girls, this never would have happened.

She thought of Clare sitting so still at the kitchen table with no toughness left in her. Christ. She wanted to speed through town; she wanted to max out the SUV, drive up Grafton's driveway and straight through their house, never slowing down, boards and glass flying everywhere then she would turn around and go back, hitting anything she might have missed. Her hands itched with the desire to destroy, so she paid attention to the speedometer, never going over the speed limit, obeying all the rules until she saw the sign that said, "Grafton's Greenhouse." She pulled into the driveway without slowing down and sped past the torn, gray sheets of plastic flapping from the wooden frame and came to an abrupt stop in front of the porch.

The house clearly had been abandoned. The front door hung open, and various items were on the porch, including a table and four straight chairs and a couch. The chairs were on their sides as though thrown there.

Annie was stepping off the running board when she saw it. A piece of white paper lying in the gravel. She hadn't even had to go in the house. It was wrinkled, but when she spread it carefully on the hood of the truck it was easy to read. A gift if not from God, then from a universe that gives as well as takes and sometimes, against all odds, drops a blessing upon us.

She carefully folded the scrap of paper and put it in her pocket, jumped into the driver's seat, and opened her purse. No cell phone. Shouting in frustration, she dumped the contents on the seat. No phone? Oh shit, oh Christ! How had she managed to leave it behind? Annie saw it in her mind's eye then exactly where she had left it. On the kitchen counter ready to be charged. She threw her purse on the floor, started the truck, and drove until she saw a phone booth at the edge of a gas station. The cement around it was buckled and cracked from freezing and thawing and the windows of the building were boarded over. A CLOSED sign hung from the door. Annie swerved and braked next to the phone booth, jumped from the SUV, picked up the phone, and put in a quarter even though she expected it to be dead. Instead, she heard a dial tone. She watched herself as though from a distance. She saw her fingers move as she punched the numbers from the white sheet of paper into the phone. An operator came on the line and said she needed to put in four more quarters. Annie dug in her front pocket and pulled out three. She tried the other front pocket, but it was empty. The woman on the other end of the phone line repeated, "You will need four more quarters, please."

"I know it," Annie snapped. She tried her back pockets.

"Got it," she said. and put the four quarters in the slot. The phone rang and rang and then a woman's voice said, "Clarysville Inn."

Annie cleared her throat and stared out the dirty windows of the phone booth. "Where are you located?"

She listened to a reply, quickly thanked the voice on the other end, hung up, returned to the SUV, and looked through the contents of her purse and under the seats. There was a pile of coins pooled on the floor in the back. Annie returned to the phone booth and dialed. Clare answered immediately.

"Tell the cops I know where the Graftons are headed."

"Where are you?"

"In a phone booth. The Grafton's are heading toward a motel in Ohio. It's called the Clarysville Inn."

"How do you know this?"

"I've been to the Graftons. I found a piece of paper. And they are definitely gone. Packed up and hit the road."

"Come back here as fast as you can."

"I will but tell the cops what I said. Can you make them believe it?"

"I don't know. Maybe you should talk to them."

Clare handed the phone to detective Guire.

"Ms. Voight," Guire said after listening to her. "We don't know this is a kidnapping. The license to the vehicle does not belong to Mr. Grafton. Which makes it unlikely that they are involved in this. The little girl is probably lost in the woods. And you had no business going out there. Yes, we will call the number you just gave me, but you must let us do our jobs and stay out of it. And I suggest you get back here immediately."

Clare needed to keep herself together. She went to the sink and splashed her face with cold water.

"What's going on?" John asked as soon as the detective hung up.

"Apparently Ms. Voight went on her own to the Graftons and found an address on a piece of paper to some motel in Ohio."

"Well, call the Ohio police. Call the fucking FBI." John's face had red splotches on his white skin.

"I'm going to, but all of you need to let me do my job." Guire went outside and detective James remained sitting at the kitchen table.

"Clare, what else did she say?" John was breathing hard.

"Nothing really."

"Let me have that paper with the number."

"Guire has it."

"Right. Do you remember the number?"

"I'm sorry, no."

Guire came into the kitchen. "The number is to the Clarysville Inn in Ohio. They wouldn't reveal if the Graftons were registered or not. Privacy issues."

"Jesus fucking Christ." This from John.

"We sent an officer to the address where the man owning the truck with the license plate number Sloan gave us lives. We called the Ohio State Police and called for back-up and have an APB out. The Ohio police are getting a warrant for the motel. In the meantime, we will wait for the dog and continue the search here. We'll get the radio station to ask for volunteers."

It felt as though the tension had sucked the air out of the room by the time Annie walked into the kitchen and looked around, a hand in her front pocket.

Guire watched her. "You had no business going out there. You could be charged with interfering with an investigation."

Annie started to speak but John interrupted her. "You got the number?"

Annie leaned against a wall, pulled out a slip of paper from her jeans, and gave it to him.

Guire shifted his gaze to the young man. "I wouldn't go there if I were you. You need to let us do our jobs. Your place is here waiting for us to find your sister."

John said nothing and turned toward the door.

"You got GPS, right?" Annie asked.

He nodded without turning around.

"Will you call us once you get there?"

"Sure." The door banged behind him. No one spoke as they listened to the car start and drive away. Guire shook his head then turned to Clare. "In these kinds of cases, it really is best to stay put. The child has generally just wandered off. And the dog will be here any minute. We are taking every precaution possible, as I said. And I don't want you leaving here tonight. Do you want a detective to stay with you and your daughter?"

A car door slammed, and Obeah sat up straight, her ears straining forward.

Guire looked out the window. "It's the dog." He nodded to Detective James. The two of them were suddenly gone, and Annie and Clare and Sloan were alone in the kitchen.

"What next?" asked Clare.

"We wait. Can I get you anything? Coffee, bourbon, something to eat?"

"No."

Eventually, Sloan fell asleep on the couch, breathing easily, lips slightly parted. Clare carefully gathered her daughter into her arms and carried her up the stairs, the puppy trotting behind her. She settled the girl on her bed, gently pulled off the child's jeans then covered her with a blanket and lay beside her. Obeah jumped up and lay on the other side, curling against Sloan. It was fully dark. Beams of lights crisscrossed the woods. It didn't matter how many people roamed among those trees tonight. They wouldn't find Colleen. After a while, Annie appeared in the doorway, holding the bourbon bottle in one hand and two glasses pinched between her fingers and thumb in another. She lifted the booze and smiled sheepishly. "I don't know about you but I could use some."

Clare sat up and patted the bed. Annie settled next to her, handed her a glass, and put the other one between her knees. She filled the glasses half full, making as little noise as possible. Clare wrapped her arms around her knees. "Where do all these people come from?"

"Town most likely."

"Townies." If she had moved to town, none of this would have happened. A whippoorwill cried, the first of the season.

"I wonder how many people are out there looking," said Annie.

Clare hesitated. "I ain't got the will to count."

"No. They are kind of pretty though, the lights. Shining through the trees."

"Do you think they'll get to that hotel in time?"

"Yes. Certainly. For sure."

"You don't know for sure."

"No."

The pup opened an eye, looked at them, and scooted to the foot of the bed and went back to sleep. The women sipped the whiskey and watched the lights, their knees pulled up to their chests. Occasionally a voice was raised, the words indistinct.

Annie said, "This is all my fault. If I just hadn't answered that damn phone."

Clare said, "Actually, if you want to talk that way, you have to lay the blame on me."

"How do you mean?"

"It all started with that bear."

Annie said nothing. There was no clock or watch in the room. They did not mark the time. When their glasses were empty, Annie filled them again. They sat staring out the window. Clare took a strand of Sloan's hair, twined it around her fingers. "John must be going out of his mind."

"Yes."

"Annie?"

"Yes?"

Outside a dog barked, a deep resounding bay. The two women looked at each other and said, "The dog," and burst out laughing, a willful laugh that took hold of them and would not let go, shook them, made them gasp and snort and caused tears to run down their cheeks. They laughed until their bellies hurt. They might have laughed until their breath was gone from them but Sloan, in her sleep, moaned, rolled onto her back, and flung her arm into her mother's lap. Annie and Clare sniffled, sighed, and turned still.

The laughter had shaken their minds open, made them porous, vulnerable, had created a space for images to enter. They tried to focus on the swaying lights, but thoughts, pictures kept sliding in and though they shoved them away they returned; sometimes vague but more often clear and terrible. As time passed, dread stiffened their limbs, turned them into brittle frozen objects caught in a spell. At one point, Annie managed to take Clare's hand, but Clare was still Clare and she pulled it away.

Chapter Thirty

When the Ohio State Police broke open the door to room twenty-four of the Clarysville Inn, Mr. Grafton was sitting on the bed holding Colleen, whose head lolled loosely against his arm. Mrs. Grafton was lying on the other bed curled in a fetal position, her face turned to the wall.

"Put your hands in the air," said the first trooper. He leveled his service revolver at Mr. Grafton, who threw his arms straight up toward the ceiling. Colleen rolled off his lap onto the floor. The second officer picked her up and she slumped, boneless, against him. He settled her gently on the bed. Even so, she lay as though flung there.

"We found her in the woods. In the mountains." His eyes blinked madly as he stared at the dark hole in the barrel of the gun. "Her mother had abandoned her. Just thrown her out of the car. She told us this. The girl I mean. She was a mess." His eyes slid toward Colleen. "Crying, sick, filthy." Then back to the trooper holding the gun on him. "We cleaned her up and then she fell asleep. Hadn't slept in days. She told us this." Mr. Grafton's cheeks quivered as he talked.

The trooper yanked the old man off the bed, onto his feet, cuffed him and read him his rights. Even so, Grafton kept talking as fast as he could. "We were going to bring her to you as soon as she was rested. The poor thing is just done in. God knows what that woman did to her. She was half starved and lost in the woods." The trooper reached behind the old man and tightened the cuffs.

"Ow, that hurts."

"Trust me. You don't even know the meaning of hurt." The trooper pushed Grafton hard, and he fell onto one knee. Jerking him to his feet, he continued, "Where you're going, you'll learn the meaning of hurt, all right."

"All we did was rescue an abandoned child. You got no right."

The cop pushed Grafton toward the door. "Shut up. Just shut up."

While this was going on, the second trooper checked Colleen's pulse, lifted an eyelid, and shone a small flashlight into her eye. The pupil was dilated. He spoke into the transmitter hooked onto his shoulder. "I need a bus immediately." He stared down at the child. He had never seen anyone so beautiful.

"You got no right!" Mr. Grafton's voice was shrill. His wife curled tighter into a ball. Two more troopers entered the room and the first one shoved Grafton roughly at them. "Put him in the cruiser and you, ma'am, get up with your hands above your head." Mrs. Grafton uncoiled and, faster than the cop would have thought possible, did exactly as she was told.

While the troopers were busy booking the Graftons and a medical staff was assessing Colleen's condition, John Avery drove madly toward Ohio. On the way, he called the police, but all they would tell him was that the Grafton's were apprehended, and his sister had been taken to the Sisters of Mercy hospital. It was late at night when he arrived at the hospital and there were plenty of parking spaces. John swerved into the one closest to the front doors, taking the turn sharply enough that he felt the weight of the car shift onto the two left wheels. Inside there was a huge cross overhead with Jesus hanging from it and the ancient part of John's brain noted the image that sent a wordless flush of guilt through his conscience. He hadn't been to church in years and thought he had put all that behind him. He stood in front of the nurse's station and stared at the middle-aged woman seated at the desk. He reached into his pocket for his wallet and handed her his driver's license. He opened his mouth but could not get the words out.

The nurse glanced at the picture and handed it back to John. "Take a deep breath," she said.

John breathed deeply through his nose. "I am, uh um…"

"Take a breath and let it out to the count of six."

John did this and then told the nurse in a burst of words that he was Colleen Avery's brother and he wanted to see her.

"She's resting comfortably."

"Is she in ICU?"

The nurse looked momentarily baffled. "Why no. Where did you get that idea?"

"No one has told me a thing," John nearly shouted.

"You need to calm down. You won't do her any good in that condition."

"I want to see her."

"Not in that condition, you won't. You have to calm down."

A young, plump and pretty nurse approached. "I'll take you to see her, but you must be calm. She's sleeping. It's the drugs."

"Drugs?"

"Yes, apparently those people who had her gave her sedatives."

The pretty nurse took hold of John's arm and steered him down the corridor. The nurse at the station called, "This is on you if he upsets her."

The young woman said softly to John, "Your sister is out of it. You are not going to upset her."

"What kind of sedatives?"

"Benzos. And apparently a lot of them."

John knew about benzos. "Is she in a coma?"

"No, but she is very sound asleep." The nurse opened a room with a single bed. Colleen lay on it as still as a porcelain doll. Her hair was combed and arranged neatly on the pillow. She looked peaceful and her arms were straight at her sides as though she were laid out for a viewing. John went to the bed, sat on the edge, and gathered her hand. It felt warm and alive.

"How long will she be asleep?"

"It's hard to say, but she is in no danger. Her vital signs are stable."

"Did anyone say what happened to her?"

"You will need to talk to the police about that."

John lay his forehead next to Colleen's. His tears wet the pillow and once the nurse had quietly left the room, his shoulders heaved with noisy sobs. In time his breathing settled into the same steady rhythm as his sister's. He might even have fallen asleep. Gray light was seeping into the room when the pretty nurse returned. "I'm about to go off my shift. I wanted to let you know," she said. When John tried to sit up, his back felt like rigor mortis had set in. He eased himself upright. The nurse pulled a chair close to the bed. "Why don't you sit? You'd be so much more comfortable."

John pulled the chair so that it touched the bed.

The nurse put a stethoscope to Colleen's chest. "Everything sounds normal. Look. Do you see her eyes moving under her lids? She's dreaming. She'll be awake soon."

"Dreaming?"

The nurse looked at John, studying him. "You know," she said kindly, "this kind of sedation usually causes amnesia for the events just preceding it. It's possible she won't remember a thing."

"Really? Not a thing?"

"That's right. Not in all cases, but there is usually some amnesia."

John looked at his sister. He wondered if the Graftons would get the death penalty. What happened to them didn't matter as long as Colleen couldn't remember anything that hurt her. He didn't care about anyone else.

"Even so, the police are going to want to talk to her as soon as she wakes up. We are to let them know."

"I don't want them asking her any questions."

"She's going to be fine. I'm sure she'll be going home today. Nurse Blake will take my place. It was nice to meet you, Mr. Avery. Take good care of your little sister."

John looked away. "Thank you," he said as the nurse left the room. When he turned back to Colleen, her eyes were open. She smiled her huge smile and held out her arms. He held her to his chest, breathing in the smell of talcum powder and innocence. He squeezed and squeezed her until she said "ouch" and wiggled away. "Where am I?"

"In a hospital."

"Hospital? Why?" Colleen frowned, looking around.

"You slipped and hurt your head. You had to come and stay here overnight."

Colleen held the sides of her head in the palms of her hands. Then she explored the top and back. "My head don't hurt."

"Doesn't. They gave you medicine so it wouldn't."

"I don't feel no bumps."

"Any bumps." John took Colleen's fingers, rubbed them across the occipital condyle. "There, do you feel that?"

"Oh, yeah." Colleen looked puzzled. "It don't hurt though."

"Doesn't. I told you they gave you medicine."

"How did I fall?"

"What do you remember?"

"Obeah." Colleen sat forward. "Where is Obeah? We lost Obeah."

"She's fine. She's with Sloan."

Colleen threw her legs over the side of the bed. "Okay, let's go there now."

"Hold it, hold it."

A new nurse, older with a dark mustache over her upper lip, came into the room. "Oh, we are awake. Very good. How are you feeling, sweetie?"

Colleen looked at John.

"It's okay. This is your nurse." The woman briskly took Colleen's pulse and listened to her lungs and chest. "Fine, fine," she said. "I'll let the police know she is awake."

"Are the police coming here?" Colleen placed her hand, fingers spread, on John's arm.

"Yes," said John. "But you don't have to talk to them." He looked at the nurse, who said nothing.

"Why are they coming?"

John didn't answer. He considered taking Colleen away with him right now. But they would track him down eventually. "Look, Colleen, you don't have to talk to them if you don't want to." He considered calling Annie.

"Are the police our friends?"

"Sometimes."

The nurse watched him.

There was a hard rap on the door, and two troopers walked into the room without waiting for an invitation. Each had blue eyes, thick slicked-down blond hair, and a bright, shining face. They looked as though they had just stepped out of a corn field. "Sir, we just have a few questions for your sister," said the one who appeared to be the oldest.

"That was quick."

"Just a few questions, sir. It won't take long and we will be very careful. Now it would be best, if you don't mind, if you would leave the room."

John wondered again if he should call Annie. "I…"

"We will be very careful, sir, we promise. And we know what we are doing."

"Can we step outside a minute?" John wasn't a bit sure they knew what they were doing. In the corridor he said, "Look, the nurse told me that the type of drugs the Graftons gave Colleen could cause amnesia. If she doesn't remember what happened, I don't want you people filling her in, okay?"

"She could be very helpful in putting the Graftons away for good."

"I have a lawyer."

"Sir, we imagine you have questions of your own you would like answered."

John didn't know that he did. In fact, he was quite certain he wouldn't want any information that would create pornographic images featuring his little sister hanging around in his mind, showing themselves when he closed his eyes or even when his eyes were open but unguarded.

"Mr. Avery, we will be very careful when we talk to your sister. If it appears she has no memory of events, we will not pursue it."

"I want to be with her. I believe it's my right. She's a minor."

"What is your relationship to her?"

"I'm her brother."

"Where is her mother?"

"She's an invalid."

"And her father."

"He's dead."

The older trooper who seemed to be in charge shrugged. "You can stay but you must not say anything. We don't want to contaminate this investigation."

The interview was brief. Though the police were as gentle as possible, Colleen said nothing. She looked at them through blue pools with her fingers in her mouth and said nothing.

The three men went back into the corridor.

"Mr. Avery, this is a very serious case. It is very important we get all the information we can. We would like you to talk to one of the SANE nurses here at the hospital."

"The what?"

"These are nurses who specialize in sexual abuse. They know what to look for. We can't say enough good about them. We are very lucky to have them. They are really top-notch."

"What are they going to look at?"

"It would be best if you talked to them yourself. They are available now."

The two nurses were young and smoothly professional. Smiling, they indicated John should sit in the comfortable chair. They introduced themselves as SANE Nurse Mahoney and SANE Nurse Wells. They showed John a series of pictures of young girls' vaginas, labia, and hymens. They pointed to tears, holes, bruising in the vaginal walls, cervixes, labia, and hymens of five- and six-year-olds after being raped. They then showed the same body parts of girls who had not been molested. They explained how prosecutors could use this evidence in court. When they finished, John leaned back in his chair. "So," he said, "you call yourselves SANE Nurses."

"Yes. It stands for…"

"And how do you get these pictures?" John interrupted.

"With very special cameras."

"Cameras that you insert into the, ah, vaginas of little girls."

The nurses said nothing.

"And you are proposing to do that to Colleen? My sister, Colleen?"

"It could be very helpful."

"To whom?"

"To the investigation. Mr. Avery, we do not want the Graftons of this world to go free to hurt other children."

John stood. He did not care about other children. "May I take my sister home now?"

The nurses looked at each other. Nurse Mahoney turned to John. "The doctor should be doing his rounds now. You may be able to catch him. He will undoubtedly release your sister today. She is doing fine. Now we know the police would like us to do a rape kit and that needs to be done as soon as possible. We would like to do that today. Now would be best. We have time. For the swab and the SANE exam."

"Mahoney. That's an Irish name, isn't it?"

Mahoney smiled. "Why, yes," she said.

"Are you Catholic?"

The smile disappeared.

"Does the Catholic church have anything to say about these exams?"

"No, it doesn't," Nurse Wells said, quickly. "Mr. Avery, we understand that family members might have concerns, but we are very well trained, very professional. Of course, we can't do anything without your consent."

"What I think doesn't matter. My mother has custody. Naturally."

Nurse Wells didn't miss a beat. "We could fax her the release. Or send it electronically and she could sign it and email it back."

"She doesn't have a computer... or a fax."

"Could she go to Kinkos or someplace like that? Then we could fax her there."

"My mother is not well."

"The child's father?"

"Dead."

The nurses looked at each other, seeming silently to confer and come to an agreement all in the space of a few seconds. They turned their attention back to John. Wells told him that in such circumstances he might be able to sign the necessary papers. She would check with the police waiting outside.

John rose from his chair. "If you come anywhere near my sister, I will take that stethoscope from around your neck and stick it up your anus."

There was a new nurse at the nurse's station. She told John the doctor had discharged Colleen. "She's waiting in her room. You can sign for her and take her home." She leaned forward and said in a softer voice, "And between you and me, good for you."

He was shaking when he entered his sister's room and when he handed her her clothes and when he walked behind the orderly, a big, heavy man with an easy manner, who wheeled his sister down the hall, and once outdoors he continued to shake as he buckled Colleen into the back seat of his car and headed back to Colton.

By the time he reached his house, John had managed to calm himself enough to keep the keys from rattling when he put them in his pocket. His mother was in the kitchen fixing dinner when he brought Colleen through the door. It was noon. Mrs. Avery was making spaghetti. She made spaghetti at least once a week. At the sound of the door, she turned slowly away from the stove, her expression as bland and empty as a sheep's until she saw Colleen. Her eyes widened, a smile started and disappeared, and she leaned heavily against the stove.

"The police were here last night, John."

"What did they want?" John pulled out a chair for his sister, who stood glumly by the door.

"They were looking for Colleen."

"Well, as you see she's right here. She's been with me. Come over here, Colleen, and sit down."

"They said she was missing."

"She was but only for a short while. She and Sloan disappeared in the woods. They were looking for Sloan's puppy."

"Who's Sloan?"

"That friend I told you about. They were just playing and got lost in the woods."

"That's it? Nothing else happened?"

"Right. Nothing else." The whole gruesome story would be in the paper, of course, but they would not mention the children's names. A small decency. John was sure he could keep the truth from the parlor where his mother lived.

"You were in the woods, precious? And you are all right?" Mrs. Avery knelt before her daughter, took her hands in her own. Colleen didn't pull away, but she didn't look happy. This perpetually sunny child had carried on the whole way home. She wanted to be with Sloan. She didn't want to go home. She wanted to go to Sloan's house. She wanted to see Obeah. She raised her voice and then began to cry. She cried profusely, wetting the front of her shirt. She even kicked the back of John's seat until he told her to stop. Now she looked at her mother warily.

"Are you all right, precious?" Mrs. Avery ran her hand along the side of Colleen's face. Her daughter turned away from her.

"Give her time, Mom. Don't push her. Come here, Colleen. Sit down. I'll fix your lunch. What do you want?"

Colleen didn't answer.

"Tell me what you want, or I will give you liver sandwiches," he said, hoping for a laugh.

Colleen scowled at him. Finally, she said, "PB and J."

Mrs. Avery's mouth opened. She put her head in her hands. "Oh, thank you God, sweet Jesus!" She pulled Colleen, who squealed and struggled, into an embrace.

"Let her go, Mom. Mom! *Let her go.* You can't react that way. You've got to act normal."

"But John—"

"No buts. You'll ruin it if you make a fuss. Now get up and go back to the spaghetti. Or have some lunch. Let go of her, Mom. Colleen, come over here and sit down."

"After all these years, John!"

"Colleen is going to be staying here now, Mom. She's not going away."

Mrs. Avery stood up with her hand on Colleen's shoulder. "Will that other little girl come here?"

"I don't know."

Colleen yanked away from her mother's grasp, spun around, and ran out the door and down the street, legs pumping and hair flying. When John caught up to her, he picked the child up, threw her over his shoulder and carried her home, the sound of his sister's wailing trailing behind him.

The afternoon consisted of tears, tantrums, Colleen's continued attempts to run away, his mother swabbing her eyes and finally shrieking, "John, just take her back there."

"I'm not doing that."

"Whyyyy?" Colleen's face was a mask of tears, dirt, and snot.

"Look, you want to see Sloan? We'll arrange for a play date."

Colleen stopped snuffling. "When?" She spoke around the fingers in her mouth.

"Sunday."

"When is Sunday?"

"In four days."

Colleen began to hiccup.

"Now go upstairs and take a bath. Wash your face."

"I'll go with her."

"She doesn't need you to, Ma. She's old enough to bathe herself. Oh, for God's sake, Ma, stop crying. Both of you just stop it. Colleen, go upstairs and take your bath. Don't make me carry you."

When she was finally in bed, curled in a fetal position and weeping quietly, John checked the nails around her window. Then he sat on the bed next to her and rubbed her back. "It will be okay, Colleen. You'll make new friends. And you can see Sloan in the park in town." But Colleen did not respond. She remained in a miserable heap, limp, still, wet with tears. It seemed there was no end to them.

Chapter Thirty-One

The two women were asleep when Sloan woke. She decided to go downstairs and see if anything had happened in the night. Perhaps Colleen would be in the kitchen. She slid out of bed and went quietly down the stairs with Obeah's nails ticking along behind her. There was no sign that anything had changed while she slept, and Colleen was not there. She let the puppy out into a sparkling sunny morning. Waiting for her to do her business, Sloan wondered why her mother was still asleep. After Obeah had finished, she brought her inside and fed her. While Obeah ate, Sloan made herself a bowl of cereal and carried it with both hands back upstairs. She managed to climb onto the bottom of the bed without spilling any milk, crossed her legs and dipped a spoon into the sweet crunchy Cocoa Puffs, all the while keeping her eyes on her mother. The noise of her chewing woke the women. Muddled by sleep and liquor, Clare slit her eyes at her.

Sloan licked the milk from her upper lip. "Where's Colleen?"

"What?"

"Is Colleen found?"

Clare propped herself on her elbows. "I don't know." The sun filled the room with bright light. Annie moaned, sat up, and shaded her eyes with her arm. "It was dawn when we fell asleep."

"Call the police, Mama, and see if Colleen is found."

Clare looked at Annie. "I ain't callin' them."

"I'll call 'em," Sloan mumbled.

"Of course you won't," said Annie. "Anyway, why don't we call John? He must know something. And the police won't tell us anything. They can't."

Sloan jumped off the bed, tugged her mother's boot. "Come on, let's go."

"Annie can call him."

"Clare, you know him so much better. Besides, it's you he'll want to talk to."

Clare swung her legs off the side of the bed, turned her back on Annie. She would not call John. She didn't know why; all she knew was an uneasy feeling, a dread that lingered on the edge of sorrow, a defeat, but in what she couldn't say. It was a new feeling to her; it watered down her limbs, slowed her thinking, and turned her stomach sour. Perhaps she was just hung over.

Downstairs, she threw bacon on to fry while Annie made coffee and Sloan played on the floor with the dog. The food only made her feel worse. "Call him," she told Annie. "Let's get it over with."

Annie dreaded the call as much as Clare, but in a different way, a specific, clearly defined way. She was afraid Colleen was still gone. Or worse. She wiped her hands on the back of her jeans and picked up the phone. It rang several times before she hung up.

"No answer." Annie called three more times. When she stepped away from a desultory game of monopoly to call the fourth time, she was watching Sloan absently when suddenly John came on the line and startled her into a stinging sweat. "Oh. Hello John. It's Annie," she managed. "I was calling to find out about Colleen."

There was silence on the line.

"Do you have any news?"

"She's home."

"Oh, thank God. How is she?"

"As far as we can tell she's fine." John's voice was flat and did not invite further conversation.

"Thank God. That's wonderful."

Sloan tugged on the phone cord. "Let me talk to her."

"Um, Sloan wants to talk to her."

"Not now."

"Well sure. I understand."

Sloan grabbed Annie's arm. "When is she coming back?"

"Where are the Graftons?"

"In jail."

"Well, thank God for that." Annie hesitated, waiting for more details, but John said nothing. Sloan continued yanking on her shirt. "I want to see Colleen," she said, loud enough for John to hear her.

"Maybe later. In a while," he said. His voice sounded very tired.

Annie gathered her thoughts then said, carefully, "I think the dangers are past. No more bears. No more foster care. No more Graftons. I think if you think about the odds, Colleen will be very safe here."

Sloan pulled on Annie's shirt. "What's he sayin'?"

Clare's boot had been tapping the floor, but now she sat very still. Annie listened to John and said, "Can I call you later?" She waited for John to answer, then hung up the phone and faced Clare, shaking her head. "He needs time. He's pretty messed up about this. Naturally."

"Of course," said Clare.

Sloan yanked on Annie's sleeve. "What does that mean? When is Colleen coming? She's not, is she? John won't let her. I'll just go get her. You can't stop me. I'll get her from school."

Clare watched her daughter, whose green eyes had hard black lines running like spokes from the pupil. "Don't even think about running away," she said, her voice sounding as tired as John's.

"Then make John bring Colleen here."

"I can't."

"Yes, you can."

"No, I can't."

"I hate you!" Sloan's hands were in fists. She pounded up the stairs and flung herself on her bed. Clare followed, sat next to her, touched her shoulder, but Sloan yanked away from her. "Go away," she cried into the covers.

Clare went into the bathroom to the mirror. She looked at her face, touched the bones around her eyes, her lips, the rough hair. Then she smiled her lone-wolf smile. She knew that animal, all right. People found them romantic, a courageous symbol of the basic aloneness of all creatures. In truth, no wolf would choose to live alone. Unfortunate circumstances damned them to this life. They spent much of the time on the outskirts of a pack picking up scraps left behind. She picked up a pair of scissors and a hunk of hair and cut it off as close to the scalp as possible. She continued until she was all but bald. Then she threw the hair in the trash and went outside to clean the manure out of the pasture, a task she always enjoyed for the physicality of it and the sense of order it engendered. However, her mind would not hold still, and she could not become absorbed by the steady rhythm of pick and throw; the healthy pull on her shoulders and arms. After an hour's work she gave it up; caught, saddled, and bridled the most melancholy horse in the herd. Sloan, seething, watched her from the stoop. "If you think your hair looks nice like that, you're wrong," she yelled to her mother. "You look like a witch!"

As Clare led the horse past the house, she kept her eyes on the ground, hoping to become invisible, hoping to avoid a fight. But Sloan jumped off the stoop, red faced and sweating. "When are you going to get Colleen?"

"I'm not. She won't be coming back for a while. Stay with Annie. I'm going for a ride."

"I'm going to get Colleen. I know how to drive."

"I'll tie you up if I have to."

Sloan bared her teeth and raised her fist. Clare ignored her and swung into the saddle. She and Scout made their way mournfully up the mountain with Sloan's shrill voice, "I hate you; I hate you!" trailing behind her.

When Clare reached Unc's place, she felt wasted, quivery, and sick. Her mouth was dry, and her voice cracked when she called to him. Unc came out of his cabin and helped Clare from the saddle, eased her gently onto the log. He sat next to her, watched silently as she took deep breaths and finally dropped her face to her hands and wept. He patted her back, touched her strange new hair, finally put his arm around her, held onto her as the sobs increased in power, shaking her till her teeth chattered. Clare tried to talk, to ask for help, but she could not. Unc took hold of her with both arms, held her tight. "Cry," he said. "Go ahead. You got reason." He stroked her hair, tucked her head under his chin. "You thought you could get away with anything. And once upon a time you could. But it goes, Clare. It always does."

Slowly the sobs subsided, but the tears would not. They washed over her, on and on until the source was empty and with a shuddering sigh she sat up. The two remained sitting shoulder to shoulder as the light turned pink and blue around them. Unc ran his hand over the bristled hair. "I like it. Makes you look like a soldier."

Clare rose, gathered the reins, mounted the spiritless horse and said, "Yeah, I'm a soldier all right."

Chapter Thirty-Two

$\mathcal{D}$r. Wittcomb helped herself to a Mounds bar. After she finished the candy, she went into the bathroom, washed and dried her hands carefully, returned to her desk, and picked up her letter of resignation and read it over. Satisfied, she put it in an envelope. She should have done this years ago. She could help no one. She didn't know if it was that her skills had dimmed or that American society was on the downward slide to decadence. Foster parents molesting their charges. Kidnapping them. According to Charles Dickens, these things had always happened. At any rate, she was done. What would she do with the rest of her days? Definitely not volunteer or start going to church. She wouldn't garden due to her old and aching bones. Perhaps she would open a bakery. Feed people. She would charge exorbitantly low prices. The kitchen would have to be certified, but she knew the health inspector. She could get a van and drive to people's homes. Colleen's. The child continued to speak. The amnesia seemed complete, but her sunny disposition was gone. She crossed her eyes and spit, wailed, and shed tears like Chukchi shed her coat. All of this because she could not see Sloan. Dr. Wittcomb wondered if the same happened with the older child. She would drive her van out there, bring that wild child some sweets. That is, if Clare would allow it.

Chapter Thirty-Three

John assumed that time would heal this wound in his sister, but it did not. After a month of tears and fits of fury, running away from school, spending way too much time in the principal's office, Colleen, having worked loose the nails that held it shut, was caught trying to shimmy down one of the poles holding up the porch under her bedroom window.

It was Sloan, however, who delivered the final blow. So estranged was she from her mother that she was able to slip away from Clare's watchful eye. The police stopped the girl as she was galloping full-out on one of her mother's training colts down Route thirty, determined to find Colleen and bring her home. She didn't know where Colleen lived but was undaunted by this trifle.

When John heard from Dr. Wittcomb about Sloan's attempt, he called Annie at her office.

"This isn't working," he said.

"I'm not sure what you mean by '_this._'"

"Look, I admit I've been totally freaked out. This whole thing has been a damn nightmare."

"Whole thing. What do you mean by whole thing?"

"All of it. It feels like no one is safe out there. Not me, not the girls. But keeping the girls apart isn't the answer. Colleen is miserable."

"Not _you_? You mean because Clare was your client?"

"Look, you can blame it all on me if you want to. I deserve it. But that isn't why I called. I know it isn't rational to not let Colleen go out there. She's miserable and the Graftons are in jail and so is that boy. And bringing Sloan here isn't the answer either."

"Listen. Have you talked to Clare at all?"

"No."

"Don't you think you should?"

"What good would it do?"

None, thought Annie. Not if you can even ask that question. "So, what exactly are you trying to say, John?"

"I won't be around here much longer. I'm going back to school, in Pittsburg, in the fall. There won't be anyone here to watch out for Colleen."

Like everyone else in town, Annie knew about Mrs. Avery. There was no surprise there, but John suddenly going back to school? "So, are you quitting your job?"

"Yes. I'm going into a different field."

"Really? What's that?"

John hesitated a moment over Annie's tone then chose to ignore her rudeness. "Environmental Health."

Well, of course. It made perfect sense to her. First there were the trees; quiet, dignified changing so slowly one hardly noticed, and then the methodical counting of animals, the testing of water, the careful study of flora and fauna. There would be no real-life witches to change your life forever, no exquisitely impossible relationships. Even a rabid raccoon was a walk in the park compared to what happened to the people in these woods.

When Annie told Clare John's plans, for one awful instant her friend looked bereft, completely caught off guard, but then she recovered herself and said, "So, Colleen can really stay with us?"

"That's what John is saying, yes."

"The girls will be fine with that."

Chapter Thirty-Four

Four Years Later

Clare was long lining a horse, a home-bred, in the round pen when Annie arrived. It was six o'clock in the evening, the time of day in the summer when the light changes, when it deepens the contrasts, making the world appear clearer. The two-year-old horse, Wild Child, was a beautifully built filly with delicate lines and the natural grace of a fine-boned cat. She would be a gift to the girls.

The new barn was made of raw lumber and the color of the wood was slowly changing from honey to silver. Several horses had their heads out the Dutch doors, calmly watching the world go by. Obeah, lying under a tree with her head on her paws, kept a sleepy eye on Clare, to whom, in a dignified way, she had granted ownership.

Clare talked softly to the filly. She now had a waiting list for training colts. She never pushed a horse too fast and knew all the old ways to bring a horse along. Annie had heard people say that she was the best trainer in the tri-state area. They had become business partners shortly after Colleen moved in for good. She parked near the house and walked to the round pen. "Hey," she called, and her friend turned and smiled, brought the youngster down to a walk and patted her neck as they approached the fence. Annie folded her arms on the top board. She loved this time of day. "Where are the girls?"

Clare rolled her eyes. "At 4-H of course. Going over last-minute instructions. They should be here riding."

"I hardly think they need practice riding."

"I know, but all them rules. That's what they have to go over. Rules, rules, rules. Can you believe a child of mine actually belonging to an organization like that?"

Annie knew that Clare was secretly pleased the girls had found their way into this organization with its emphasis on animal husbandry and was also relieved that it gave them a social life that demanded little socializing from her.

"What time are we leaving for the show tomorrow?"

"Around seven." Clare coiled the lunge line into a tidy oval.

Annie watched her for a minute. "Do you mind if Marshall comes for supper tonight?"

"I don't but Unc might. Maybe. Actually, now that I think about it, maybe he would like it. I can see him and Marshall peacefully having nothing to say to each other. Sure, ask him to come."

"Is Unc's lady friend coming?"

"God no. Can you just imagine it? Someone from the Holler sitting in a stranger's house, eating stranger's food, surrounded by strange people."

"What was I thinking?" Annie smiled and touched the filly's muzzle.

Clare ran her hand along the graceful neck. "So, it will be you, Marshall, Unc, the girls, of course, and May Wittcomb with her truckload of food." She laughed. "Let me cool this baby off and I'll come in and help you get ready."

A black new model Jeep Cherokee made the turn in the driveway and stopped. It was the 4-H leader, Mrs. McKurty. Colleen and Sloan clambered out of the back seat, turned, and gave the woman a cheery wave. They had grown lean and strong in the last four years. They ran across the yard and nearly flew over the fence. After landing, they both suddenly grew languid and draped an arm over Wild Child's neck. They kissed her before turning their tanned, smiling faces to the women. Sticky with sweat, their hair had taken on a life of its own. Sloan leaned against the horse. "What's for dinner?"

"Roast chicken and potato salad," said Clare.

"And Auntie May's famous spaghetti and cheese?"

"Of course."

"Awesome."

"And hot dogs?" This from Colleen.

"Yes, hot dogs too."

Colleen smiled her wide grin. "Cool."

She must know, thought Annie. Even at only ten years old, (when she was kidnapped four years ago, she was six) the girl could maintain a cool silence on subjects she didn't want to discuss. Annie took Colleen to see her brother two or three times a month, and they talked often on the phone, so it was very likely she knew, but chose to remain mute on the subject. She probably was even going to the wedding.

Sloan straightened and pulled one of her strawberry blonde curls in front of her eyes, crossing them for a better look, examined the strand closely, rubbing it between her fingers then released it to go springing back in place. "Let's go wash our hair," she said, and the two girls sprinted off in a flash of elbows, knobby knees, and the undersides of muddy sneakers.

Clare smiled at Annie before turning to go back to the barn.

Annie hesitated and called, "Wait a sec."

"Yeah?"

"John called me to say he was sending me a letter to give to you. He told me not to let you tear it up before you read it." She pulled a small envelope from the back pocket of her jeans.

Clare stepped forward and took it from Annie's outstretched hand. She stuck her index finger under the flap and opened the single notebook page without hurry.

Dear Clare,

Please read this before destroying it. I have news and I wanted you to hear it from me first, not someone else. I know it's been four years but not a day goes by that I don't think of you. Cheap words, I know. I loved you and always will, but I can't live with you. We come from different worlds. Speaking of which, Colleen obviously does well in your world. She entered it at a young and impressionable age. I can see that she benefits from the company of Sloan and the rest of you. I will always be grateful to you for keeping her.

I hope I am not hurting you when I tell you I am getting married. To a girl I met at college. I'm sure you've heard that I went back to school. After all that happened with Sloan and then Collen, I couldn't continue doing in-home therapy, or any kind of therapy. I'm not cut out for intensity. I had to walk away before it destroyed me or somebody else, and that meant walking away from you.

Please take care of yourself and the girls. I hope you can forgive me for just disappearing from your life, but if you can't, I understand.

Love always,

John.

Clare's cheeks turned ruddy as she read, and when she looked up, her eyes glistened. "Well," she said. She handed the letter to Annie.

She stared at it for a while. Finally, she said. "Oh Clare. I'm so sorry."

"Oh, it's not so bad," Clare said, the blush fading from her cheeks.

At the sight of her friend standing so straight and strong next to her horse, Annie felt her chest go tight. Marshall would be coming to dinner. Unc's lady friend would stay at home. May would be here on her own. But she had been on her own for a long, long time. It was just a year that Clare, apparently giving up on the company of men, had stopped going to her usual haunts. "You should go out more," Annie blurted. "See people. Start dating again. You'd have no trouble meeting someone. You know that."

Clare smiled and shook her head. "Oh, Annie, I swear. I love you, but you can be so naive sometimes. Happy endings don't last. There is no such thing as happily ever after." With a gentle laugh, she appeared to shake herself free. "Now come on with me to the barn and help me brush this horse down. And feed the others. They haven't had supper yet."

Annie started to object but changed her mind. Clare's eyes no longer glistened. Wasn't it this woman's stubborn, even at times foolish refusal to compromise that she loved about her? Annie slipped through the fence rails and the two friends walked together across the round pen.

About the Author

E. Compton Lee began her writing career as a freelance writer of nature and human-interest articles for magazines such as *Mother Earth News, Practical Horseman, American Country and Horseman.*

Her first novel, *Native,* takes place in the backwoods of Appalachia, and portrays a woman struggling to overcome misogyny and bigotry to find her place in the cutthroat world of the horse industry.

My Name Is Sloan is a companion to *Native,* and is followed by *2026,* the story of what happens to a nation when the unthinkable occurs.

Born and raised in the Hudson River Valley, she left that region at the age of eighteen and embarked upon a journey which immersed her in a multitude of cultures. The knowledge gained from those experiences is what is used when she writes her novels.

E. Compton Lee lived in the Allegheny Mountains of Pennsylvania and western Maryland for fifteen years, where she worked as a therapist and ran a horse business. She currently lives in Williamsburg, Virginia, where she writes full time.